KAKADU DAWN

Annie Seaton

Porter Sisters 6

Porter Sisters series

1. *Kakadu Sunset*
2. *Daintree*
3. *Diamond Sky*
4. *Hidden Valley*
5. *Larapinta*
6. *Kakadu Dawn*

Standalone Books

Whitsunday Dawn
Undara
Osprey Reef
East of Alice
Porter Sisters Series
Kakadu Sunset
Daintree
Diamond Sky
Hidden Valley
Larapinta
Kakadu Dawn

Others

Four Seasons Short and Sweet
Deadly Secrets
Adventures in Time
Silver Valley Witch
The Emerald Necklace
An Aussie Christmas Duo
Ten Days in Tuscany

Pentecost Island Series

Pippa
Eliza
Nell
Tamsin
Evie
Cherry
Odessa
Sienna
Tess
Isla

The House on the Hill series

Beach House
Beach Music
Beach Walk
Beach Dreams

Sunshine Coast Series

Waiting for Ana
The Trouble with Jack
Healing His Heart

Second Chance Bay Series

Her Outback Playboy
Her Outback Protector
Her Outback Haven
Her Outback Paradise
The McDougalls of Second Chance Bay

Richards Brothers Series

The Trouble with Paradise
Marry in Haste
Outback Sunrise

Love Across Time Series

Come Back to Me
Follow Me
Finding Home
The Threads that Bind
Love Across Time 1-4 Boxed Set

Bindarra Creek

Worth the Wait
Full Circle
Secrets of River Cottage
Bindarra Creek Duo
A place to Belong

The Augathella Girls Series

Outback Roads
Outback Sky
Outback Escape
Outback Wind
Outback Dawn
Outback Moonlight
Outback Dust
Outback Hope
An Augathella Surprise
An Augathella Baby
An Augathella Spring

KAKADU DAWN

To my husband, Ian . . . and to the beautiful family we created together. I am blessed.

Out of suffering, strong souls emerge…

Chapter 1

McLaren Mango Farm – early May
Dru and Ellie

'She's a cheeky little thing, Ellie. And gorgeous.' Dru smiled as Matilda, her sister's third child, tugged at her blonde curls.

'You mightn't say that if you were up with her at three o'clock in the morning and all she wanted to do was giggle and play. Even before she has a feed! Matilda Susan McLaren, let go of Aunty Dru's hair.' Ellie took her daughter's fingers and untangled Dru's hair from the chubby fist.

'Well, she looks like she's getting plenty of food. We were lucky with Ruby. She's always been a good sleeper. Slept through the night her second week home from hospital.'

'James and Verity were a bit like this one when we first brought them home, but they started to sleep well around six months, so I've got a month left, hopefully.'

'I'm the one who can't sleep these days.' Dru's voice was tight, and she looked past Ellie out to the mango plantation. The sky was cloudless on a glorious autumn afternoon, and Dru had driven out for lunch while Ruby was at daycare.

Ellie frowned. Dru was the most together of the three sisters, and she'd handled being a mother with a natural calm that Ellie and Emma had had to learn.

'The new baby?' Ellie glanced down at Dru's very pregnant tummy. 'I'm sorry we'll be overseas when you have him. Is he kicking a lot?'

Dru shook her head and bit her lip, and for a minute, Ellie thought she was fighting back tears.

'Dru?'

'I'm okay. Just pregnant.' She straightened and seemed to pull herself together, but her voice still didn't reassure Ellie. 'Now tell me, how long are you going for again?'

'We'll be gone at least six weeks, possibly eight, but I want lots of FaceTime with you.'

'Are you organised?' This time Dru smiled. They all knew that Ellie, who'd once been super-organised, surprisingly struggled with running their home and looking after three children.

Ellie rolled her eyes. 'Let's say that Kane is helping me, thank goodness. But I am so excited about simply going overseas, and James and Verity are excited about going on a big plane.'

'How will you go with Matilda?'

'If Tilly sleeps, I'll be fine, but I can't complain. She's such a happy little soul.' Ellie tickled her baby under the chin and got a giggle. 'You're a cheeky girl, but Mummy loves you. I'll sleep on the plane when she does. Kane can entertain the other two, and at least I won't have to cook and wash for twenty hours.'

'Sounds like you're in the right frame of mind anyway.'

'It will actually be a break. I find organising the day so much harder than flying.' Ellie sat down and unbuttoned her blouse when Matilda started to grizzle. 'How's Ruby settling in at daycare?' she asked.

'She loves it.'

'I honestly don't know how you do it. Your apartment is always spotless, Ruby is clean and happy, and you work as well. Will you keep the part-time work going when the bub arrives?'

Dru shrugged. 'Depends on how he behaves.'

'You're sure he's a he?'

'I hope so. I'd like Connor to have a son. I'm silly. I tell myself if I call him, he, he will be. Unlike you, I'm not going back a third time. If we have two girls, so be it.'

'As long as the baby is healthy and happy,' they both chanted with a grin.

'Bless, Mum. She's been a fabulous granny. And listen, how's Connor? We haven't seen him for ages.' Ellie was taken aback when her strong sister lowered her head and stifled a sob. She widened her eyes, quickly taking her baby off her breast and laying her on her playmat. She stepped over to her sister, put her hands on her shoulders, and was surprised when Dru lifted her hands and covered her face.

'Dru? What is it? Is Connor sick?' Ellie asked.

'I don't know. He never talks to me anymore. He's barely home.'

'What do you mean?'

'He's always at work, and as soon as he gets home, he has to go out and see someone. Ruby's probably forgotten what he looks because he's gone when we wake up, and then she might see him for five minutes at teatime before he goes out again if she's lucky.'

'Have you talked to him about it?'

'I tried early on, but you know me. I can shut down too when I'm cross or worried.'

'That's the worst thing you can do. If he's shut down and you've shut down, you won't sort anything out.'

Dru lifted her head and dug in her pocket. She pulled a tissue out and dabbed at her eyes. When she finally held Ellie's gaze, the uncertainty and fear on her face were something Ellie hadn't seen for a long time. Dru had healed since they'd discovered the truth behind their father's death. And since she and Connor had met and married, she'd been a different person. Happy and open, the suffering she had carried within for many years had been replaced by happiness. The final step for each of the three sisters in getting over their father's death had been seeing Mum's happiness when she'd married Graysen.

'What are you worried about?'

Dru's voice trembled. 'I'm worried that if I probe too deep for the truth, I'm going to find out a truth that I don't want to hear.'

'What do you mean?'

'I mean, I think . . . I'm wondering if he's met someone else. If he's seeing someone else.'

'No way! That is not Connor at all. Connor is straight and true and upright, you know that.'

'I thought I did know that.'

'You need to talk to him, Dru. You've got to get to the bottom of this. You can't keep worrying. It's not good for you or Ruby or the baby. I wish we weren't going away next week, now that you've told me. Have you talked to Emma? Or Mum?'

'Shit, no. I'm sorry I lost it. I shouldn't have told you either, Ellie. I don't want you worrying, and please don't say a word to Mum or Emma or Dee. Please?'

'You can't carry this by yourself.'

'I know. It's been about three months now. That's why I broke just now. I'll talk to Connor. I suppose if there is someone else, I need to know.'

'Don't say that, Dru.' Ellie shook her head again. 'No, I just can't imagine that. That is so totally not Connor. He adores you. And Ruby. You can see it every minute he's with you.'

'I think you'll find many women who could say the same about their relationships and husbands. And be stunned when the truth hits.'

'No, I still can't believe it.' The first tinge of doubt rippled through Ellie. Even though she was reluctant to believe it, there was obviously something wrong. Dru's usual inner strength was no longer there. 'I know. How about I get Kane to have a word with Connor? Go out for a beer, not be obvious.'

Dru pulled a face. 'No, Ellie, I'll handle this myself. Promise me you won't say anything to anyone. Okay?'

'Okay,' Ellie said reluctantly. 'But you know I'm here if you need to talk to me. You call me if you need me and I'll come to Darwin. Or when we're away, we can FaceTime privately. Gosh, I wish we weren't going away now.'

'Don't be silly,' Dru said. 'It's probably just a rough patch, and he and Greg are really busy. They've had a lot of work on.'

'I still wish I was here for you, or that you would tell Emma.'

'Ellie, this opportunity that you and Kane have been offered is incredible, and it's got the potential to put your mango farm on the international map.'

'I know, but—'

'No buts.' Dru leaned over the sofa, picked Matilda up, and kissed her cheek. 'Goodbye, sweet Tilly. It's time I was going.' She passed her across to Ellie. 'Have you heard from that girl who's coming to do that research?'

'Yes, Tarni Morgan. She was surprised when we told her about the opportunity Kane's been offered and that we'd be away for quite a while, but she was quite happy to house-sit while she does the research.'

'That worked out well. She can look after the animals for you.'

'It did work out, but there's been a bit of a complication.'

'Complication?' Dru picked up her bag and took her car keys out. 'What sort of complication?'

'Do you remember Cy?'

'Cy?' Dru frowned.

'Yes, Ryan's cousin. He was best man at their wedding.'

'I remember now. That was the only time I met him.'

'Yes, we haven't seen him since the wedding either. I think he's stayed away because of his father going to jail.'

'So, what's the complication?' Dru glanced at her watch. 'Walk with me to my car and tell me.'

Dru held the door open as Ellie held Matilda, and followed Ellie as she walked down the front steps overlooking the circular drive.

'Kane ran into him a couple of weeks ago in Darwin. He was working at the Berrimah cattle yards, the quarantine place where the cattle go before they're exported. Apparently, he lost his job as a supervisor. Anyway, to cut a long story short, he hired him to manage our place for the couple of months we'll be away. He didn't think of Tarni being in the guest room while she's here doing the research for the International Horticultural Association. Anyway, when I pointed that out to Cy, Kane rang him and Cy said he was happy to bunk in the work shed with his swag. The problem is that I feel awkward about them both being there. At least there's a small bathroom in the shed, but they'll have to share the kitchen.'

'I think you're worrying about nothing. Two adults can share a kitchen without a problem. I'm sure everything will work out for you. You worry too much.'

'Probably.'

Dru unlocked her car and hesitated. She turned to Ellie.

'How about I talk to Connor, and we get all the family together at our place before you and Kane and the kids leave? Maybe having all of you there might make a difference. Maybe he'll go back to being the husband I'm used to.'

'I think that's a wonderful idea. If you're sure you're up to it?'

'I'm only pregnant, not ill.'

'Okay, that would be great. I'll wait to hear from you. You stay in touch.' Ellie hugged her sister with her spare arm. 'You promise me you'll take care of yourself.'

'Okay, big sis.'

Dru beeped the horn as she turned out of the gate onto the Arnhem Highway.

Ellie stood there for a long time, her cheek against her baby's soft skin. Her throat tightened as she remembered that dreadful day when sixteen-year-old Dru had rung her at work to tell her Dad was dead. Ellie and Emma had grieved too, but Ellie had never understood the depth of pain that Dru carried inside; they hadn't realised that Dru had found him hanging in the shed until a few years after he'd died.

It was hard to see Dru struggling again, and Ellie vowed to herself that she would get to the bottom of it before they left for Mexico.

Chapter 2

Darwin Correctional Centre – early May

Russell Fairweather looked across the table at the young man sitting opposite him. Mayonnaise ran down his bristled chin as Dean crammed a whole sandwich into his mouth and then picked up the second one. Russell suppressed a shiver of distaste and kept his expression bland.

'So, tell me again exactly what you want me to do. I think I've got it right.' Dean spoke between chewing.

Russell picked up his ham and pickle sandwich and examined it. The bread was a day old and the ham was processed. One of those artificial squares full of salt, sugar, and antioxidants. The pickles were an unnatural yellow. Some nights he dreamed of being in his luxury penthouse sipping on a glass of the finest shiraz with a plate of gourmet pate and imported cheese sitting on the marble table in front of him. Since he'd been in prison, he'd lost a lot of weight, but that was the last thing Russell worried about. His attention was focused totally on seeking revenge on the bitch who'd put him in this hell hole and trying to find a way to get out earlier than the fourteen-year sentence he'd been given by a female bitch of a judge. No more views over the harbour, no more silk shirts or Gucci loafers.

'You tell me what *you* understand is your role.' He pushed back the rage that sometimes clenched his chest in a vice. He'd held a picture of that fucking Porter girl in his head for the seven years he'd been incarcerated. With good behaviour, he could be out in another three years.

'Okay.' Dean had been two years into his nine-year sentence for sexual assault when Russell's incarceration began seven years ago. He would never forget the rage that consumed him that first day. He'd been treated like a lowly criminal, stripped of his belongings, and dressed in prison-issue clothing. He had held his rage in and spent the first night vomiting as his body reacted to his new situation.

Russell's behaviour in prison had been impeccable; he'd pleaded not guilty in court, but unfortunately, there had been enough evidence for him to be found guilty. He had hired the best defence and if it hadn't been for that Porter girl shooting him, he would have gotten off the conspiracy to commit murder charge on a factual defence.

Dean put the second half of the sandwich on his plate and placed his hands on the table. Russell wondered if the guy copied his movements consciously. 'There will be a work ute waiting for me at my parents' house the day after tomorrow.'

'That's correct.' Russell still had contacts outside. Having one of the correctional officers in his pocket had made his incarceration slightly more bearable.

'And if I'm successful, I get to keep it.'

'That is correct. And how will you explain it to your parents?'

'It belongs to a bloke I met inside. His name is Jerry and he organised for someone to drop it off. We were good mates in prison and Jerry wants me to get it serviced and drive it until he gets out in a couple of months. He's going back home to Western Australia.'

'And then?'

'I have to find out how I can get work on the McLaren Mango Farm on the road to Jabiru. Either as a worker or as a tradesman of some sort. Even if it takes a couple of months.'

'Good. Keep going.' They had had this same conversation each day for the past three months.

'And then I watch and wait until I get the perfect opportunity to kill the woman who owns the farm.' He smiled and Russell knew why he had taken this young man under his wing. His eyes were cold and the smile on his face held anticipation. He reminded him a little of Mick, the best employee he'd ever had.

'And how will you kill her?'

'I watch what she drinks, get access to her fridge when she's not there and add ethylene glycol.' He beamed. 'Anti-freeze. Although Russ, I'd still rather knife her.'

'Don't even be tempted, Dean. Slowly, slowly. This death is to appear to be from natural causes. Do not divert from our plan. She will be dead by the time the poison is identified and by then you will have a new identity and be on your way to Western Australia.' He chuckled. 'And then you can kill and rape to your heart's content.'

Dean was unaware that as soon as he'd carried out his task someone on the outside had been lined up to take care of him. The poor young man would die in a fiery crash on the highway. Russell left no bases uncovered.

'It's gonna be fun. Thank you.'

'The dose?'

'I have the dose inked on my arm.'

'And if anyone asks you what the number is?'

'It's my girlfriend's birthday so I don't forget. Ten zero six. Tenth of June, drop the six, and it means one hundred mls on the last day and six doses of ten mls whenever I can get to her drink.'

'I've chosen well. Thank you, Dean.'

'It's great how you've looked out for me, Russ. I wouldn't have made it in here if you hadn't looked out for me. A man probably would have topped himself. And the things you've taught me.' The ingenuous expression was back and Russell cringed at the affection in the young man's voice. If the stupid fool only knew that it had been solely to get Dean indebted to him, he would be asking for much more than a work ute and a new identity. Although there had been a positive and unexpected offshoot of the relationship that Russell had fostered; teaching him to read good literature and scientific magazines, and listen to decent music had helped pass the long days a little more easily.

Three years to go.

The rage rose again. He wished he could be there to see her die. She would suffer before she went into a coma. The headache would come first with a lack of coordination, then the slurred speech and then nausea and vomiting, and most importantly, pain, excruciating pain as her kidneys disintegrated.

His only regret was that she wouldn't know he was responsible. But he did, and that's all that mattered.

When Ellie Porter was dead, he would focus on getting through the remaining length of his sentence. Maybe he'd let her bastard of a husband know when he was out. He'd certainly do everything he could to make his life miserable. Russell's non-parole period had been set at ten years and he had already served seven of them. Seven soulless years. Mindless years with no luxuries. He had been a model prisoner, working in the library, running lessons on business management and, God forbid, helping in the prison gardens.

Ellie Porter deserved everything that was coming her way.

'Drummond! Why are you still here?' The loud voice ran through the dining room like a shotgun and Dean jumped to his feet.

'I'm out tomorrow, sir.'

'That's not what I mean, you deadshit,' the officer yelled. 'I know you're gone tomorrow and what a pleasure it will be not to have your ugly face in my sight. I mean, why aren't you out in the kitchen? Your clean-up shift has started. No need to be slack because it's your last day. I can soon change that.'

Dean hurried off to the kitchen without a backward glance and the officer winked at Russell. He leaned forward and whispered.

'Ute's been delivered and Jerry White's papers are in the glove box, including some references from his "previous employers" on mango farms in North Queensland. Brought you the paper to read seeing as you've done your gardening shift for the day.'

'Excellent,' Russell murmured.

He hid a smile as Dave Whittaker, the officer on his payroll, put a firm hand on his shoulder and raised his voice. 'That's enough of the bloody smart chat from you, Fairweather. You might have been a toff once, but you're not anymore.'

There were glances and titters from the dozen or so prisoners who remained in the dining room. The officer swung around and surveyed those remaining. 'I hope the lot of you have done your work shift for the day. If not, get hopping.'

Russell stood and sauntered out of the dining room with the newspaper tucked under his arm. He made his way to the library and chose a seat under the window to settle in and read the newspaper. It was quiet and the chair was comfortable; if he closed his eyes, he could almost imagine he was home in his apartment. When he arrived at the prison, he'd been allowed to make supervised calls to cleaning and home maintenance companies to arrange to have his apartment routinely cleaned and the outdoor garden on the balcony attended to.

Ten fucking years on non-parole. Ten years of being locked away with criminals. He was above them all, and he should not have been locked away. So far, he hadn't encountered anyone of his intelligence. He was in the medium security section. Perhaps those in the high and maximum-security areas might hold more intelligence than the lowlife criminals he was forced to associate with. Peter Porter and Panos Sordina were dead, but they had been nothing to him, apart from a step on the way to making his fortune, and he felt nothing about their deaths. The only death he regretted, was Mick, and that bitch had been directly responsible for his death. Russell hadn't cared if Mick's cool disregard for human life came from his military experiences, or whether he had genuine psychopathic tendencies, but he had proved a loyal employee over several years and followed orders without asking questions.

And that poor bastard had been eaten by a crocodile. All due to Ellie Porter. And what did she get? Nothing but praise in the bloody media.

The only emotion Russell held was the rage to which he knew he was so, so entitled. If that daughter of Peter Porter hadn't interfered, he could have made his first billion by now. He swallowed and opened his eyes as he reached for the newspaper. His hands were shaking as he sat straight and laid the *NT News* on the table in front of him. It was Wednesday so it was a thicker than usual version, with more classifieds that would keep him occupied. He shook his head.

What have I come to? Looking forward to reading the classifieds. Watching people shed their detritus, and looking at the positions vacant as if he'd have to look for a job when he was released. At least the investigators hadn't unearthed his Swiss bank account, and Russell had volunteered nothing.

Despite the boredom of the local paper, he kept up with the markets and territory politics because Russell fully intended to go back to his old life when he was released. Dean had spoken to him once about trying to escape when a few of the inmates had formulated a plan to overpower the correctional officers, but Russell had told him that was foolish; he wanted to leave with a clean reputation and not be on the run.

He had many to seek revenge on, and the hours passed as he lay on the hard bed at night planning retribution.

The first article that sent his blood pressure skyrocketing was about the McLaren Mango Farm.

He had to take a deep breath and calm himself, his fingers on the pulse point on his wrist before he allowed himself to read the whole article.

International award-winning researcher comes to the Territory.

As many of our local mango farmers will tell you, breeding mangoes is a long-term endeavour, typically taking up to twenty years to produce a new breed. Upcoming local farmer, Kane McLaren, who has developed his farm to become a leader in the hybrid field since purchasing the property seven years ago, has had outstanding success in shortening the breeding time frame.

He applied for and was successful in having a horticulture research officer allocated to work with him on his breeding program.

International award-winning researcher, Tarni Morgan arrives in the Territory this week to commence work on improving the efficiency of the successful hybrid that Kane has developed. The new variety has been named Susan Goldie. The hybrid variety can range in colour from pink to yellow and is round or oblong in shape. The flavour is sweet and sour with tropical fruit notes and the first crop available for market will be released later this year.

Kane McClaren said that Ms Morgan's knowledge will be a huge addition to their research program, and he and his wife, Ellie, who is a daughter of the original property owners, are looking forward to hosting her on their property.

He informed us that the main area of Ms Morgan's research will be the investigation into the new hybrid's susceptibility to the disease anthracnose. This is currently managed with an integrated approach: orchard hygiene, fungicides and nutrients. Ms Morgan's work in genetic tolerance will be highly beneficial to the McLaren program.

The McLarens are also working with the Mexican Mango Growers' Association whose program to develop and evaluate breeding systems and technologies that improve the efficiency of mango breeding has seen them take the position of second highest exporter worldwide.

Russell slowly folded the newspaper and left it neatly on the table. He stood, picked up his chair and threw it at the wall.

Luckily, the security guard was in the other room, and by the time he came into the reading room to see what the noise was, Russell had collected the chair and was standing by the table.

'What was that?' he demanded.

Russell frowned innocently. 'What was what?'

'That bang.'

'I didn't hear anything.'

The guard stared at him for a moment and then went back to the other room.

Russell calmed his breathing and focused on what was ahead. It appeared that Dean was ready to carry out his instructions. His mouth was dry and he craved a Glenfiddich in one of his crystal glasses. With a frustrated sigh, he headed for the communal area where he could make himself a cup of tea.

A smile finally lifted his lips as he told himself over and over, the day he read of Ellie Porter's death in the *NT News* would be the day his life began again.

Chapter 3

McLaren Mango Farm – early May
Cy

Cy Prescott drove in through the gates of the McLaren's property, and when he reached the house, he drove over to the shed about a hundred metres further on. As close as he'd been to the Porter family before he'd moved away, Cy had never been to the mango farm. He'd been closer to Ryan until Joe—he couldn't think of him as Dad after what he'd done to Ryan and Dee—had tried to burn down the donga he'd thought Dee was in, and then had shot at them from a cliff high up in Hidden Valley. Joe had been charged with a number of offences, both current and historic, and had been sentenced to twenty years in prison.

Having a father who'd been convicted of murder was a stigma that Cy had trouble living with. When he was the only manager who was laid off at the wharf, he was sure it was because of his old man being in the Darwin Correctional Centre.

His cousin, Ryan Porter-Carey, half-brother to Ellie and her two sisters and brother-in-law to Kane McClaren, had tried to convince Cy on a number of occasions that he should bear no responsibility for his father's actions.

'Mate, it's nothing to do with you,' Ryan had insisted when he'd called him about the job at the mango farm. 'And no one will judge you. It's your father's guilt, not yours.'

'What if it's in my genes? My old man shot at your Dee and Ellie McClaren and left her baby on the road.'

'How old are you now, Cy?'

'You know I'm twenty-nine.'

'And how many crimes have you committed?'

Cy hesitated. 'I smoked dope once when I was at school.'

'So did I,' Ryan said.

'Get away,' Cy said with a chuckle. 'I thought you were a model student.'

'You were a right pain in the arse when you worked here, whenever there was a female around, trying to be the tough guy, but you grew out of that.'

'I'm pleased you noticed.'

'Seriously, Cy, I want you to consider this job. It's only for a couple of months and Kane really needs someone he can rely on, and I vouched for you. The job's yours if you want it.'

Cy had hesitated. 'I was heading back to the Kimberley, and it pisses me off that I feel as though I have to stay around here.'

'Why do you have to stay?'

'Because the old man's crook.'

'I'm sorry. I didn't know that.'

'Don't be sorry. He deserves it after what he did in his lifetime. The prognosis isn't good. As much as I hate him, I think I should do the right thing and hang around until . . . until, you know.'

'You're a good man, Cy and don't ever let anyone tell you any different.'

'All right. Tell Kane I'll take the job.'

'Great. Now, when can you start?'

Cy chuckled but it held no mirth. 'Today. Would you believe I've finished up at the wharf and moved out of my flat? The lease was up for renewal and I couldn't see the point.'

'Where are you staying?'

'In a cabin in a caravan park at Howard Springs. It's the closest to the jail. Money's not an issue. I managed to get a fair bit away when I was working for the export company.'

'You'll enjoy looking after Kane's place, and he told me even though he'd pay you a salary, he's happy for you to come down and give me a hand, a couple of days a week.'

'That's awesome. I've missed the cattle work. It'll be good to get in the saddle again.'

'Rightio. Turn up there late tomorrow afternoon. It's just past Marrakai, so not far for you to go back to the jail, if you need to. Are you visiting Joe?'

'I've been twice and it looks like he'll be sent to the hospital in town. Has to have a prison guard, but he's so bloody crook, he couldn't hurt a fly.'

'I'm sorry to hear that, Cy.'

'Don't bother.'

There was silence for a few seconds, and then Ryan spoke again. 'I'll give you a call in a week or so when you get settled.'

So, now here he was, at the mango farm. When Cy had called Kane to formally accept the job, Kane had described where the farm was and where to find the key to the shed in a magnetic box underneath the water tank.

'We'll be home late afternoon. I'll see you then, Cy, and thanks so much for taking on the job. Just to fill you in, there'll be another worker in the shed with you. A horticulturist, Tarni Morgan, but your roles won't overlap. I'll tell you more tomorrow.'

Cy wasn't impressed that he was working with a woman. Ryan had nailed it on the phone. Cy knew he'd been a bit of a lair when it came to women. Up until a few years ago, anyway.

Growing up without a mother had made things tough for him as a kid; he and Joe had lived rough. They'd moved around a lot and when Joe had gone back to Ryan's place to work as station cook when Cy was in his late teens, Cy had headed far west and worked as a ringer on a few big stations near Lake Argyle. He'd sown his wild oats, and he'd been a cocky little bugger. He'd been sat on his bum a few times over those years when he'd overstepped the mark. Not knowing any better, he thought he had to big-note himself and make himself obvious before anyone would take any notice of him.

He knew that Ellie McLaren hadn't been impressed with him when he'd met her out at Ryan's *Wilderness Station* a few years back. She'd been flying the helicopter for the muster and he'd been a smart arse, cracking his whip, showing off, trying to get attention.

Embarrassment flooded through him.

He'd apologise to Ellie when he saw her in a couple of days and tell her that he wouldn't cause any trouble on their farm; he'd grown out of that stupid behaviour.

What Joe had done had made him grow up virtually overnight, and had changed him; Cy felt as though he was adrift in the world. Ryan had been great and kept him grounded as best he could, but no one could understand what he was going through unless they'd been there themselves.

His doctor had suggested counselling, but Cy had seen that as a weakness. When he'd lost his job at the export company his self-confidence had taken another huge hit. He might look like a tough cowboy; all those years in the sun had weathered his face and he'd refused to let his body go soft when he had an office job. He'd worked out at the City Gym every night after work and weekends to fill in the time, and been pleasantly surprised at how quickly he'd bulked up. So, the image of the big tough guy remained. But it was all a front.

Sometimes inside, he felt as weak as a kitten.

Working with this horticulturalist woman and sharing the kitchen with her was going to be a pain; he'd just keep to himself. Maybe get his butane stove and his camping fridge out and set them up in the shed if there was room. He'd check it out when he got back.

Then when she arrived, he'd speak when he had to, put his head down and do his job.

Cy locked the car and pocketed his keys and the key to the shed. Kane had warned him about keeping everything on the place secure and locking up when he was down in the orchard. The property was on the Arnhem Highway, the main road from Darwin to Kakadu, and was always busy. Cy understood; he wasn't prepared to risk anything after what Joe had done. He knew how people could appear innocent and hide murderous and criminal intent. After the experience with his father and with Kane's experience eight years ago, he could well understand his need for security. Cy was willing to oblige.

He headed off down into the trees to check out his new workplace. At the back of the shed was a pen with two dogs. He crouched down and let them sniff his hand and soon both tails were wagging.

How good would it be to own fertile land like this? Cy was used to the red dust of outlying stations. As he walked through the avenues of healthy trees, he marvelled at the lush green grass beneath them. He headed down to a dam he'd spotted at the back of the property and noticed irrigation pipes heading underground, they must go to the orchard. The land was almost coastal with its lush grass and healthy trees, and smelled fresh and clean. He was more used to the smell of cattle.

Cy turned and had a good look; sure enough, there was a rise along each side of the avenues. Just far enough in to allow a vehicle or a tractor to drive through without damaging them. The pipes were buried and now that he looked more closely, he could see a circular black sprinkler every thirty metres or so. The pipes were buried and ran from the dam down every avenue of about fifty trees.

A slick setup. Tidy, he liked that. Cy was keen to see what the brief for his job was when Kane met with him later. Maybe a property like this was something to think about. He could run a few cattle on fifty acres. Anticipation rose at the thought of trying something new as he walked back through the trees to the shed.

At the homestead end of each avenue of trees, a flowering rose bush climbed an arch-shaped frame, and he raised his eyebrows in surprise. He didn't think things like that grew so well out here, but when he thought about it, Ryan's mother, his Aunty Suzanne, had had a rose garden at *Wilderness Station* when she was alive. When Joe had taken him to visit Ryan when they were kids, he and Ryan had been banned from playing in the front garden, but the soft green grass had been too much of a temptation for two young boys who were more used to red dust and dirt.

Cy stared at the pink rose bush. If she'd still been alive, Aunty Suzanne would have been devastated to know her little brother was in jail for murder.

Chapter 4

Makowa Resort – Saturday afternoon, mid-May
Tarni

Tarni Morgan waited in the queue at the reception desk of the Makowa Resort. A tourist coach had driven in as she turned off the Kakadu Highway on the second last leg of her long journey, and by the time she'd parked her Jeep and taken her suitcase out of the back, the passengers on the coach had disembarked and raced over to reception.

With a sigh, she joined the end of the queue of people asking questions and booking tours, patiently waiting her turn. She'd driven almost four hundred kilometres from Mataranka today and exhaustion crept through her entire body. All she wanted was a cup of tea, a shower, and a soft bed. She'd stayed the night at Mataranka because she'd heard of the restorative properties of the hot springs, but when she'd walked through the bush to Bitter Springs, she'd been disappointed by the smell and the floating moss in the water and had decided not to go in. She couldn't afford to get sick again.

She'd opted to spend two nights at the Makowa resort to recharge her batteries. Over the last week, she'd traversed the country from Adelaide north. She'd almost completed the bottom-to-top highway and when she took a day to go into Darwin from the McClaren's farm, she would have made it from coast to coast. Almost four thousand kilometres; her body felt every one of them tonight.

Strange how a bad life experience could affect you physically. When Jonty had been killed, Tarni had been numb for weeks. She'd refused any medication because she saw that as weak. She kept going to the research centre and buried herself in work. She didn't have to face sympathy there, because she'd never shared any personal details with the staff. They hadn't known she'd once had a partner, and they didn't need to know that he was gone now.

Unusually, tears welled in her eyes and she blinked. This afternoon her body was weak, and she knew she needed rest and meditation. Finally, she reached the head of the queue and the check-in process was quick and trouble-free.

'Ms Morgan, I'm so sorry you had such a long wait. Can I organise for a hot drink to be waiting for you in your room?' the pretty young indigenous receptionist asked.

'Oh, that would be wonderful.' She glanced at the woman's badge. 'Thank you, Heather, for being so thoughtful.'

'My pleasure. Would you like me to book you into the restaurant for dinner?'

'No. I'm going to have an early night.'

'A word of advice. If you are going to use room service for dinner, order before five, and you won't have to wait long.'

'Are there any tours I can assist you with?'

'Thank you, but no. I'm just passing through. A rest stop on the way north.'

Once she was handed the key and an outline of the resort services had been passed over, Heather gestured to the concierge.

'Adam will show you to your room, and carry your luggage. Enjoy your stay.'

'Thank you. A two-night stay will be good.'

As she turned to follow the concierge, Heather called after her, and she paused. 'If you don't want to take a tour, there are several walks in the brochures I've given you. Stay on the boardwalks and you won't have to be wary of crocodiles.'

'Crocodiles? This far inland?'

'Yes, that surprises a lot of our guests. But don't worry, we've never had one in the grounds.'

'I'm very pleased to hear that.'

Tarni covered a yawn as she followed the young man to her room.

Chapter 5

Dru and Connor's apartment - Darwin Harbourside - Saturday afternoon, mid-May.
The Porter family

Ellie glanced into the back of their Sahara Land Cruiser as they pulled up in the guest parking area at the back of the harbourside apartment block in Darwin. As promised, Dru had organised a family barbecue. It was the same apartment she'd bought before she'd met Connor after moving back to the Territory from Dubai.

James was trying to undo his seatbelt; Verity was talking to her doll, and Matilda was sound asleep in her car seat.

'That'd be right.' Ellie grumbled as she turned to Kane when he switched the ignition off. 'Tilly's finally gone to sleep and now we have to get her out of the seat. Neither of the other pair hated being in the car like she does.'

The last fifteen minutes of the drive had been in peace apart from James' constant questions. 'What's that, Dad? Why does that happen, Mummy?'

Ellie wondered how much longer he would call her Mummy. He was growing up too fast.

'She might stay asleep if I lift her out carefully,' Kane said.

'And what world do you live in?' Ellie chuckled. 'She's waking up already.'

'But she'll be happy as soon as she's out of the car, won't you sweetie?' He leaned over and tickled Matilda under the chin, and she gurgled back at him.

'Was that a *Dada*?' he asked with a smile.

'No, it wasn't. Tilly's too young to talk yet, silly.'

'I'd disagree,' Kane said with a wide smile. 'She's very advanced for her age.'

Ellie grinned at him, unclipped her belt and climbed out. She opened the back door and James slid out, and then she reached over to the middle and unclipped Verity's belt.

'Can I bring Adora, Mummy?' Verity held up her baby doll.

'Of course, you can, sweetie. Wait beside the car until Daddy's unpacked our gear.' She glanced over at Kane. He'd taken Matilda out and was unloading the back of the car one-handed. Sometimes Ellie felt as though she was living a surreal life. After her days as a helicopter pilot, and the horrendous times they went through after Dad's murder, she occasionally felt as though she was now living in a fairyland. A gorgeous husband she adored, three beautiful children, and a successful mango farm, not to mention leaving for the United States and Mexico on Monday. Her nightmares about those times and Russell Fairweather were mostly in the past now. When she got into bed now, she slept soundly until Matilda woke up.

Kane almost had everything out of the car: the stroller, the bag of toys and spare clothes, and most importantly, the pavlova that Ellie had spent most of the morning baking and decorating—when she should have been packing. He clicked the remote to bring the back door down and then when he was sure everyone was out, he locked the car.

'Quick, Els. Take your pav before it overbalances.' After he passed the domed Tupperware container to her, Kane juggled holding James' hand, Matilda, and the stroller with the bags loaded into it.

'I can take something else for you,' Ellie said as she checked that Verity was still standing beside the car.

'You look after that pavlova. It has to get upstairs without sloshing.'

'My pavs don't slosh!'

'Well, without getting dropped,' he said with an apologetic smile. 'I'm addicted to your pavlovas, my love.'

'You're forgiven then.'

Kane nodded towards the cars that drove in as they started walking, and they both paused. 'Here's Emma and Jeremy now.'

'And Mum and Graysen. Great timing.'

'You've got a bit of a load there, McLarens,' Jeremy, Emma's husband, called through his open window.

'I bet you've got more.'

Jeremy laughed. 'We travel light.'

'I wish,' Kane said.

Between the three sisters with Dru's Ruby, Emma's Akasha, and Dee and Ryan's twin boys, Angus and Wyatt, Ellie's three: James, Verity and Matilda, Ellie knew Mum would be in seventh heaven this afternoon. They didn't get together as often as they should.

She grinned over at the Lexus parked at the back of the car park. Just as well there were a few visitor parking spots allocated in the basement car park; the family had filled it up today.

Mum opened the passenger door of their luxury Lexus sedan and hurried over. 'Hello, my baby. I've missed you so much.'

'Mum, it's only been five days,' Emma said as she lifted Akasha out.

'Yes, but you all get to see them every day and I don't.' Sandra grinned as she swooped down and kissed Akasha, and then turned her attention to Ellie's three.

'James, I'll swear you've grown since last weekend.'

'He has; plus, Mum, you get to talk to them on the phone every day, *and* FaceTime too.' Ellie leaned over to kiss her mother's cheek and smiled at Graysen as he relieved Kane of some of his load. 'How are you anyway, Mum?'

'I'm good. We've been busy packing and I'm so happy to see all of my munchkins together before we leave for Africa.'

'How long now?' Ellie asked as Sandra took Matilda from Kane.

'We tried to time it to coincide with your trip so we'd be back by the time you get home. You're gone for six weeks, aren't you?'

'Could be a little bit longer now,' Ellie said as they all headed towards the lift in the basement. Jeremy buzzed the security intercom, and Dru answered immediately.

'I'll unlock the gate for you.'

As they waited, Sandra bent down to James. 'Can I have a cuddle, Jamie?'

'Nan! Cuddles are for girls. I shake hands.'

Sandra shook her head. 'Nanny's not going to see you for ages and ages, so I need a big nanny cuddle.'

James pulled a face. 'Later, when you put Tilly down.'

'I'll look forward to that, young man. Oh, and wait until you see the present for you in my bag. I thought I'd better get it early, seeing as you'll have your birthday while you're away.'

'Oh wow, Nan, I do love you heaps.' James wrapped his arms around Sandra's legs as they waited for the lift to arrive.

Ellie grinned over his head at her mother. 'You used the magic word, Mum.'

Sandra chuckled. 'You used to love your presents too.'

Emma smiled as they waited to get into the lift. 'Do you think we'll all fit in? At the rate they're all growing we're going to need a second lift when we come to visit Dru and Connor.'

'When they grow, my love, we won't have to carry bags of clothes and strollers and toys,' Jeremy said. 'I'm pleased that Dru and Connor organised lunch here today. I haven't seen Connor for ages.'

Worry rose in Ellie's chest; she'd spoken to Dru on the phone a couple of times since Dru had shared her worry, but without asking outright, she hadn't been able to get any indication if Dru had spoken to Connor.

It wasn't any of her business. She knew that couples went through their ups and downs, and Connor was a hard worker, and he had a very stressful work-intensive job with his security firm. Dru mentioned in one of the calls that Connor was in a complex investigation with Greg, his former colleague. Greg and Connor had been in the Federal Police together before Dru had met him; they'd met when Connor had been hired to investigate a diamond theft at the mine in the East Kimberley where Dru had worked as an engineer.

Greg lived out in the bush at Wyndham so she could understand that Connor would often be away in Western Australia. Even though they had an office in Darwin where Connor met clients, Greg had preferred to remain a hermit in his shack at Wyndham where he had the most incredible array of computers. They had built a solid reputation and were always busy. His work was complex and Ellie hoped that that was all that was taking up his time.

She was going to check Dru and Connor out surreptitiously today and see what their interaction was like. She'd kept her word to Dru, and not mentioned a word to Kane or her sisters.

As much as she loved her sister, and Connor as well, their relationship wasn't any of her business. If they were having issues, it was up to them to sort it out, and she and the rest of the family would be there to support them if needed.

'Pingggggg!'' James made a high-pitched pinging sound when the lift slowed before it stopped at the top floor of the apartment block. The real ping followed immediately.

'I knew we were here. I beat the ping. I beat the ping.'

Sandra ruffled his hair. 'You are such a clever little man, James McLaren.'

'I wonder if Ruby's here, I like playing with her.'

'Of course, she will be,' Ellie said. 'It's not a kindy day. You know that.'

Dru must have heard the lift arrive because the front door was open. Even though they were in a secure block, she was still super-conscious about safety after her experiences in Dubai and Darwin before she and Connor got married. Dru had taken a long time to recover; she was fine with the family, but as she had always been since they lost their father when she was in her teens, Dru could be a bit of a loner.

Connor had been great for her and had pulled her out of her introspection, and Ellie knew that he would never let her sister down.

She hoped he wouldn't anyway.

'Come in,' Dru called from the balcony. 'We're out here. Oh, and Ryan rang. He and Dee can't make it, unfortunately. Something about a pump problem somewhere.'

'That's a shame, but we saw them yesterday. They called in on their way back from Darwin. They'd been to buy a new pump for the house water, so I hope it's not that one,' Kane said.

Ellie walked through the apartment marvelling at her sister's efficiency. The minimalist space was always so clean and tidy, with everything in its place. She tried hard at their new house out on the farm but there were always toys scattered around the floor, piles of clothes for folding, and Vegemite finger marks always on the kitchen cupboards and fridge, no matter how many times she seemed to wipe them.

When she reached the living area that led out onto the deck, Mum was hugging Dru. She stepped back and frowned. 'Have you lost weight, Drusilla?'

'I always know I'm in trouble when you call me Drusilla.'

'*You've* lost weight.' Sandra followed her arms. 'But your baby bump has grown.'

'I think the baby is going to be a big one. He's taking all the food I eat,' Dru chuckled but to Ellie, it sounded forced.

'Where's Connor?' Sandra asked looking around.

'He got called to a meeting in Casuarina with Greg and their client,' Dru answered. 'I figured you could all stay for dinner as well as lunch if you wanted to see him too.'

'Oh, you should have changed the day,' Sandra said. 'We could have come tomorrow.'

'No, it would've been too hard for Ellie and Kane.'

'That's right, we leave Monday, Mum. And we can't stay late, Dru. We've got a heap to do, and the horticulturist is arriving in the morning.' Dru met Ellie's eyes and she noticed Dru had more makeup on than usual. She couldn't see her sister's eyes through her dark glasses, but she suspected Dru had been crying.

Damn. That didn't bode well.

'Do you need a hand in the kitchen?' Ellie asked.

'All good. You keep an eye on Ruby for me, and I'll call when I need a hand to carry dishes out. Kane, would you fire up the barbeque for me?'

'Sure. Come on, Jeremy. We'll be the barbeque kings.'

Half an hour later, they were all sitting around the large table on the deck overlooking Darwin Harbour. The table was covered with enough food for a dozen more guests with steak, sausages, and onions on a big tray, and several salads, as well as two trays of fresh baked bread. Dru had set two small tables for the children, and Ellie had Matilda on her lap.

'You amaze me, Dru. Is that homemade bread?' Emma asked.

'Nothing amazing about that. It's time management, Em. Connor left at about six and I stayed up after we had breakfast together. I insisted that he had the omelette I cooked because he's got a bad habit of eating on the run. So, I was able to cook the bread and make the salads before Ruby woke up.'

Ellie wondered what sort of meeting would start in the suburbs at six in the morning, but didn't comment. She glanced at Dru but the sun was behind her and it was hard to see her expression. The sunglasses had stayed on, even when Ellie had gone into the kitchen to help her carry out the salads.

'I bumped into Connor in town a couple of days ago. I thought he'd lost a bit of weight,' Graysen commented.

'Yes, that's why I'm feeding him up,' Dru said. 'He works too hard.'

'Graysen, tell me about this African project you've picked up,' Ellie asked, with another glance at Dru. She didn't want her to break into tears in front of everyone.

'I'm quite excited about it.' Graysen leaned forward. 'I've been contracted by *National Geographic* to do a series on lions. Have you heard of the tree-climbing lions?'

'At Lake Manyara. They climb the trees apparently to get away from the wet ground,' Sandra chimed in. 'We're going on a personal safari in Tanzania. Sorry, love.' She touched Graysen's hand. 'I didn't mean to interrupt, but I haven't been this excited since I set off for the Larapinta trek.'

'Are you camping out?' Emma asked with a shiver. 'All those wild animals!'

'No, we stay in lodges and have all our meals—' Sandra broke off as Dru's phone rang. Dru picked it up off the table.

'Oh, it's Connor. Excuse me for a moment.'

Ellie watched as Dru hurried inside, phone pressed to her ear and talking quietly. 'If you hadn't done that trek, Mum, you wouldn't have met Graysen. I had so much trouble imagining Mum in a tent in the bush, Graysen,' Emma said.

'Your mother's learned a lot of new skills,' Graysen said.

Emotion overwhelmed Ellie; she thought back to the years after their father had supposedly committed suicide when Mum had been a shell of her old self. Ellie and Emma had cared so much for Sandra and assisted her through some dreadful times. It was only when they discovered Dad had been murdered and justice was served that Sandra had begun to heal.

Ellie looked up and held Graysen's eyes. She spoke quietly as conversations swirled around them. 'Do you realise how much you've done for Mum? You've brought happiness back to her life. We watched her heal, but after she met you at Larapinta, she's back to the woman she was before. She's strong and involved in things now, but most of all, Graysen, you have absolutely brought her back to that happy and loving mother I had when I was growing up. And I'd like to thank you for that.'

'It's a two-way street, Ellie. I wasn't in a good place when I met your mum either, but I think we've both done okay and being accepted and welcomed into your family has been wonderful for me. I feel like *my* life is complete now. I have a woman I love with all my heart, four wonderful stepchildren and their partners, not to mention seven grandchildren.'

'And one on the way,' Sandra said.

'And one on the way,' Ellie said as Emma smiled and nudged Jeremy. He gestured to Dru and shook his head a little.

Hmm. Maybe two on the way, Ellie wondered. She really hoped so. Emma had a hard time falling pregnant with Akasha. She turned back to Graysen. 'Now we've done all the soppy stuff, tell us more about this safari you're taking Mum on.'

As Graysen filled in the details of the African safari, Dru came back to the table and sat quietly, focusing on the salad on her plate. She jumped up again when the intercom buzzed.

The balcony was noisy with children and the conversation of the adults.

'Mum, can you hold, Tilly please?' Ellie said. 'I'll go and help Dru get the pavlova out.'

Sandra smiled and took her youngest grandchild onto her lap and Ellie followed Dru inside. Her sister was standing rigid by the intercom, one hand over her eyes. Ellie hurried across to her,

'Dru? Is everything okay?'

'Yes, it was just someone who wanted to visit, but I told him I had visitors.'

Ellie's eyes narrowed.

Dru's voice rose. 'Oh, God, Ellie, don't go thinking I'm having an affair too. It was Greg. Connor told me they were together today. From six o'clock this morning.' Her voice was bitter, but strong. 'Connor was lying to me, and I think that's the final proof I need.' Her lip quivered and her eyes filled with tears, and Ellie reached out and put her arms around her.

'Dru, don't jump to conclusions. I'm sure there's a very good reason. He's probably on some super-secret case or something he's involved in through that agency that hires him sometimes.'

'No. Greg wanted to come and see me and find out what was going on with Connor. And for Greg to do that, it's big. You know what he's like. A loner, but he stands by Connor; he's as loyal as. Connor could do anything and Greg would stand by him, but he's shutting Greg out too. I'm right, he's having an affair. That's the only explanation. If Greg is asking *me* what's wrong, there is something very, very bad happening. And the phone call? That was Connor and he told me that they hadn't finished and that he and *Greg* had to go away tonight. He said to say hello to everyone— 'her voice finally broke— 'and to apologise for being away. He *lied* to me, Ellie. He doesn't love me anymore. I've just got to toughen up and get over it.'

'No, Dru.' Ellie kept her voice calm as her emotions swirled tumultuously. She was starting to think maybe Connor was guilty of something. He was certainly acting strangely. 'You have to talk to him.'

'We've always talked. He's always been up front with me about what he's working on, Ellie. He knows he can trust me. I don't say anything to anyone. He shut down about six weeks ago and I can't reach him, no matter how hard I try. He doesn't even come into our bed some nights. He says he has to work late and then I wake up alone the next morning. He says it's because I need my sleep and he didn't want to disturb me when he came to bed. He's never ever done that before so I know there's something wrong.' She closed her eyes and her lips drew together for a moment. 'And you know what doesn't happen when you're not in the same bed, don't you? I haven't even seen him with his clothes off for weeks, and he's started locking the bathroom door when he's showering. It's got to be my fault. I'm too cold for him. I mustn't be a good enough wife or maybe I'm not a good enough mother either.'

'Dru, stop it! Wake up to yourself. You need to sit down with him and find out what's going on. Ask him straight out. Please promise me you will, or I won't go away.'

Dru wiped her eyes and stood straight. She took a step away from Ellie, and the old closed-down Dru looked back at her.

'You will and you'll forget everything I told you. I'll confront him tomorrow.'

'Call me.'

Chapter 6

McLaren Mango Farm - Monday
Ellie

Ellie was quiet on the way back to the farm. The three kids were asleep in the back of the car, tired out from playing with their cousins.

Kane reached out to her and put his hand on hers. 'You okay, love?'

'Yes, just thinking about everything I have to do.'

'Your pavlova was good. Did you see Graysen had three serves?'

She forced a smile. 'I did. And did you see Mum's ecstatic smile when Emma announced she was pregnant?'

'I did.' Kane frowned. 'Was Dru okay today? She seemed a bit quiet this afternoon.'

Ellie hesitated. She'd promised, but she was also used to telling Kane everything. Finally, she spoke slowly. 'She wasn't very happy. Disappointed that Connor was working, I'd say.'

'There's nothing wrong with the baby, is there?'

'No, all good there. It's a personal matter.'

'Okay. I won't ask, but I've got a fair idea. I wasn't going to say anything because it didn't seem right.'

'What weren't you going to tell me?' Ellie turned sideways in the seat to face him. Kane's expression was troubled.

'I was in town a couple of weeks ago and I saw Connor.'

'You met up with him?'

'No. I saw him in a coffee shop. I still don't know if I should say anything. I could be jumping to conclusions.'

'Kane, tell me.'

'He was sitting with a woman, and she reached out and held his hand across the table. She looked very unhappy.'

Ellie's heart pounded painfully and her throat closed. 'Oh, shit,' she whispered. 'Did you recognise her?'

'No, she was dressed up, though. Like a professional.'

'Maybe she was a client.' Ellie turned away and looked out the window. They were not far from home and the bush flashed past as she tried to calm herself.

Dru was right.

'It's not our business, and I could be way off the mark, so please don't say anything to Dru.' Kane's voice held concern.

'She already suspects he's seeing someone else. I shouldn't tell you, but you had an idea too, so it's okay.'

They were quiet for a while, and Kane reached for her hand again. 'You okay?'

She nodded.

'I'm not going to be much help to you when we get home. Cy texted me; he's arrived and he's having a wander around the trees.'

'Oh, I thought he was coming tomorrow. I guess I'd better cook a decent meal tonight.'

'No, Els. He won't expect it. He's here as an employee and as much as he's connected to the family, you don't have to entertain him. We've got to make a start on the packing tonight.'

'I know, or we're going to miss the plane. Did you organise with Jeremy to drive us to the airport on Monday morning?'

'I did. All you have to worry about is what clothes you need to pack for you and the kids.'

'And get the house clean for the horticultural lady.'

'I'm sure she'll understand if she has to throw sheets on her bed on Monday.'

'It was such bad timing, wasn't it?'

'It was, but we can't pass up an opportunity like that. Having Tarni Morgan work on the hybrids is a coup. It's just a pain that her availability coincided with our trip to Mexico.'

'It'll all work out. I haven't even had time to ask you what exactly we'll be doing there yet.'

Kane's smile was slow and Ellie felt that familiar tug of love in her tummy.

'I've booked us into a swish hotel, and you and the kids will be relaxing every day. There's a children's playground, six swimming pools, four restaurants, room service and a laundry service. So, make sure you pack a book to read for when I'm out touring the farms.'

'Ha, ha. I don't think I've read a book since before James was born.'

'So, it's time to start.'

'I'll buy one at the airport but I'll bet you it comes home unread.'

Ellie was still amazed that they were flying overseas on Monday. She had been shocked a few months ago when Kane had come into the kitchen one night. 'How would you like a trip overseas?'

She'd replied jokingly, 'To Bali?'

'No, Mexico. It's a combination of a course and a tour for growers worldwide. They're doing so well in Mexico. The second biggest exporter of fruit in the world after Thailand now. It's a perfect time. It's the quiet time of our growing season, and we could make it a family holiday and take the kids, but it's also a business trip and I could claim it on tax.'

'Always thinking, Kane McLaren.'

'That's me,' he'd said, twirling her around in the kitchen. 'I thought we could take the kids to Disneyland in LA on the way home.'

'Let's do it!' Ellie said.

'And not only will we have a great time, but I'll also learn more about hopefully improving the hybrid fruit I've been working on. I've been reading these articles about developing and evaluating breeding systems in Mexico for the last couple of months and it sounds really good. It seems to address all the problems we have here with the hybrid. Reading about it and going to conferences isn't good enough. When I saw this tour, it fitted what we need. I can go out to the plantations and see what they're doing firsthand.'

'It sounds perfect. Yes, let's do it.' Ellie had put the tea towel down and slipped her arms around his neck. 'Wow, we're going on a trip!'

'We are.' He grinned back at her, and slipped his warm hands beneath her loose T-shirt, and then put his lips against hers.

'Whoever would've thought eight years ago,' she murmured, 'when you climbed into my helicopter, and I took an immediate dislike to the grumpy engineer, that here we'd be with three children, a successful business and talking about going overseas?'

'We've come a long way, Els, and I'd do it all over in a heartbeat.'

'So would I.' Ellie knew he was talking about how they'd purchased the farm she'd grown up on and demolished the old farmhouse before building the lovely home they now lived in. She closed her eyes and let the memories roll over her as Kane held her close. Mum making the annual winter batch of mango chutney, the yellow-stained walls above the old gas stove, her bed on the back enclosed veranda where she dreamed of learning to fly a helicopter. Sunbaking by the dam in summer with Emma and Dru, as small waves on the water made the blue plastic drums slap against the wooden short piers at the end of the jetty. The smell of Reef Oil always brought that memory back and always made her smile. Growing up with her sisters on the Porter Farm had been wonderful until Dad's dreams had become unrealistic.

The original sign from the gate had been replaced by **McLaren Mango Farm**, but the original charred timber **Porter Farm** sign graced the entrance to the work shed. Kane had retrieved it from the rubbish pile at the back of the shed where his stepfather, Panos Sordina, had thrown it. Sordina, a man whom Kane had never respected, had bought the farm from Sandra after her first husband had died. Sordina had been in Russell Fairweather's pocket.

Ellie and Dru had made the sign the first winter after Emma left for medical school. They'd almost caught the packing shed on fire, giving the sign a charred edge with Dad's blowtorch. She remembered how the wood had glowed orange and one of the mango cartons on the bench where they'd been working had burst into flame. Dru had laughed as she'd run for a bucket of water from the dam and then doused the small fire.

But the memories weren't all good. Dad hadn't been a good manager and his dreams had been bigger than his pocket. Even all these years later, Ellie could still remember the exhaustion on his face, the leaden despair that had eventually driven him to the pub most nights. It had been the beginning of the end, and when the coroner's verdict had been death by suicide, the financial and drinking evidence supported the verdict.

Mum had never believed that Dad would take his own life, and Ellie and Emma had supported her, finally uncovering the intricate web of deception and murder that Fairweather had spun. They didn't talk about those dark days very often now. Ellie knew she'd come a long way since those days.

She and Kane had both had tragedies in their lives. Russell Fairweather, the wealthy industrialist responsible for the murders of Ellie's father and Kane's stepfather, was still in jail. In the back of her mind, she always worried about when he was released, because she knew what Fairweather was like. A man who would seek revenge and would never let it go; that was the only negative in her life. She would never forget the look in his eyes when she shot him in the leg.

'You can't hide from me.' His laugh had chilled her blood and the memory never left her. She'd just learned to deal with it and not let it affect her everyday life.

The lingering worry sitting in the back of her mind was that one day he would harm her family. His greed had led to many deaths, and the disintegration of more than one family; she knew Fairweather would never let it go. One day he would seek revenge.

Ellie shivered in Kane's arms and he lifted his head. 'Second thoughts?'

'No . . . no, I think a family holiday is a fabulous idea.'

'I'm pleased. It will be a great break for you. Don't worry about packing tonight. I'll help you tomorrow. I'll spend some time with Cy when we get home, make sure he's got everything he needs, and give him a key to the house so he can use the kitchen. I'll have to make sure he sees the part of the shed I've set up for Tarni's lab, and I've put in all the equipment she needs.'

'Has Cy got any experience with our sort of farming?'

'Ryan assured me he can turn his hand to anything. He said Cy's a hard and loyal worker, and that's enough for me. You're not judging him by his father, are you, Els?'

'No. Not at all. You know I trust you with our farm, Kane.'

##

Two days later, Ellie woke early and rolled over onto her back, staring at the ceiling. She came out of sleep slowly watching through half-closed eyes as the first fingers of dawn crept through the window.

Her eyes flew open. This morning they were leaving for the airport to catch their flight to LA! Excitement rushed through her, followed by the immediate realisation of the chores she still had to do. The first one was to make up the guest bedroom and pick some roses to put in there. Then the last of the folding, ironing, and packing.

She smiled, unable to believe that she, Kane, and the three kids were doing this. She rolled slowly onto her side and looked at her sleeping husband beside her. The wrinkles that had started to surround his eyes were less defined in sleep, and his long lashes lay on his cheeks as he breathed deeply.

A rush of love for Kane, her soul mate and the father of her children, overwhelmed Ellie. He was her world.

Life was good.

Stop mooning over your husband of eight years and get moving, she told herself. If she didn't hurry up and get out of bed, they wouldn't be ready when Jeremy came. She was almost ready, just the last few items from yesterday's wash to deal with.

Quietly slipping her legs over the edge of the bed, she stretched slowly before reaching for a light robe. Padding barefoot on the polished timber floors, she left the room silently without disturbing Kane. He'd been up late last night, spending a few hours in the shed with Cy. He'd been happy when he'd joined her for a late cuppa.

'Cy's go it all under control already. He's a fast learner. He's going to finish digging the irrigation trenches. I told him to hire a labourer to give him a hand.'

'I hope he and Tarni get on. He was always a bit of a ladies' man.'

'Apparently, he's settled down since Joe's been in jail.'

'Hmm,' Ellie said.

'They're grownups, stop worrying. Just focus on our trip.' Kane had wagged a finger at her.

On her way to the kitchen, Ellie paused in the doorway of each of the children's rooms.

James was sound asleep, still clutching the teddy that he always slept with.

Note to self, pack Teddy.

Verity was on her tummy with her bottom stuck up in the air, the way she always slept when she was sound asleep.

Best of all Matilda's hands were curled into little fists, each thumb tucked inside her curled fingers. Ellie knew that meant her baby girl would sleep for at least another hour.

She filled the kettle in the kitchen and slid open the door to the side veranda. As she stepped outside the first shards of gold tinted the clouds to the east, and the sky was a soft apricot.

Kane always called it a mango blush colour. Dawn on the farm had always been her favourite time.

The shed was in darkness, so it looked like Cy wasn't up and about yet. Ellie stood there and breathed in the fresh cool air. There was a chill of late autumn there now, and she pulled her robe around her a little bit more tightly.

Even though they had demolished the original farmhouse that she, Emma and Dru had grown up in, the land was still the same. As she looked out, she could picture Dad out there, pruning the trees, his battered old hat sitting on the back of his head and his work pants held up with his favourite leather belt.

If she closed her eyes, she could imagine Mum walking down to the trees with Dad's cuppa. It had been the first thing she'd done every morning. Like Ellie, Dad had loved the dawn and in the early days that was when he'd started work.

'Best time of the day, Ellie,' he'd told her, and she'd always followed the same routine. Even after a rugged night with all of the kids when they were babies, she was still up before sunrise.

Even though Dad had passed, there was still a sense of him on the farm, and Ellie knew how hard it was for Mum to come out here. When she was with Graysen she still had the memories of those happy years.

A door closed quietly in the house and she went back into the kitchen; there was too much to do, and she couldn't stand outside daydreaming all day. Jeremy was coming down from Darwin to collect them around ten a.m., leaving his car here and taking them up in their Land Cruiser to the airport. Excitement bubbled up, and Ellie smiled as the jug boiled and she poured the hot water onto a teabag in her favourite teacup.

Chapter 7

McLaren Mango Farm - Monday morning
Ellie

Kane ran up the steps where Ellie was waiting on the veranda with the children. She shaded her eyes with one hand as she juggled Matilda on her hip. There was no sign of a car coming down the driveway. The only sound was the soft purr of the Land Cruiser's motor as Jeremy waited, and James' constant questions as he ran up and down the steps.

'How long will it take to get to the airport, Mum? Dad, how does a plane stay up in the air? It doesn't have blades to do the gravity thing like Mum does in her helicopter. Will Uncle Jeremy bring our car home?'

Kane brushed his fingers over Verity's hair as he passed her on the top step where she was playing with her Adora. 'At least we have one quiet child.'

'Should we keep waiting for her, or should we leave?' Ellie asked.

Kane shook his head. 'We're going to have to leave now. If we don't, we're going to be late.'

'I wonder where she is.' Ellie turned. 'James. Go and get into the car. In one of the dickie seats in the back. Have you got your book?'

'Woo hoo. I have!' He shot past his parents and took the stairs two at a time.

Kane held his hand out to Verity. 'Come on, sweetie. Time to go. Tarni's probably been held up on the highway. There's a lot of smoke on the horizon. I'd say they're burning off down on the highway on the other side of the Mary River National Park. She might have got away late too.'

Ellie followed Kane and Verity down the stairs. 'As long as she hasn't had an accident or something.'

'I've tried to call, but it's going to voicemail. The service drops out around the park. I spoke to her last night and she was at Makowa Resort, so at least we know she's close by. I've texted and told her Cy will show her around.'

'Maybe she had a leisurely breakfast,' Ellie said as Kane opened the back door behind the driver's seat for her.

'Whatever it is, everything will be fine. Our focus is getting to the airport.' Kane lifted Verity into the middle seat and secured her seatbelt.

'Did you and Jeremy load all the suitcases in the back, and the stroller?'

'We did. Jump in, Ellie. Hang on, here comes Cy. I'll just quickly let him know that Tarni's late.'

'Morning, Jeremy. Thanks for driving us.'

'We're going on an aeroplane, Uncle Jem,' James interrupted from the back of the wagon.

'I know, buddy. I wish I was too.'

'Why don't you come with us?'

'Because I have to go to work.' Jeremy turned around to the back seat and grinned at Ellie. 'Excited?'

'I am. I just have to clear my head and get into the mindset that we're actually going.'

Ellie had tried to stop worrying about Dru. She'd spoken to her on the phone last night, and Dru had seemed calm.

Kane climbed into the front seat. 'Okay, guys, we're off. Cy's fine.'

'There's a black Jeep coming down the drive,' Jeremy said as he put the car into gear.

'We've got time to say hello, haven't we, Kane?' Ellie leaned forward. 'It's a bit rude if we just get in the car and pass her on the drive.'

Kane glanced at his watch again. 'Okay. We've got three minutes. We can't risk any hold-ups along the highway into Darwin.'

'You're such a worrywart.' Ellie lowered her window and Matilda started to grizzle as the Jeep approached.

'Verity, can you play peekaboo with Tilly, sweetheart, please?'

'Adora can.' Within seconds, Matilda's grizzle had turned to her delightful giggle as Verity hid her doll around the side of the car seat and started playing a game with her baby sister.

The vehicle came to a stop beside the Land Cruiser as Kane jumped out and came around to Ellie's window. The Jeep door opened, and a tall, thin woman jumped out and hurried across to them.

'I'm so, so sorry I'm late. I was stopped at least fifteen times on the highway. They're burning off the bush.'

Ellie considered getting out but decided to greet the visitor through her window. Time was fast running out and not only that, if she got out Matilda was likely to start crying.

'It's okay,' Kane said. 'We thought that might have happened. It's that time of the year. When they burn off the savannah woodlands the highway traffic can be disrupted. Local knowledge, but look don't worry, you've caught us. I'm assuming you're Tarni Morgan. Welcome. I'm Kane and this is my wife, Ellie.'

Ellie gave the young woman a small wave through the open window. 'Hi, Tarni. I'm strapped in so I won't get out. It's great to meet you. Thanks so much for agreeing to come when we were away.'

The dark-haired woman seemed flustered. Her cheeks were pink as she shook her head. 'It's good to meet you too, but I don't want to hold you up.'

Kane held out his hand and looked over to the shed. 'We will have to leave now. Cy Prescott's our manager. He'll show you around, and get you settled. He's working at the dam down the back behind the trees.'

Tarni took the hand that Kane held out and shook it briefly. 'I'm truly regretting I didn't come down last night, but I was so tired after driving from Mataranka, I decided to stay there two nights.'

Ellie had only seen Cy briefly since he'd arrived on Saturday night. He'd been extremely polite and seemed to be a very different man to the brash cowboy she'd met mustering at Ryan's place a few years back. She hadn't seen him since Ryan and Dee's wedding.

Tarni wasn't what she'd expected either. She'd imagine someone more outdoorsy. The newcomer was so fair it looked like she hadn't ever been in the sun. Dark shadows sat beneath her eyes, and she was very thin. She looked as though the first puff of wind would blow her away. Ellie wondered if she'd been ill.

'Cy's looking after the place while we're away,' Kane said. 'I've asked him to show you the work shed where you can set up all your gear. He knows the trees you'll be working with. I've taken him around the last couple of days and he's got a good handle on it. He's sort of a relative of the family, but he's going to bunk in the shed so you'll have your own space in the house.'

'I hope it suits you,' Ellie chimed in. 'He'll be sharing the kitchen with you. I've stocked up the fridge and cupboards for both you and Cy, so just make yourself at home.'

Tarni's flush deepened. 'Really, you didn't have to do that.'

'We're a long way from the shops.'

'I'll replace what I use when I go to the city.'

'Don't worry about that,' Ellie said. 'Honestly. Make yourself at home. Get yourself settled inside before Cy comes up.'

'I'll give you a call before we take off in case you've got any questions,' Kane said. 'We've got to hit the road.'

'Have a great trip,' Tarni said. 'I'll be keen to hear what you see over there.'

'We've left the front door open for you, so make yourself at home. The guest room is at the far end of the hall,' Ellie said as Kane went around to the passenger side of the vehicle. 'And you have an ensuite.'

'Thank you. Um . . . again, I'm so sorry I was late. It's good to meet you, Ellie. I look forward to seeing you when you get back.'

Ellie raised her eyebrows. 'So, you'll still be here when we get back?'

'Yes, the Institute has extended my research to a three-month secondment until the end of winter. Of course, I won't stay in the house when you come back, I'll move into town and travel down.'

'Don't worry about it,' Ellie said. 'We'll sort all that out when we get home. You just enjoy living here.'

'Um . . . I'm sure I will.' Tarni's voice shook as she glanced past Ellie to Verity and Matilda, and a flicker of sadness crossed her face. 'Thank you so much for being so welcoming.'

Ellie wondered if Tarni *would* still be here when they got back. Tarni Morgan wasn't at all what she had expected.

Chapter 8

McLaren Mango Farm -Monday morning
Tarni

Tarni felt totally out of her comfort zone as Ellie and Kane brushed off her apologies for being late. She felt even more foolish as she stumbled over every sentence that she uttered. Ellie and Kane McClaren welcomed her warmly and brushed off her apologies. How unprofessional and what an awful first impression to make. She'd known they were flying out today, and she should've left even earlier, but the last thing she'd expected was the fires on the highway and the numerous stop-and-go signs that had made her arrival an hour and a half later than she'd calculated. She bit her lip and turned her attention back to Ellie who was still talking to her.

'The coffee maker's on and there's some fruitcake in the pantry for morning tea. The washing machine is easy to use. There's washing powder in the laundry. I've made your bed up and there's spare linen and towels in the hall cupboard outside your door. Please make yourself totally at home.'

'Thank you. I'll find my way around. You didn't have to put me up in your house.'

Kane leaned forward and called to her out of the driver's window. Tarni smiled at Ellie and moved around to the passenger window on the other side.

'I forgot to say your supplies arrived about four days ago. The boxes are just all stacked up there. Stay in touch by email. If you have any questions about the mangoes or where I've been working just email me. I'll be online every day. Wi-Fi password is on the fridge.'

'That's fine, Kane. I know exactly what you're up to from your application, and I know what our objectives are. If I do need to know anything, I'll email you. Thank you so much for providing your farm as an opportunity for me to further my research.'

Finally, she managed to sound coherent.

Kane went to speak, but the driver interrupted. 'Hi, I'm Jeremy and I'm going to have to be rude and take this lot to the airport now if they want to go to Mexico.'

She smiled and stepped back as he started the vehicle and a throaty roar surrounded her.

'Thank you for coming,' Kane called as the car pulled away. 'If we can achieve what we're aiming for, it's going to be a game changer for mango production at our farm.'

His words faded as the vehicle pulled away.

Tarni stood there and watched as the bronze four-wheel drive disappeared over the hill. Silence surrounded her and all was still. The anxiety of being in a new place tugged at her as it always had recently, and she pushed it back. It wouldn't take long to settle, and she would be fine once she was immersed in her work.

I will be.

There was no sign of the manager; Tarni stood there for a long time before she turned to the house. As she opened the screen door, a puff of dust rising from the drive near the highway caught her eye, and she wondered if they'd forgotten something. She waited on the veranda, with the house keys in her hand; a large black ute crested the hill between the house and the highway. She frowned; Kane had indicated that the dam was in the other direction. Tarni waited as the vehicle approached. A short and stocky guy climbed out and looked up at the house. Tarni walked across and stood at the top of the steps.

'Hi there,' he called up the steps.

Feeling uncomfortable, she walked down the stairs. 'Cy?'

Tarni was reassured when he grinned at her. He was a young guy about her age, dressed in clean work clothes. 'No, I'm Jerry White. Sorry to interrupt you.'

'What can I do for you? My husband is just a little way into the orchard,' she said, not wanting him to know that she was alone there.

'I'm working my way around the Territory. I'm looking for work wherever I can pick it up and I was wondering if you had anything going here at your farm.'

Tarni nodded. 'I can ask my husband for you and certainly take your details. I know he was talking about hiring somebody for some trench digging.'

Jerry had a pleasant face, and he smiled back at her. 'Sounds right up my alley. Anyway, I'm staying at the Marrakai pub so I'll give you my card. No problem if there's nothing. I'm just moving from property to property putting my name down in case someone is looking.'

Positivity shone from his eyes and Tarni couldn't help smiling back. 'Well, Jerry. I'll certainly pass it on.'

He handed her a small card with his name and mobile phone number on it. Tarni glanced at it; there was a list of the sort of work that he could do.

Tarni nodded. 'I'll pass it on for you.'

'Much appreciated, Mrs McLaren.'

She must have looked surprised because he gestured at the road to the gate. 'I saw your name on the sign at the gate. My mum always taught me to be polite.'

With another nod, she stood in the doorway and watched as he went back to his car. He turned and waved, climbed in and drove out.

Slipping the card in her pocket, she made a mental note to give it to the manager when she met him.

Chapter 9

McLaren Mango Farm - Monday morning
Cy

Cy unloaded the last pipe from the back of the ute and looked around; it would probably take him about three days to dig the trenches and get all those pipes in. One established avenue of trees needed irrigation pipes added, and Kane had also drawn him a plan for more trenches to be dug, where pipes were to be laid for the spring planting of more trees.

'We'll be putting in the new hybrid seedlings that the research assistant will be propagating. Hopefully, we'll get them in this spring. It'll be a great help if you can get the new irrigation pipes in and prepare the soil.' Kane had gone on to explain the various fertilisers to be added to the soil.

Cy was pleased he had a physical job to begin his time at the farm while he got his head around the other stuff that needed doing. He was hoping he handled it well; looking after trees was very different to looking after cattle. He'd thought it would be a lot easier, but following Kane around the farm yesterday had been an eye-opener. There was a lot to be done; maybe he wouldn't have time to help Ryan out when he was mustering.

'Don't worry, Kane. If I have any questions, I'll be in touch. I'll make your place a priority.'

'There'll be time to help Ryan out. Go over to the Marrakai pub, and put a sign on the community noticeboard when you're ready for some labouring help. For a small job like that, cash in hand will be fine. It'll save you the problem of going through all the forms and tax stuff. What's your birth date?'

Cy had frowned at him. '*My* birth date?'

Kane grinned at him and pushed his Akubra back with one hand. 'I've left enough cash in the safe for you to pay someone, and also the farm credit cards are in there with the PIN. I'll change the safe combination to your birth date so I don't have to write it down anywhere.'

'Good plan.' Cy nodded. 'But what if you forget my birthday and I'm not here when you get back? I'm sure you're going to have a lot of new stuff crowding your head when you get back. Anyway, it's the twenty-sixth of June.'

'I'll write "Cy's birthday" on the calendar and that will remind me. As far as getting some labour, there are a couple of blokes you can leave a message for at the pub. Just ask to leave a message for Jonesy and Kimbo. Rod, the publican will pass it on.'

Cy decided he'd see how he went before he hired anyone. He wasn't afraid of hard work. After spending a couple of years office-bound. It was great to be out in the fresh air. Even though it was autumn, sweat poured off him as he dug to see how hard the ground was below the ripped surface.

Hard enough. It would be slower than he'd expected. The crowbar clanged as it encountered rock, and the impact jarred. Digging could wait until he measured up how far from the trees the trenches would have to be dug.

Cy glanced at his watch. He'd said goodbye to Kane earlier and loaded the pipes onto the ute. He hadn't wanted to be in their way as they packed up and headed off. They had enough on their minds, getting organised and dealing with three kids without having to worry about final instructions for the farm. Email or text would suffice. It was just after ten, so they'd be gone by now and it was time for a cuppa, and he probably needed to be around when this research person arrived.

He would've much preferred being on the place by himself, but that wasn't his call.

As Cy drove back to the shed through the avenues of trees, he admired the lush glossiness of the leaves and the brilliant green of the grass beneath. It was an absolute showpiece of a farm and the desire to have land of his own grew a little bit more. He'd have a look around the area one day when he'd got the irrigation finished.

He'd ask Ryan if he did go over to *Wilderness Station*, but the amount of work that he had ahead here might make that happen later than he'd hoped. He'd give Ryan a call tonight; it had been a while since they'd had a good catch-up.

As he approached the house over the hill, Cy was surprised to see a black Jeep parked next to the shed. Looked like she was here already.

He drove up slowly and parked behind the Jeep.

Running his hands through his hair, he brushed the dirt from the front of his shirt and climbed out of the ute.

There was no sign of anyone and the shed was still locked, and then he remembered he still had the keys in his pocket.

Wiping his boots on the mat at the end of the paved path, he quietly walked up the dozen steps that led up to the veranda at the front of the McLarens' house.

'Anyone there?' he called out. 'Hello?'

He was met by silence, which was soon broken by his work boots on the timber floor. As he passed the kitchen, a face appeared at the window.

'Good morning, I'm Cy,' he called.

Eyes wide, a woman looked out of him. Then she nodded and pointed to the door.

Slow footsteps sounded down the hall, and for a moment, he thought she was walking the other way, but after a moment, she appeared at the screen door.

'Hello. You're Cy? The manager?'

'You're Ms Morgan?'

'Tarni Morgan, yes,' she said through the half-open window. An aromatic smell was drifting from the kitchen, and Cy's mouth watered. 'I'll just unlock the door and come out.' She walked back inside, returned with a set of keys and unlocked the screen door.

Looked like she was security conscious, which wasn't a bad thing. That was the one thing Kane had stressed to him a couple of times. Cy had wondered if it was their past experiences that made them distrustful or if being so close to the highway created security issues.

Crime could happen anywhere as he well knew from his father's misdemeanours. The woman stepped outside, and Cy was taken it back to see how tall she was. She was almost as tall as he was and he cleared six feet by a good inch or two.

She held out her hand, her voice quiet and cold. 'Hello, Cy. I want you to know I'll keep to myself and won't interfere with your work or be a bother to you with whatever you're doing on the farm. I'll be working in a small area of trees and then I'll spend most of my time in my makeshift laboratory. I don't expect we'll see much of each other.'

And that suited her fine, was the message Cy picked up immediately. Well, that would suit him just as well.

'I've made a roster for the kitchen, for breakfast, lunch, and dinner so we don't have to bother each other at mealtimes.'

Cy raised his eyebrows; she was pushing his buttons after a two-minute acquaintance. 'I'm afraid I can't stick to a roster; my days will depend on weather and workload.'

Her forehead creased in a frown. 'Oh. Well, I'll have to be flexible then.' The smile that slightly tilted her lips appeared forced.

'No, you don't need to worry. I don't need to come into the house at all. I've got a butane stove and a camp fridge so I don't need to bother you.'

'Oh no, you can't do that.' Her cheeks coloured a bright red and Cy got the feeling that this woman was used to calling the shots.

Well, she wasn't going to tell him what to do. She wasn't going to organise his life within a day of her arrival.

'Kane and Ellie were quite definite that you were going to be using the kitchen. And Ellie said she's filled the fridge and cupboards for both of us.'

'Look, love,' he said, hiding a smile when she cringed at the "love". 'There's no need for me to come in there. I'm used to camping out in the paddocks working with cattle, with no electricity, no running water, so that little shed over there is five-star luxury to a cow cocky like me.'

She didn't need to know that the apartment he'd rented at Cullen Bay in Darwin had been in a five-star luxury complex.

'Well, if you're sure then. But I'll pack some of the food she's left for your fridge.'

'Whatever. Suits me fine. You do your thing, I'll do mine. The shed's locked now, so I guess you haven't been there to see your gear.'

'I tried to but the door was locked.'

'I was down the back and I took the keys with me. There is the second set inside that I'll give you. Did Kane fill you in on the security here?'

'The security? No.'

'If you're in the shed, lock the house and vice versa. There's a lot of traffic on the road, and Kane is very security conscious.'

There was no need to tell her the McLaren's history. Tarni Morgan was only here a short time and it was none of her business anyway.

'How about I take you there now, and then we won't have to bother each other again,' Cy asked

'That would be good, thank you. I'll turn the stove off and put some boots on. I'll meet you down there.'

Cy shrugged. 'No rush. Have your lunch. I'll be down there for an hour or so.'

He turned on his heel and left her standing by the door.

He'd worked with some difficult ringers and cattlemen over the years, but Miss Horticulturist had made her dislike obvious from her first words.

Cy shrugged as he headed across to the shed. Hopefully, the three months would go quickly.

Chapter 10

Darwin Harbourside Apartments - Monday
Dru

Dru's worry had been replaced by anger. Last night, Connor had been home for dinner for a change. After Ruby had gone to bed, Dru delayed clearing the table, determined to speak to him. The problem was she had no idea how to broach the subject which was making her sick with worry.

Should she just ask him outright? Simply ask, "Hey are you having an affair, Connor?"

Or should she say, "Oh by the way, darling, I've noticed you don't seem to love me anymore and don't want to spend time with me. Do we have a problem?"

They certainly did have a problem and she was just going to say what was on her mind. Mum had always taught them that honest communication was the key to relationships. Mother and daughters, sisters, and husbands and wives. But Dru's experience had made her wary of telling anyone—even Connor, at times—what she was feeling or thinking. Sure she'd mellowed since they'd got together, and she truly loved her husband, but she'd had a traumatic few years before she'd met and fallen in love with Connor.

But the past was just that. It was past and it was over and now done with. Connor knew all about Zayed. Hell, he'd even met him when they'd been investigating the diamond theft when they'd first met.

Dru's lips tilted slightly in a bitter smile. Where had that Dru gone? That kick-arse engineer who wasn't afraid to take anyone on. She'd softened, and until Connor had turned from her, she'd been happy in her gentler role as wife and mother.

So, she sat there waiting quietly at the dining room table, and she could sense that Connor was waiting for her to get up and clear away. She didn't mind doing it because he'd always come into the kitchen and help load the dishwasher and make a cup of coffee after dinner, but she realised he hadn't even done that for a few weeks.

It was now or never. She opened her mouth ready to say, "Connor, I've been worried about you the last few weeks. Is everything all right?"

Before the words came out, he stood suddenly and pushed his chair in. 'Excuse me, Dru. I have some work to do. I don't want a coffee tonight.' Her husband walked up the hallway and his study door closed quietly. That was the sum total of the words that he had spoken to her since they sat down to eat dinner, she'd been so focused on trying to think of how to phrase her concerns that she hadn't noticed that he hadn't spoken at all.

Dru lifted her hands and covered her face, tears wetting her fingers as she finally gave in to the emotion that had been building for weeks. When her tears were spent, she stood, putting a hand to her back, the nagging ache that had been there all day hadn't gone away.

With a sigh, she reached for their plates and noticed that Connor had barely touched his meal. Anger began to build again; he even left half of his dinner, so he could leave the table early and not have to speak to her.

That was it. He'd pushed enough.

Going into the kitchen, she filled the kettle and banged cupboard doors and clattered cutlery in the sink, but there was not a sound from the study.

Tomorrow she was going to find out what was going on once and for all. If he was having an affair, he could damn well pack his bags and get out.

Dru barely slept that night and was awake when Connor crept out of bed just before dawn. She lay there in the dark as the shower came on in their ensuite. A few minutes later when he walked into the bedroom, he was fully dressed. She closed her eyes and pretended to be asleep, and when Connor quietly opened the bedroom door, it barely made a snick as he closed it slowly on his way out. Dru lay there, waiting to hear the kettle go on, but there was silence. Perhaps he'd gone into the study.

She climbed out of bed and slipped her gown over her shoulders and opened the door. The apartment was in darkness. Taken aback, Dru flipped the hallway light on and glanced into Ruby's room. She was still sound asleep.

The kitchen was in darkness, and she turned the light on to see a note propped against the fruit bowl.

I left early. I didn't want to wake you. Have a good day. Connor

Well, that was progress at least; a few words written on a piece of paper, wishing her a good day.

Have a good day! *I'll show you a good day, Connor Kirk.*

Dru's anger simmered until it reached boiling point and as she crashed around in the kitchen, she realised all she was doing was waking Ruby early.

She made a cup of coffee and slid open the doors to the deck. The harbour was bathed in mist and the smoky horizon glowed a pale orange from the burning off of the savannah to the south-west.

She would go and see Connor in his office. Take the personal out of it, not have the confrontation at home, because if he told her something she didn't want to hear she didn't want to find out about it in their home.

It might sound silly, but if Connor wanted to go, she would stay in her apartment.

And it *was* her apartment. He'd moved to her place after they'd got together during the investigation of the diamond theft at Matsu diamond mine. He'd suspected her to start with, and then they'd worked together. It hadn't taken her long to fall for him.

How can you do this, Connor?

How can you do it to me and Ruby?

As she walked around the apartment, Dru gradually realised there was very little of Connor in it, all the furniture, all the prints, and all the colours were her choices. She'd expected to live alone when she'd decorated it. But to be fair, he had paid off her mortgage when they married.

Until she met Connor, there was no way that Dru had been looking for a relationship. She was a loner, and she wasn't prepared to give her heart because she'd seen what that had done to Mum when Dad died. She'd sworn she would *never* depend on anyone, and now, because she'd broken that promise to herself, here she was in the same situation because, damn him, she loved Connor with everything she had, and if he left her, she would be broken-hearted.

'Mummy, can I have some brekkie now, please?' Ruby stood in the doorway, holding her special blanket under one arm and her Lambsie in the other.

'Of course, you can, darling, and what lovely manners you have. Come out and cuddle me.' Ruby climbed into her lap and Dru put her arms around her little girl and nuzzled into her soft, sweet-smelling skin.

'Mummy, are you crying? There are tears on your cheeks.'

'Are there? Goodness me. I don't know where they came from. My eyes must be very tired.'

Her heart broke as she imagined a life where Ruby was in shared custody.

After taking Ruby to daycare, Dru turned back towards the city. Connor's office was in Mitchell Street not far from their apartment. She parked her car in the basement car park and headed through the waterfront precinct and across the esplanade.

To build her courage she set straight out along the path through the park that ran along Lameroo Beach. The day was bright and sunny, but there was a chilly wind blowing off the water. She pulled her cardigan around her shoulders, wondering if she dressed Ruby warm enough for the day.

After walking for half an hour Dru's mind had eased a little and she took a deep breath.

She'd planned her approach. She was going to tell Connor that she'd been going for a walk in Bicentennial Park and decided to call in and see if he'd come for a coffee with her. Just the thought of having to make up an excuse had those blasted tears threatening again.

Before Ruby was born, coffee together was a regular day date, but now being home with a child, her walking habit had slipped.

Guilt began to rise in Dru and her stomach churned.

What else had she let slip? How much could she blame herself for Connor's lack of interest in her? Has she focused too much on Ruby? Had going back to work part-time and the energy that took maybe taken away from the time she'd given to Connor? Maybe she'd brought this on herself.

Maybe he'd been lonely and maybe he'd met someone else who'd made him the centre of *her* world.

Connor was still the centre of her world along with Ruby, but she knew that she could be cold, and she could shut down. When she was tired after a day at work, and then coming home, cooking dinner and bathing Ruby, and then spending time reading her a story, and being a good mum had her attention to Connor slipped?

A rogue tear trickled down her cheek and she brushed it away angrily. All this second-guessing was doing her head in, but she couldn't help it. The regret added to the guilt now burning in her throat. Dru strode out, determined to get there more quickly, but a sudden stitch in her side had her catching her breath. She stopped, put her hands on the timber rail and looked out over the water. Maybe walking first hadn't been such a smart move. The baby kicked and it felt as though his heel was stuck in her rib cage. She rested both hands on the fence and lowered her head, taking deep breaths as the stitch intensified.

She dragged in another deep breath as the baby kicked again.

'Are you all right?' A concerned female voice had her straightening up.

Dru lifted one hand and wiped the remaining tears from her cheek. 'Oh, yes, I'm fine, thank you.' Somehow, she found a smile for the two women who were standing close by looking at her with concern. 'Just the baby kicking. I think I was walking too fast.'

'Are you sure?' the other woman asked. 'You look very flushed.'

'Yes, I'm fine.'

'Why don't you sit down for a while? We'll walk with you to the next seat and make sure you're all right. Do you have a phone with you?'

'I do. Thank you, but really, I'm fine.' Nevertheless, she let the two older women walk her to a seat, and she sat down.

Once they were satisfied Dru was all right, they continued. She put her head back and closed her eyes, letting the sun dry her tears.

She should've talked to Ellie about all that sort of stuff before they'd left for Mexico. How did Ellie balance being a mother, and a part-time helicopter pilot, and still give enough attention to Kane? They had three kids for goodness' sake.

But Dru knew she and Ellie were different personalities. Even though Ellie did have a hard streak too. Emma was the only one out of the three sisters who hadn't developed that hard core after Dad's murder.

Maybe it was because Emma was a doctor and had more ability to look after herself.

But Ellie seemed to still have a close relationship with Kane. She thought back to last weekend when they came for lunch. When Connor had bailed and Greg turned up.

Kane and Ellie had presented a united and loving front. Dru had seen the way Kane had touched Ellie's shoulder on the way past, and given her a smile and how their eyes had stayed connected. All the things that she and Connor had done when they had first been in love. How long had it been? Had it only been two months or had there been a gradual creeping of distance between them since Ruby arrived?

Greg's words confirmed her belief that Connor was lying to her about where he was that afternoon. The acceptance of that truth had shattered Dru, and she had no idea how she had kept going in front of the family. That was proof that Connor couldn't deny and if he wouldn't talk to her today, she'd be telling him just that. Greg had told her the truth, and he was just as worried about Connor as she was.

Pushing herself to her feet once the stitch had gone, she crossed the Esplanade again and turned up Knuckey Street towards the building where Connor's office was situated on the fourth floor.

The lift was waiting in the foyer downstairs, and she stepped in, pressing the button to go up. Her mind was churning as she tried to get her opening words right.

How hard was it to go to your husband's office and ask him to come out for a coffee with you? If he said no, then she'd just have it out with him there.

The door opened silently, and she stepped into the deserted corridor; the carpet muffled her footsteps as she approached the door of Kirk Francis Security.

The glass door to the office was closed, and there didn't appear to be a light on inside.

Dru's heart kicked to a pounding rate as she read the small type font of the note stuck on the frosted glass.

CLOSED FOR A MONTH. PLEASE CALL THE NUMBER BELOW FOR URGENT ENQUIRIES.

She recognised the mobile number typed below. It was Greg's.

If the office was closed, where was Connor going every day?

Did he have a hidden life?

Did he have another home?

Was he with whoever *she* was during the day?

Dru's worry dissipated as a strong surge of anger consumed her.

How dare he?

How dare he treat me like this?

Turning swiftly, she strode back to the lift, jabbed at the button, and waited. Seething when she stepped in and the lift headed downwards, Dru waited impatiently for the doors to open before she strode out, only to come to an immediate stop.

Through the foyer, she could see the loading bay in the street directly outside the double glass door.

A car pulled in and her husband appeared from the side of the building. Connor opened the passenger car door of a low-slung red car that looked very expensive. Dru narrowed her eyes as she quickly crossed the foyer and stood at the side of the window. A woman was sitting in the driver's seat.

Dru's heart almost stuttered to a stop as her husband reached out and took the woman's hand.

##

Dru opened her eyes when their apartment lift came to a stop. She blinked and looked up at the green numbers lit up on the panel. She couldn't even remember coming into their apartment block or getting in the lift. Her mind had been in a red haze of grief and anger as she'd run from Connor's building. The stitch in her side was still pulling and stretching, and the pain was running down her leg now. Her lower back was clenching, and one small part of her mind remembered that same pain from when she'd given birth to Ruby.

Oh God, no. Please no.

Her body shivered as her confusion cleared and she stepped out of the lift, clutching her handbag with one hand and her right side with the other; she'd run all the way home from

Connor's building, and the stitch had got worse and worse. She'd put her bag over her shoulder and cradled her hands beneath her pregnant stomach when it became unbearable.

The pain intensified and she gagged, putting her hand over her mouth as she walked towards the front door of their apartment.

Dru blocked what she'd seen from her mind, hoping and praying that somehow she'd imagined it, but the ache rose from her stomach to her chest and her throat as she visualised Connor reaching for that woman's hand.

Her anger had disappeared as she had fled, replaced by a feeling of total inadequacy. She was his wife and the mother of his child, soon to be the mother of their second child.

How could he do this to us?

This was not the man that she'd believed Connor Kirk to be. The man she'd *known* him to be. That Connor Kirk, the man she'd fallen in love with, was strong and true, and he had integrity and *he* wouldn't leave her for another woman.

Even if he'd stopped loving her and had met someone else, the Connor she loved would have told her the truth. He would have been sorry, but he would have been honest. *Her* Connor would have told her. Not that the telling would have made it any easier.

Dru's hands shook as she tried to open the door, but her fingers felt numb and her vision was blurred; she couldn't see well enough to press the security code. She lowered herself into a crouch and put her hands over her face.

What was she going to do? There was nobody to talk to. Mum was in Africa, and Ellie was in Mexico. Emma was sure to be working at the hospital.

Dru wrapped her arms around herself, still crouched outside the door of their apartment. A harsh gasp escaped her lips as the stitch became a tearing pain on her right side.

It was her fault. She'd run too fast, and she hadn't given one thought to the baby.

No, *if* she lost their baby, it would be Connor's fault. She still had eight weeks to go.

How dare he lie and cheat?

How dare he act as though I don't even exist anymore?

The pain seared through her and her belly spasmed. She breathed through it and knew she had to get inside the apartment. But there was nothing to hang on to, to pull herself up. She tried to stand, but her legs were too weak. As she slid back down, a gush of water ran from between her legs and her panic built. She would not have her baby on the floor outside their apartment. There was no one else around because their entry was on a private floor.

Dru had dropped her bag on the floor when she'd first crouched and now between pains, she unzipped it and tried to find her phone. As her fingers finally closed around it, another wave of pain hit and she realised how close the pains were. When that one passed, she focused on the buttons and hit #3 on speed dial to call Emma.

Closing her eyes as the pressure built again, she groaned as the call went straight to voicemail. She disconnected, in too much pain to listen and leave a message.

Who to call? Dru had been a loner since her teens, until she'd met Connor, and she still had very few acquaintances. She could call triple zero, but the building was secure and unless she could get into the apartment, she wouldn't be able to let them into the foyer.

There was no other way. She would have to call Connor, and if he didn't answer, she'd call Greg and get him to call Connor. He'd answer Greg's call; his priorities had changed.

Dru unclenched her fingers from the phone and lifted it. Connor was speed dial #1. Her fingers hovered over the numbers as another contraction built.

Yes, she finally admitted to herself, *I brought on premature labour by my stupid running.*

Before she could press the button, she jumped as her phone first vibrated in her hand and then rang. Emma's photo appeared on the screen and Dru pressed the connect button and held the phone to her ear.

'Hey, Dru, sorry I missed your call. I was driving and you know how much I hate using Bluetooth. What are you up to? I'm in the city and I was going to give you a call. Have you got time for a coffee? Seeing it's only the two of us in town now.'

Dru tried to speak but the words wouldn't come.

'Dru? Are you there? Blasted Bluetooth. I'll get out of the car. Hang on.'

Dru groaned. 'Em. Help me.'

Immediately her sister's voice was professional. 'Dru, where are you? Are you at home? Are you by yourself?'

'Yes.'

'Is it the baby?'

'Yes. My fault.' Dru started to cry.

'How far apart are your pains? Do you need an ambulance?'

'Probably. Can't get inside. Outside my door. On the floor,' she managed to get out between jagged breaths.

'I'll call security at your apartment to let me in. On my way. I'm only a couple of minutes from you.'

Dru sagged back against the front door and her legs slid out in front of her. Her maternity slacks were soaked and she could feel the cold tiles through the thin cotton. The pain had eased for a few minutes; maybe it was because she knew someone was coming to help her. For the first time since she'd seen Connor, her thoughts began to form a coherent pattern.

Ruby. Ruby had to be picked up from daycare at twelve-thirty; it was her half day.

Dru's hands shook as she reached for the phone. She didn't want to do it, but there was no choice.

She pulled up Connor in messages and typed.

Pick up Ruby. I can't.

It was only about ten seconds before her phone beeped.

I can't either.

You bastard, she thought.

Organise something. I'm waiting for an ambulance.

Dru's phone rang almost instantly. Her husband's photo appeared on the screen.

Ah, so that's the way to get his attention.

She looked up as the panel beside the lift lit up. Emma had been true to her word. The lift was on the way to their floor.

Dru looked down at her phone as it rang. Anger resurfaced and she pressed the red button to end the incoming call.

Chapter 11

McLaren Mango Farm - Monday
Tarni

Tarni went back to the kitchen. She turned the stove off, gave her veggie stir-fry a quick stir and put the lid on the frying pan. The McLaren's kitchen was beautifully organised, and she'd had no trouble finding anything that she needed. As Ellie had said, the fridge was well stocked, and there was so much fresh food, Tarni couldn't ignore it. She'd decided to cook a hot lunch and then go down to the shed and see where her gear was and get herself organised.

She certainly wouldn't be able to eat everything that was in there, and she hated waste. She'd ask the manager if he would take some. One thing that she had tried to do well over the past eighteen months was to eat properly. She knew how much weight she'd lost; it was strange how the mind could take over the physical side of your body. Even though she ate well, she could only handle small meals and the weight still dropped off her.

Tarni had noticed Ellie looking at her, and she knew that she didn't look well. With her height, losing weight did make her look painfully thin. She was tired because she didn't sleep well at night; it was too hard to let go of the memories.

Time. It would take time.

And focus. This was the opportunity to fill her mind with something more than memories and what could have been.

She found two green Woolies bags under the sink and opened the fridge, putting more than half of the fresh meat into one, and then about a third of the fresh veggies and fruit into the other.

Ellie McLaren must have been expecting her to have the appetite of a horse. Then again, she was just being thoughtful. The house was immaculate, and there were little welcoming touches throughout.

It was nothing like Tarni had expected at a working farm. The house appeared to be fairly new, and it was in immaculate condition even with three children. The walls were spotless, and the carpet looked new. Her bedroom—the guest bedroom—was stylishly decorated with a colourful red and black doona cover, matching lampshades and cushions, and a vase of fresh flowers sat on the chest of drawers beneath a large circular mirror.

The ensuite bathroom of the guest room was tiled in pale grey and white with red and black accessories, fluffy white towels, bottles of bath gel, and another vase of flowers on the vanity. Ellie had gone to a lot of trouble to make it welcoming for her, and in a small way, that thoughtfulness made Tarni feel more settled.

It had been eighteen months since anyone had cared about her feelings. Unless you counted Sally and Tamika's attempts to cheer her up.

As she stood at the open door of the fridge, looking to see what else she could take down to the shed, she thought back to that night a year ago when her friends had taken her out. They hadn't understood the depth of her grief. Both Sally and Tamika were divorced and believed Tarni should be able to move on without a partner, the same as they had. They'd called constantly asking her out with them.

'Come on, Tarni, it'll do you good. It'll get you out of that head of yours,' Sally said. 'A few drinks to relax, some dance music and you can let your hair down.'

Let my hair down? No, thank you. She'd made many excuses.

'I'm just in the middle of some pretty important research at the moment and I can't spare the time but give me a few weeks and maybe I'll join you when I have more time.'

'I know you, Tarn. You're happy in your cave. Just like you were before Jonty. Now remember who introduced the two of you? Good Old Sal. Now come out and we'll cheer you up. It's time to move on, honey.'

Tarni felt mean by saying no to every invitation, but she simply wasn't capable of going out into the world. She carried her grief with her like a stone every minute of the day.

Sally's persistence finally won out and they took her to Dr Gargles, a retro nightclub in Adelaide city. Keeping an interested and pleasant expression that night, and fielding dance invitations from strangers had worn Tarni out.

She couldn't see the point in drinking to bury your feelings. An upset stomach the next morning from a couple of wines, and a headache from the loud music as well as being surrounded by cigarette smoke when she decided to go and sit outside wasn't her idea of getting over her grief. She needed isolation—open spaces and fresh air. A change of scene to one where nothing reminded her of Jonty.

When the offer of a research placement to complete her PhD in the Northern Territory was offered by her supervisor at the Institute, she accepted without hesitation.

Packing up their apartment had been the hardest part of moving away. On the drive north Tarni detoured to the Barossa

Valley. She'd put a sandwich and a thermos of tea in the same picnic basket Jonty had filled with delectable food and a bottle of champagne two years ago. He'd taken her to Tanunda; to a windswept ridge overlooking the vines and told her how much he loved her.

On a chilly autumn morning last month, Tarni climbed that ridge and sat staring over the misty valley. She closed her eyes and tried to feel Jonty's presence, but only the wind surrounded her. 'Goodbye, my love. Thank you for the life we shared.' Tears rolled down her cheeks as she relived that day in her thoughts.

The man she had loved was gone; she would try to make a new start.

Tarni came back to the present as the fridge door beeped from being left open for too long. Tears lingered on her cheeks, and she used the back of her hand to wipe them away.

Checking that she had turned the stove off—her memory had been shocking since Jonty had died—she went into the laundry, where she'd put her work boots and pulled them on.

Conscious of what Ellie and Kane had both said about security she checked her pocket for the house key as she walked down the hall. She did wonder if it was a bit of an overreaction because it was a good kilometre from the highway to the house.

The keys were in her pocket. She pulled them out and locked the screen door behind her and then carried the two bags of food down the steps. Breathing in the clear air, her mood lifted as she walked across the drive and along the fence line towards the shed which was about fifty metres from the house.

Tarni straightened her back as she approached the large shed. The roller door was closed. Cy had been gruff and distant, and it hadn't seemed to bother him that she didn't want to have him in the kitchen at the house.

She did feel a little bit guilty. Maybe she'd come across too hard, but the last thing she wanted to do was to have to make small talk and socialise with somebody she didn't even know. She hadn't seen him all day.

Cy's white ute was parked there, and she remembered that she'd forgotten to tell him about the man who called in earlier looking for work.

She walked around to the back of the shed and was surprised to see there was another roller door there; this one was open.

She stood outside, put the bags down, and peered into the semi-darkness, but there was no sign of Cy.

'You were quick,' he said from behind her, and she jumped and spun around. 'Sorry, I didn't mean to give you a fright. I was in the tool shed. Come on in, and I'll show you where your gear is.'

Tarni picked up the bags and followed him inside. Cy flicked a switch and the shed was flooded with light.

The space was divided into three areas with internal walls breaking up the shed, and Cy led her to the back far righthand corner. Four large windows let natural light in, on each side of the corner, and on the back wall and the right-hand wall. Two long benches ran along each side of the corner with a sink set in the benchtop at each end. In this work area, the floor was concreted and it looked new, although the rest of the shed had a dirt floor. She wondered if Kane had had it concreted because she was coming. Cy was standing quietly watching her check out her new workspace and Tarni made an effort to be a little bit more friendly.

She held up both bags.

Cy's eyebrows rose and he looked at the bags as Tarni held them out to him.

'What's that?'

'I brought you some meat and fruit and vegetables from the kitchen. It's way more than I need. Ellie's left the place stocked enough for an army, and it's all fresh. There's no way I'll be able to use it before it goes bad so I've divided it and brought it down.'

'Thank you,' he said with a smile. 'That was very thoughtful of you.'

She shrugged, not wanting to seem too friendly. 'Better than wasting it.'

'Okay, I'll leave you to it. I'm going to head back to the dam.'

'Oh, I meant to tell you. A guy looking for work called in before. He gave me his card.' Tarni dug in her pocket. 'Oh, drat, I left it in the kitchen.'

'I'm looking for a labourer to help me. What did he seem like?'

'Clean cut, friendly enough. His card lists his skills. Do you have a key to the house?'

'I do. Do you want me to go up and get it?'

'Yes, if you need it now. Save me a walk back to the house. I'm keen to start unpacking my boxes.'

He nodded. 'Okay, as long as you don't mind.'

'Not at all. It's under the fruit bowl at the end of the kitchen bench.'

'Are you sure?' he said.

She nodded. 'Of course. Oh, and Cy, I didn't want him to think I was alone here. I was very aware of what Kane said about security, so I told him my husband was working in the orchard.'

'Smart thinking.'

She turned to the boxes underneath the bench. There seemed to be the right number there. 'One question.' She turned back to Cy.

'Yes?'

'Do you have a Stanley knife handy in the shed? Mine's packed in the boxes which wasn't real bright for unpacking them.'

'I'll grab mine for you on the way to the house. It's in my ute.'

'Thank you.'

She turned and looked around to the other side of the shed. A small tractor and bobcat filled the space.

'Where do you bunk?' she asked.

'Just over the other side of that half wall, so don't worry if you're ever working when I'm here. It's not going to bother me if you work late. I'm a sound sleeper. Or do you prefer to start work early?' He put his hands in his pockets and leaned on the post in the middle of the concrete floor.

'Sometimes I do,' she said. 'And often late at night too. I hope it doesn't disturb you. If I turn the big light on it'll shine over your side of the shed.'

'Don't worry about that. I'll be having early starts too.' He straightened up and pushed himself away from the post. 'So, is there anything else I need to show you?'

Tarni turned her attention back to the workbenches. There were plenty of power points for the incubators and the light was excellent.

'No, this all looks fine. Thank you for showing me.'

'I'll get you the other set of shed keys,' Cy said.

As he walked across the shed, Tarni couldn't help looking at him. He was a wiry, fit-looking man. He'd been kind, even though she's been distant to him. She chastised herself. She'd been downright rude to him; he might have been distant, but he was still pleasant and polite.

Cy was back quickly and handed her a set of keys. 'There's a tractor key there too. If you need to use the tractor.' He looked at her quizzically. 'Do you know how to drive one or if you don't, will you need me?'

Tarni nodded. 'Yes, I can drive a tractor and a bobcat and all sorts of things. I have a ticket for most farm machinery.'

He chuckled. 'I didn't know. I didn't think a researcher would get outside much.'

'You'd be surprised,' she said, realising they were having quite a normal, sensible conversation without any angst on her part. 'Thank you again for showing me everything. I'll be right and if I do need anything, don't worry, I won't hesitate to ask. I'll go out in the orchard tomorrow morning and have a look at the trees Kane described to me.'

'I'll be working down the back near the dam for the next couple of weeks.'

'Okay, thanks. I've got plenty to keep me going here for a couple of hours, so I'll see you sometime,' she said, turning her back on him.

'Thanks for the food drop,' he called to her back, and she could hear the smile in his voice. 'I'll get that Stanley knife for you.'

Tarni smiled as she lifted the first box to the bench. She felt settled already. A comfortable place to live, with a great little lab setup, exciting hands-on research ahead, and decent company on the place to make her feel secure.

A surge of anticipation filled her, and for the first time in a long time, the heavy nagging grief didn't weigh her down.

When Cy came back with the Stanley knife, she was humming under her breath as she lifted the boxes onto the benchtop.

'Have a good afternoon,' he said as he put the knife beside the boxes.

'You too,' she replied, and the smile came naturally.

***

Cy put the fruit and veggies in the small area where he had his fridge and had set up the cooktop. He'd have to rearrange the camp fridge to get all of the meat in there. The fruit and veggies would have to stay out; it was cool enough in the shed for them to last for a while. He could cook up a feed tonight and put some containers into his camp fridge.

It had been very thoughtful of Tarni to divvy the food up, and equally thoughtful of Ellie to leave enough for both of them.

Tarni seemed prickly, and he'd picked up quickly she was a very private person. That suited him fine. She'd been spare with her words and shared nothing about herself apart from the fact that she was aware of security and that she wouldn't bother him.

Well, he could do the same He reached in his pocket for his keys and headed towards the house, feeling as though he was intruding on her space. He shoved that thought away; it was Kane and Ellie's place. There was no need to feel like that. Tarni Morgan was employed by the McLarens, the same as he was.

Pulling out the keys, Cy quickly unlocked the screen door and went to the kitchen. The card was where she'd said, and he picked it up.

Jerry White, it said above the mobile number, and he'd listed trench digging in his skill set.

Excellent.

He'd give him a call in the next day or so, once he'd finished measuring up. If he could get those trenches dug twice as quickly with an extra set of hands, he'd give Ryan a call and let him know that he was available for some cattle work one day a week, maybe even two.

As long as he kept the water up to the trees and kept the grass tidy and trimmed below them, he'd be able to give Ryan some days once the irrigation pipes were in.

It would also mean he would be well and truly out of Tarni Morgan's way. Satisfaction filled Cy; he was happy he'd taken this job—independent work with no boss, no schedules to meet, and no blasted reports to fill in every day, as well as the prospect of being on horseback at *Wilderness Station.* His spirits lifted.

At the end of the week, he might even make the effort to go to Darwin and visit Joe.

Might.

Chapter 12

Darwin Harbourside Apartments - Monday noon
Dru

The ambulance and Emma arrived at the same time because when the lift opened, the paramedics stepped out, followed closely by Emma.

Her big sister hurried over and crouched beside Dru. 'Oh sweetie, what's happening?'

'I ran too hard.'

'Why were you running, Dru, is it?' The paramedic crouched on her other side.

Dru nodded. 'Yes. Dru Kirk. I was . . . just running.'

'My name is Santo and he's Brett. Let's have a look at you.'

'Do you think you're in labour, Mrs Kirk? Dr Langford here thought you might have been.'

'I don't know. The pains have eased since I called my sister. I think my waters have broken,' Dru had managed to have a quick look at her maternity slacks before the lift door opened, and she couldn't see any blood and that had allayed some of her fears. She'd been worried that she was haemorrhaging, but it appeared it was her waters that had broken. She remembered that gushing whoosh from when Ruby had been born

The paramedics quickly took her observations and nodded. 'BP is a little bit high, Dr Langford. We'll get her to the hospital for some tests.'

'I'll stay here with my sister while you go down for the trolley,' Emma said. They obviously knew her from the hospital.

'Lucky to have a doctor in the family, hey?' Brett said. 'We'll be back shortly.'

Emma sat down beside Dru. 'What did you mean when you said it was your fault?'

Before Dru could answer, her phone rang again. It was Connor's ringtone. She glanced down and pressed the red disconnect button.

Emma's gaze followed hers to the screen. 'Connor? Why didn't you take it? He'll be worried. Do you want me to call him and tell him what's going on?'

Dru shook her head, and the room swam. 'No.'

Emma's eyebrows raised in question. 'What do you mean, no? Have you already talked to him?'

'No, and I'm not going to talk to him.'

'What? Why won't you talk to him?'

'It's his fault.'

'Dru, you're not making sense.' Emma put her fingers on Dru's wrist to feel her pulse.

Dru moved her arm away angrily. 'What's wrong? Connor's having an affair, that's what's wrong. I went to see him and I ran all the way home, so this is on his head.' she said bluntly. 'I guess I'm going to be a single mum with two kids unless this one doesn't make it.' A raw sob broke from her throat and Emma put an arm around her shoulder.

'Absolutely no fucking way,' she said.

Dru widened her eyes; Emma never swore.

'Emma!' Her voice was ragged from holding back more sobs.

'I want you to tell me exactly what's happened,' Emma said gently. 'No, on second thoughts, not now. I need you to stay calm with your blood pressure a little bit high. How long since you've had any pain?'

'Probably a good ten minutes now.'

'How close were they before we arrived?'

'Probably a couple of minutes apart.'

'Maybe you've just pulled a muscle and they're Braxton Hicks.'

'I don't think so,' Dru said. 'I've had a lot of them lately and they don't hurt. What about my water breaking? What does that mean, Em?'

'We'll sort that out when we get to the hospital,' her sister said. 'You're with Dr Rickard, aren't you? He's your obstetrician?'

'Yes.'

'I'll give him a call. Sounds like the paramedics are on the way back up now. I'll get whatever you need from inside and I'll follow you to the hospital. Is the security code still Ruby's birthday? Tenth of April?'

'Yes. One, double zero, four, twenty-one. Thanks, Em. I want to tell you what happened. So you know. I promise I won't get upset.'

Emma took Dru's hand again. 'It can wait.'

'No. I want to talk about it. Just in case anything happens to me. I want you to know.'

'Nothing's going to happen to you, sweetie. You might have the bub today, but I know Dr Rickard will do everything he can to stop that.'

'Emma, please listen to me.' Dru glanced up at the lift display. It had gone back to the bottom floor so they weren't on the way back yet. She spoke quickly. 'I haven't told anybody. I've sort of told Ellie that I suspected, but today I had proof.'

'Proof?'

'I went to Connor's office when Ruby was at daycare. Oh God, I still have to organise someone to pick her up.' She put her hand to her chest. 'I texted Connor but he said he couldn't.'

'What! Where is he?' Emma asked with a frown.

'I don't know. Last I saw, he was getting into a car with his woman.'

'Dru, what makes you think that?'

'I know, Emma. I know.' Dru squeezed Emma's hand tightly. 'Where's Jeremy? Could he collect Ruby?'

'He's home with Akasha. I'll give him a call and he can get Ruby.'

'Thank you, I'll have to call daycare and let them know he's coming. At the moment it's only Mum and Connor and me who can pick her up.'

'Okay, you do that now, while I call Jeremy.'

Dru managed to make the call and was pleased her voice stayed calm. Her breathing had returned to normal, and her heartbeat had settled down now the contractions had stopped and she knew that she was being taken care of.

'Okay, Dru. The lift's on the way up again, so tell me quickly why you've got this God-awful, stupid, ridiculous idea that Connor is having an affair.'

'Well, he's barely spoken to me for the last six weeks and he's been very distant. We haven't slept together. He comes out of the bathroom fully dressed. We've barely had a conversation so I headed off to his office today when I dropped Ruby at daycare, determined to have it out with him. You know what Mum always says? Communication is the key. Well, it's something we haven't been doing and I set off to make it happen.'

'What happened?' Emma asked. 'What did he say?'

'Would you believe my husband's firm is closed for a month? He's been going off to work or somewhere every day, and I've had no idea where he's been.'

'What about Greg? Does he know?'

'Do you remember Greg came here on Saturday when we were having the barbecue?'

Emma nodded slowly.

'Well, he came looking for Connor too, because he hasn't been answering Greg's calls either.'

'Maybe there's something wrong with his phone.'

'And would that explain why he's treating me the way he is, and why does it have a closed sign on the office with Greg's number that I don't think Greg even knows about?'

'There must be an explanation.'

'No, Emma, he doesn't love me anymore and he's found somebody else.'

'I still can't accept that. Your husband adores you. You've only got to look at the pair of you together.'

'How long since you've seen us together?'

'At Mum's birthday in February.'

'That's three months ago. I think that was the last time that Connor spoke to me properly.'

'Why are you so certain there's another woman?'

'I saw him. He got into her car this morning. And he held her hand. Maybe he even kissed her. I couldn't watch. I took the back way out of the building because I'm a coward. I should have marched out and confronted him then.'

'That's not proof. It could've been a client. And how silly would you have felt, if she turned out to be a client? Or it could've been a friend? A new office person? There are heaps of possibilities.'

'We don't have any friends,' Dru said. 'You know what we're like. We're both loners.'

'No, not loners. I know what you're like. You're a couple who enjoy spending their lives with each other, the same as Jeremy and I; family is enough for us at this stage of our lives. Between work and kids, we don't have time for a big social circle.' Emma folded her arms. 'It *must* be a client.'

'Oh, dear, sweet Emma, you've inherited Mum's happy genes, didn't you? You're more like Mum than Ellie and I. We're the ones with the hard centres who see harsh reality and you're our Pollyanna.' Dru squeezed her sister's hand again. 'Don't be offended. I do love you the way you are, and I love you for trying to find a happy answer.'

'I'm going to find out the truth, Dru.'

'No, Em. Please leave it.'

Emma stared at her and shook her head and for the first time in her life, Dru saw a glimmer of a hard core in her sweet, older sister.

'No, you're going to be in hospital for at least a few days. We'll keep Ruby at our place until I find Connor.'

'Good luck with that.'

The phone rang again and Dru stared at the phone on her lap, as the lift door opened, and the paramedics wheeled the trolley out.

Emma picked it up and held it out to Dru. 'You have to tell Connor, Dru. He's your husband and the father of this child.'

Chapter 13

McLaren Mango Farm - Saturday
Tarni

Tarni filled her drink bottle from the royal blue stoneware water purifier on the kitchen bench. How wonderful would it be to have a kitchen like this? Since her parents died and she'd sold the family home, she'd lived in small impersonal apartments as she'd finished her degrees. The closest she'd got to decorating in a style she liked had been after Jonty had moved in.

They'd had plans, but life didn't follow the plans they'd made, and the dreams they'd shared. Her life had changed, and now she lived day to day without thinking ahead. There was no way she would ever leave herself emotionally vulnerable again. Tarni picked up the sponge from the kitchen sink and wiped the pale marble-coloured stone benchtops

Ellie's kitchen was a delight to work in; one day Tarni was going to make a home like this. She could see herself in a little cottage on the side of a hill overlooking paddocks, sitting in her chair on the veranda, bread baking in the oven.

A rocking chair?

An unbidden smile came to her lips. She'd probably need a rocking chair by the time she could save enough money to buy a place of her own and then she'd be too old to enjoy it.

Didn't hurt to dream, though. It was the first time she'd allowed herself to do that for a long time. Being out in these wide-open spaces had been therapeutic.

White tiles lined the walls and the pale colours were relieved by splashes of red and royal blue in the accessories. Even the tea towels and hand towels matched.

Her mind turned to the day ahead, and she went to the fridge and put two apples and an orange in her cooler bag, along with her filled water bottle. She already had her small laboratory set up and had started work on the first seeds that Kane had left for her. Today she was putting together the seed boxes ready to go into the incubator, and she wanted to experiment with the propagating heat pads, and the light box to see which one was most effective.

She was already into a good work routine and hadn't laid eyes on Cy since Monday. She'd heard his ute come and go a few times and noticed a light on in the shed last night, and had seen his shadow cross the window a few times, but it had been peaceful.

Even if a little lonely.

Maybe she'd been a bit harsh; she had this wonderful kitchen to herself and he was down there with a small butane stove and a camping fridge on a concrete floor. Now that she'd met him, and knew he wasn't going to intrude on her space, maybe she'd make the offer for him to share the kitchen in a few days.

From what she'd picked up from him so far, he didn't seem the type to be plying her with questions and wanting to know her background. He was a worker and seemed to be a bit of a loner. The night before last she'd heard him drive out, and he hadn't come back until late. It was strange, but she'd felt a little bit lonely here on the property by herself. She was used to the city where there was always someone around, even if she was cocooned in her world at work, and in her apartment. At the Institute, she'd had several co-workers with her in the laboratory and that was very different to being on a large property in the middle of the Northern Territory.

It hadn't taken long to shake that strange feeling off and focus on her work. Each day this week, she'd immersed herself in the research and before she knew it, the sun was setting, and she headed back up to the house for the night.

Tarni picked up the cooler bag and took the keys off the hook next to the phone. She locked the screen door but left the front door open to let some fresh air into the house. She'd cooked another vegetable curry last night and the aroma lingered.

There was no sign of Cy or his ute, even though she hadn't heard him drive out. She hadn't seen him to talk to since the day she'd arrived. She'd only been aware of his ute coming and going. It was a perfect arrangement. She unlocked the shed door, and as it was such a lovely morning, she used the remote to put the large roller door up to let some fresh air in. Switching on the fluorescent lights she headed across to her workbench. She was enjoying this work and making progress more quickly than she'd anticipated. By the time Kane and Ellie returned, the new hybrid plants might be almost mature enough to plant.

Even though she'd worked in a heated environment in the city, the warmer ambient temperatures that occurred naturally here were making a bigger difference than what she'd expected. Even in only a couple of days of late autumn. It would be good to be here in the warmer months and see how quickly the seeds sprouted.

Tarni examined the two glass jars she'd left on the propagation heat mat overnight and compared them to the control without heat. The development was identical and she nodded with satisfaction. The more natural the environment was, the better for Kane's future work, and knowing she didn't have to worry much about stable temperatures meant she could concentrate on the chemical composition of the fertilisers. With luck, she'd have enough of these seeds propagated to plant out before he came home. She lifted her head and listened as a car engine broke the silence.

That was strange; Cy usually came up from the direction of the dam at the back of the property when she was up having her lunch at the house. She'd got into the routine of staying in the house for a long break until he headed out again, although there was probably no need to do that because she now knew that he wouldn't bother her while she was down here.

The motor stopped, and a car door slammed; Tarni looked up as a shadow crossed the doorway. Cy paused just inside the doorway, the sunshine behind him shadowing his face. Tarni was surprised to see him so early; it wasn't morning tea time.

'Morning, Tarni. I hope I'm not bothering you. I forgot to pack my thermos this morning.'

Tarni took her gloves off and put them on the bench and walked over to him. Now that she could see him clearly, she realised that there were dark shadows beneath his eyes, and she felt guilty that Cy was sleeping down in the shed.

She smiled. 'Look, Cy, there's no need to stay down there and have your morning tea. You might as well come up here. That's not going to bother me at all.'

'Are you sure?' he said.

'Positive. It would be nice to have some company now and then.'

'Thanks, that's great. I need a new thermos. This one usually goes a bit cold by morning tea time anyway. That's why I come back here for lunch. I must make a note to myself to buy one next time I go to town.'

'I'll be going into town later if you'd like me to pick one up for you. As crazy as it sounds with all that Ellie left, I do need to shop.'

Surprise filled her; they were having a normal conversation, and Cy looked relaxed.

'Will it bother you if I put the kettle on?' he asked.

'Not at all,' she said. 'I was about to have a break in the sun, eat my apple and have a drink too.'

'Would you like a cuppa? Seeing as I'm boiling the kettle. I've got coffee here too if you prefer that.'

Tarni thought for a moment and then decided a cup of tea would be nice and it would be rude to refuse his gracious offer. 'A cup of tea would be great.'

'What sort of tea do you like?' Cy looked pleased that she'd accepted.

'You have a variety?'

'I do.' He grinned at her. 'I love my tea and not just a bushie's billy tea. I have green tea and Chai, plus I've got some normal teabags for when I go mustering over at my cousin's place. Ryan pays out on me for drinking "that green shit" as he calls it.' It was the longest sentence he'd spoken to her since she'd arrived. 'Sorry for swearing.'

Tarni chuckled. 'Not a problem. Even though I worked in a lab, most of my colleagues were male, and I've heard a lot worse than that. A cup of the "green shit" would be great.'

Cy's grin stayed and she was surprised to see what a difference it made to his face. He looked a lot younger than she'd first thought he was. With his tanned rugged face, she'd picked him as well into his thirties, but now she wondered if he was closer to her age.

'I've got two apples here if you'd like one.'

'It's okay,' he said. 'I've got some of the fruit that you gave me.'

'I've cooked up most of the vegies and made some meals ahead, to save me time at night,' she said.

'That was a good curry I could smell last night.'

'I'll give you a container of it. That is if you don't mind eating vegetarian.'

'If you've got enough that would be great,' Cy said. He turned and headed to his side of the shed, and paused at the edge of the half wall.

'I'll bring our cuppas outside. There are a couple of chairs around the other side of the shed.'

'Thanks. I've got a couple of things to switch off. I'll meet you out there in a couple of minutes.' Tarni was still smiling as she walked back to her seeds. It would be good to have some company.

A few minutes later, she put her hand to her eyes as she stepped out into the bright autumn sunshine. It was the first time she'd walked around here. There was a patch of lawn on the eastern side of the shed, and two camp chairs and a small table sat on the edge of the grass in front of a circular brick fire pit. In front of the chairs, two small half-logs were turned on their sides to make footstools. In between the sitting area and the fence were a small trampoline and a set of swings.

The fire pit was still glowing with embers; Cy must be sitting out here at night, and cooking on the tripod that sat over the coals. Tarni was surprised she hadn't noticed the fire or smelled the smoke the past few nights. Then again, she'd locked up securely and the kitchen faced the other direction, so that probably explained it. It would be nice to sit out here at night under the stars; if there was one thing she loved, it was sitting by a campfire.

She settled into one of the chairs, put her feet up on the log and munched her apple. She tilted her head back and let the autumn sunshine warm her face. Contentment filled her as she relaxed, and the feeling was good. Only a minute or two later, Cy walked around the corner of the shed, carrying two huge mugs of tea, with a packet of biscuits tucked under his arm. He placed them on the table between the two chairs and glanced at Tarni before he sat down.

'You look settled.'

'I feel good,' she said. 'It's a nice spot out here.' She gestured to the south where the morning mist still hovered over the tops of the mango trees. 'I brought the other apple out in case you wanted that after your cuppa,' she said.

'Thanks, I'm okay. I've eaten more fruit and veggies this week from that stuff Ellie left than I have for a long time. Healthy eating. Better than the takeaway I lived on in Darwin.'

Surprised that Cy had volunteered personal information, Tarni smiled. 'Good for you. I try to avoid processed food.'

'Yep, I'm feeling pretty fit,' he said.

Silence descended for a couple of minutes and Tarni picked up her tea and sipped the steaming liquid. 'Thank you, that's good.'

His grin reappeared. 'Doesn't taste like green shit, then?'

'No, it tastes like very nice green tea, I appreciate it. And if that's what you drink, that's healthy for you.'

Cy chuckled. 'It never quite tastes the same after a Macca's hamburger or KFC, though.'

'Oh yuk. I can't remember the last time I ate fast food. It would have to be at least fifteen years ago.'

'Sounds healthy to me. I'm lazy when I'm in town. I eat too much of it.'

'But if you're active, you'll burn it off. Mind you, it would take as long to burn up those calories as a healthy meal.'

'I hear you.'

The silence that surrounded them as they both sipped on their drinks, deep in their thoughts, had lost its awkwardness. Maybe Cy was thinking it wasn't too bad to have company too, Tarni thought.

'I hope I haven't been imposing on your living space too much being in the shed all day. I've noticed that you don't come there during the day,' she finally said. 'If you ever want to come back and have a rest or anything during the day when I'm there, let me know. If I'm in your way, please feel free to tell me to give you some space. My hours are flexible. I've made incredible progress in just a couple of days.'

Cy put his mug back on the table and reached for a biscuit. 'Me too. Must be in the air this week. I've finished measuring up for the new pipes and now it's time to start the digging.'

'Did you get onto that guy who was looking for work?'

'Yes, he's coming for an interview tomorrow afternoon.'

'He seemed pretty keen when he was here,' Tarni said. The conversation flowed easily between them.

'Bickie?' Cy held out the packet. 'Not homemade sorry.'

'Why not. I've earned it today. I'll save the other half of my apple for afterwards to clean my teeth.'

'Is that really true?' he asked.

She shrugged. 'I don't know. My mum always used to tell me to eat an apple at school after my lunch and I always did what I was told without questioning it.'

'Sounds like you were a good kid. I wasn't.' Cy's grin was roguish, and Tarni could well believe that.

She gave a self-deprecating laugh. 'I'm a rule follower.'

Cy looked past her into the distance down the back through the trees. 'Probably a good way to be. I've never been one for that, but I find as I get older, I'm finally growing up and getting myself a bit more organised. Doing the right thing. Not that I've ever done anything really bad. I was just a bit of a mouthy lair in my youth.'

'If it's not rude to ask, how old are you' Tarni asked. 'I'm just curious because I first thought you were older.'

'Ah, my mature face,' Cy said. 'I'll be thirty soon.'

She nodded. 'That's about what I guessed.'

'Okay, I'll be rude too. What about you?'

'I'll be thirty soon,' she parroted his words.

'1993 was obviously a good year.' He reached for the biscuit packet. 'Another one?'

'I will.' Tarni surprised herself as she reached for another cream biscuit. Her appetite had improved since she'd arrived. She ate it slowly, savouring the sweetness and then brushed the crumbs from her T-shirt. 'Thank you. I guess I'd better think about getting back to work. It's too nice sitting out here in the sun.'

'This is the best time of the year up here. The traditional owners call the season "Yegge", one of their six seasons. The weather cools down and we get these misty mornings. You'd probably like to see the water lilies. There's a big billabong on the way out to Hidden Valley where my cousin has his cattle station. It's like a carpet of flowers. And this time of year, the country is burned off to "clean the country". You've probably seen the smoke hanging around. It makes for some spectacular sunrises and sunsets.' Cy stopped and looked a bit embarrassed. 'Sorry, I got a bit carried away there.'

'No, it was great to hear about it. I know nothing at all about the Territory apart from how the mangoes grow. I've been getting up early and watching the sunrise. Dawn is very different here than in the city.'

'You came from Sydney?'

'No, Adelaide. I grew up in Sydney, but I've been in Adelaide for a few years now. What made you think I was from Sydney?'

'Most people who come here are from the east. Kane told me most of his seasonal workers come from the orchards and vineyards down around southern New South Wales. To be honest with you, this is my first time working on a farm like this. I usually work with cattle.'

'Are you enjoying the work?'

'It's very different.' Cy spread his arms wide and gestured down towards the avenue of mango trees. 'But I'm enjoying it so much, I've been thinking that I wouldn't mind getting a small property like this one.'

'Change is good.' Tarni's voice was quiet as she looked out over the trees. 'Once I get the first seeds going, I'd like to have a bit of a look around. Speaking of which, I'd better get back to work.'

'Me too.' Cy stood and threw the dregs of his tea onto the grass. Thanks for the chat. I'll be around the shed a bit later. I have to order some more pipes and do some work on the bobcat.'

'Thanks for the tea and the biscuits.' Tarni said. 'How long does it take to get into Darwin? Is it reasonable to go after lunch? I'm not fussed about driving back in the dark.'

'About an hour. Depends how long you stay in there.'

'Is there anything you need?'

'No, I'm pretty right. I've got plenty of fruit and veggies.' His grin was wide and the tanned skin around his eyes crinkled as he held her gaze.

Tarni smiled back at him but was shocked at the sudden surge of attraction that ran through her. Chatting to Cy, and sharing his morning tea, had relaxed her and her usual angst had receded as they'd talked.

'No. I only want a couple of things. Where's the best place to go shopping that would be open tomorrow?' Tarni looked away from him and started walking back to the shed.

'What sort of shopping?' Cy walked beside her.

'Nothing flash. Just basics. Aldi or something like that. And maybe, a bookstore.'

'If you don't want to do any touristy stuff, the shopping centre at Casuarina should suit you. All the shops should be open on Sunday. It's about ten minutes off the highway. Once you see the RAAF base, turn right and it'll take you there.

'Are you sure there's nothing you need?'

'A new thermos if you're near that sort of thing.' He paused as he reached the door and turned around. 'Drive safe. That highway can be a bit dodgy with all the smoke.'

'I will.'

A warm glow, suffused Tarni; it was unusual to have someone to tell her to drive safe, or keep safe. Even though she had conversations with her colleagues at the institute, they were all work-related. She'd not shared any of her tragedy at work. She hadn't even told anyone she was heading off on this project, and she doubted that she'd even been missed. As for Sally and Tamika, they'd not been in touch since that night she'd gone to the nightclub with them.

'See you around, Tarni Morgan.'

Tarni headed for her workbench and Cy took the mugs and remaining biscuits back inside. A moment later, she heard his ute start up and head down towards the dam. He was a worker. Maybe they could do morning tea again.

Maybe she'd even ask Cy to the house for dinner one night.

Chapter 14

Royal Darwin Hospital - Sunday
Dru

Even though Dru's waters had broken, a raft of tests and a visit from her specialist had resulted in the decision to keep her in hospital. She'd been in here six days and had not yet spoken to Connor in person, but they had exchanged texts each day. His excuse was that he was on a case and out of phone range.

The texts she sent in reply were impersonal and didn't encourage a dialogue. Dru was not going to find out the state of her marriage by text. That seemed to suit him because Connor's replies were also very impersonal. No emoticons, kisses or love hearts, and none from her either.

Connor said he was working, but his texts had been vague and evasive and reinforced her belief that he was moving away from their marriage.

Her phone was beside her on the white cotton blanket, and Dru glanced down at it. So far today, there had been no texts exchanged. When she looked up Emma was standing in the doorway.

'Hey, Dru,' Emma said as she walked across and stood by the bed. Dru saw her big sister's eyes drop to the phone.

'Morning. Are you here as my sister or are you on duty?'

'Both. I'm on duty, but not on maternity. I'm on a quick break. How are you feeling?'

'Bored, frustrated, and wanting to go home. I can't get anything out of the nurses. When will I be able to go home?'

'That's up to Dr Rickard. There's a much greater risk of infection with your waters breaking.' Emma sat in the plastic chair beside the bed. 'But the good news is your baby's heartbeat is strong, and there is no foetal distress.'

'So how long will I have to stay in here?' She looked at her sister and Dru's heart sank. 'Come on, Em, tell me the truth.'

'It's up to Dr Rickard, but if you were my patient, I'd be keeping you in here until the baby's born. You've had the forty-eight hours of steroids to help mature his lungs, so if you go into early labour again, you won't need them. You can decide to go home, but you need to know the risks. Has the fluid stopped leaking?'

'Yes, nothing for a couple of days.'

'Do you have someone at home to look after you and Ruby? And to drive you to the hospital if your contractions come back?'

Dru looked down. 'That's an unfair question.'

'No, it's a common-sense question.' Emma folded her arms. 'If you have any contractions or more fluid leakage you have to come straight back. How would you get here? As a medical practitioner, I would advise you to stay here. So far so good, with the baby's health, so here is the sensible course of action.'

'For eight weeks?' Dru almost squealed. 'I can't stay in here for eight weeks!'

'Prepare yourself, love. I think you'll find you have to stay in here until at least thirty-eight weeks, or until they decide on a Caesarean depending on how you go over the next few days. You're still only thirty-two weeks, another six weeks will give the baby a much better chance.'

'I can't stay in hospital.'

Emma raised her eyebrows.

'I have to be there for Ruby,' Dru said emphatically.

'Ruby is fine at our place. I told you. When Connor gets back, we'll work out something with him.'

Dru muttered under her breath, but Emma ignored her.

'When Jeremy picked her up from daycare on Monday, she was very excited to be coming over to play. And she slept well the last three nights.'

'Better than me.' Dru folded her arms over her pregnant stomach and sighed. 'I'm sorry, Em. It's just so frustrating. Will you bring Ruby in to see me?'

'That's the main reason I came now. I knew you'd want to see her. Now that you've stabilised and the test results are all back, Jeremy is going to bring her in this afternoon. I'm not sure yet how late I'm working tonight. There are a lot of staff off with COVID.'

'Okay. Thank you. I do appreciate you looking after her,' Dru said. 'How is she really?'

'She's fine. She keeps mentioning her little brother. I do hope it's a boy for her.'

'As long as the baby is healthy, we'll all be happy.' Dru's voice shook a little and she cleared her throat. 'I told Ruby I was in here to get her little brother or sister. When you were at work last night, Jeremy called and I had a chat with her. She sounded fine.'

'Yes, Jeremy said you had a good chat and that Ruby went off to bed happy.'

'He's a good dad, Em.'

'He is. With us both working part-time, Akasha always has one of us there.' Emma's voice was careful. 'Have you spoken to Connor yet?'

'Only by text. He's "on a case" and has little phone coverage, he says.'

'Okay.' Emma's expression stayed blank. 'I'll go over and get some more clothes and toys for Ruby this afternoon. Is there anything else you want from home?'

Drew felt her heart rate increase as a wave of frustration took hold. 'I don't want to stay here, Emma. Ruby can't be away from home for that long.'

'She won't be. Like I said, when Connor gets back from his case, she can go home with him, and we'll help out when he has to work. I'm sure he won't take on any new cases with you in here.'

Dru shrugged. 'Well, he is going to have to step up, isn't he? But I'd prefer she stay with you. Who knows where he'd take her?'

'Now you're being silly. How much did you tell him, Dru?'

'Just a little bit while he insists on texting me. I told him I was in the hospital. If he wants to come and see what's wrong, he knows where to find me.'

'For goodness' sake. You're as stubborn as each other. Then again, I don't recall Connor being as stubborn as you.'

'Thanks heaps, Emma. You're supposed to be on my side. So, you're saying that I'm the difficult one in our relationship? You don't know anything about us.' Anger filled Dru and the baby kicked. She put a hand on her stomach and took a deep breath.

'Calm down. I'm not taking anyone's side. I'm simply saying that you both need to be receptive. You need to listen, and he does too. He needs to know how you're feeling and what you're assuming.'

'I will assume what I saw to be true until I get out of here and Connor can explain otherwise. Until he does that to my satisfaction, I'll ask you to keep Ruby at your place.' Dru's eyes filled with tears. 'Oh God, I wish Mum and Ellie were here too.'

Emma moved her chair closer and put her hand on Dru's.

'Come on, sweetie. Stay calm.'

'I am.' Dru sniffed.

'You're putting us in a difficult position. What if Connor wants to pick up Ruby and take her home? He's her father and that's where she needs to be while you're in here.'

'No, I'm her mother and she needs to be with me. If you don't want her, isn't there some sort of creche or a stretcher or something where she can sleep in here with me?'

Emma pursed her lips. 'Now you're talking rubbish. You know we'll have Ruby as long as it takes. Your job is to focus on your health and the baby.'

Drew leaned her head back and closed her eyes. 'I'm sorry. I just feel so bloody stuck.'

Emma squeezed her hand. 'Listen, Dru, you know—'

Dru's phone started to ring cutting off Emma. It had been silent since she'd briefly answered Connor's last text.

She ignored it and as she opened her eyes, Emma reached down and held up the phone. 'It's Connor. Do you want to speak to him or do you want me to?'

Drew folded her arms, a little bit more tightly and nodded. 'You can.'

Dru closed her eyes as Emma answered.

'Connor, it's Emma.'

Emma listened for a while and Dru wondered what he was saying. Her stomach began to churn.

'Yes, she's on bed rest. She had started some early labour signs and her waters have broken. Ruby is at our place. Yes. she's fine. Just a moment, Connor.'

Emma held the phone away and asked quietly. 'Do you want me to put it on speakerphone?'

Dru shook her head, knowing she was being stubborn, but she didn't want to talk to him. To be honest, she didn't think she was capable of it, and if she heard her husband's voice, she knew she'd go to pieces.

Emma lifted the phone again. 'I'm back now. Like I said, Ruby's at our place and she's fine.' She waited a moment and listened. 'Okay. Yes, the maternity ward at the public hospital. First room on the left after the lift. Yes, a private room.'

Dru shook her head and mouthed to Emma. 'No, no visit.'

Emma looked at her and let out a soft sigh. 'Listen, it might be better if you wait a day or two—'

Connor cut her off. Emma listened and then started talking again.

'Because Dru's tired and the doctors are going to be around a lot.' Emma stared at Dru and held up crossed fingers.

Good, she was putting him off.

'Okay, Connor, not a problem. I'll let you know if there are any developments. I'll check that I've got the right number for you.' She listened again. 'Okay, fair enough. Right, okay, I'll do that too, but I'll keep in touch by text and then when you're in service you'll be able to get it okay? Rightio, Connor, take care. Bye.'

Emma ended the call and put the phone on the stand next to the bed without making eye contact with Dru. When the phone was on the stand, Emma looked down at her folded hands in her lap.

'Well?' Dru said. 'What did he say?'

'Connor said to tell you not to forget one important thing.'

'What thing?'

'He said even though it's hard for him to talk to you or come and see you this week, he said to remember he loves you.'

Dru's throat clogged and she found it impossible to talk.

'He was a bit taken aback that he couldn't come and see you. I hope I didn't sound *too* unbelievable saying that the doctors were going to be with you all the time, but then he said he couldn't come anyway. You put me in a difficult situation, Dru. You need to speak to your husband.'

Dru shook her head and her bottom lip quivered.

'Anyway, he can't come to see you because he and Greg are out of town.'

Tears began to roll down her face. Emma stood and leaned over and pulled a tissue out of the tissue box beside the bed. She gently wiped her sister's cheeks.

'Oh, Dru. What's going on?'

Chapter 15

McLaren Mango Farm - Sunday
Tarni

After the pleasant morning tea break yesterday, the day had passed quickly, and the next morning, Tarni had her control tray of seeds ready. They sat in the sunlight pouring through the window at the end of the bench when she heard Cy's ute pull up outside. She picked up the pipette of the hormone mix and slowly placed two drops beside each seed, and then carefully lifted the tray of seeds and placed it in the incubator. She breathed out a sigh of satisfaction as she closed the door and set the timer. One to go.

She was grateful to Kane and Ellie McLaren for the opportunity of finishing her research on their property. It was good for her and fitted well with Kane's research trip to Mexico. Together, she hoped they would get some great results. Kane would increase the efficiency of his crops, and Tarni would complete her doctorate.

A win-win situation, but the other spin-offs for her, even before the first week was up, had been unexpected. She guessed she hadn't given much thought to what being on the farm would be like. Even those last two days at Makowa Resort, she'd been too tired to wonder about it. She'd been focused on the long drive up from Adelaide, planning and ordering the equipment she needed, rather than wondering what it would be like to be on the mango farm.

Being away from the city and away from crowds and away from people who knew her was a new experience. Her work at the institute was interesting and it complimented her university studies well. Her work and study had been her salvation when Jonty died.

Tarni had known for a few months it was time to make a change to her life. To move on to something different, and to stop brooding on what might have been. Sally and Tamika had given her the usual platitudes, that it was time she needed, but staying in the same apartment in Adelaide, and going to the same job every day, Tarni had felt no different than she had the day the police had knocked on her door nineteen months ago.

She'd wondered if time was the answer. Maybe a change of scenery would help. One thing that she had learned from it; she would never trust anyone to stay with her. She would never give her heart again.

Tarni's parents had been killed in a car accident when she was in her mid-teens, and she'd gone to live with her grandparents. Within a year, her grandmother got sick and passed away, and then the next year when she had been in her final year of high school, Tarni was left alone with no family when her beloved Pop died.

Sure, there were aunts and uncles and cousins somewhere, but they were scattered across different states. Tarni left the small country town she'd grown up in and moved to university in Adelaide and focused on her study.

Meeting Jonty in her honour's year had been a life changer for her; and even though he was gone now, she didn't regret one moment of their time together.

She was happy that he loved her, and she loved him.

When she was cooking last night, Tarni realised she hadn't thought about Jonty or Adelaide all day. Time hadn't done it; the complete change was making her feel like a new person.

She hummed under her breath as she reached down and pulled out another tray, ready to fill with the treated seed-raising mix, and the last remaining seeds.

When it was done, she'd have a quick lunch and head to Darwin. She'd read about the tropical city last night and was interested to see if it was what she was expecting. Hearing it was only an hour away had motivated her to go today.

Tarni reached for the last empty tray and frowned. It was broken on one corner, so she discarded it and rummaged in the cardboard carton on the floor hoping there was a spare kit to put another tray together. The last batch of seeds she had propagated were fragile due to the chemical mix and she needed a sturdy tray to plant them in.

She reached for the drill and added a larger bit than the one she had used to put the last tray together, carefully matching the four marks before she drilled the holes. She focused intently as she drilled the timber, but a movement on the rafter above the workbench took her attention as she drilled.

She screamed as the biggest rat she'd ever seen ran across the low rafter just above her head; she'd swear she could see its teeth as it stared back at her. As she jumped, the drill slipped from her hand and dropped to the bench. The box she'd been drilling fell to the floor as she stepped back. As Tarni caught her breath and lifted her hand to her chest, the skin between her thumb and forefinger pulled and stung.

'Ouch,' she said looking down at her hand. The skin in the V between her fingers was torn in a ragged tear, and blood began to well out and run down to her wrist.

'Bloody heck, that hurts,' she muttered as she examined the damage. Her head spun and a surge of nausea hit her as the blood welled. 'Oh my God, that really hurts.' She looked around for something to stop the bleeding but there was nothing within reach. She didn't even have a handkerchief or any tissues in her pocket.

'Are you okay, Tarni?' Cy walked around the half wall at the end of the shed. 'I thought I heard you yell out.'

'I'm okay. I think.'

'You think?' He hurried over.

'There was this huge rat up there'—she went to point above the workbench, but the room shifted, and she grabbed for the bench with her good hand. 'Oops, a bit woozy.'

Cy put his arm around her waist. 'Come around here and sit down.' Tarni was barely aware of him taking her around to his section of the shed. He pulled out a plastic chair at a table. Putting his hand on the back of her head Cy gently pushed it down to her knees. 'We don't want you fainting and hitting the concrete, I think there's enough blood on you already by the look of things.'

'The drill slipped when I saw the rat,' she murmured through her hair as it fell on both sides of her face. 'I need some tissues or a Band-Aid.'

'I think you need more than a Band-Aid,' he said quietly, as she lifted her hand by her side. 'Keep your head down. I'll be back in a minute,'

'I'm okay. It was just seeing the blood. I'm a squib when it comes to blood.' Tarni could hear Cy rummaging through a box, and he was soon back. He pressed a wad of tissues against her hand.

'I can sit up now,' she said. 'The dizzies have gone.'

'Okay slowly,' he said, supporting her as she sat up. 'You've done a bit of damage. It looks like you might need stitches, I would say.'

'Damn,' she said. 'I have to get that last box of seeds in today, or the control will be useless.'

'Once we get you sorted, you can tell me what to do and I'll do it for you if you like.'

'I'm okay. Just get a Band-Aid on it, and I'll get the job finished.'

'Just let me clean it up first and then we'll take a look at how much damage you've done, but I'm pretty sure it wouldn't be wise to get dirt anywhere near that cut.'

'I wear gloves when I'm working with the seeds so I don't contaminate them.'

'I was thinking more about dirt getting in the wound,' Cy said as he carefully removed the wad of blood-soaked tissues and examined her hand.

Tarni stared past his head and didn't look at the cut. Cy's breath was warm against her cheek as he moved closer and a funny quiver—not from the injury—ran down her back. It was the closest she'd been to another person for a very long time.

'Are you okay with me washing it and seeing how deep it is?' His voice held concern.

Tarni nodded. There was a small bathroom in the corner of the shed that she hadn't used; when she needed one over the past few days, she'd gone up to the house.

She sat there as water ran and a cupboard opened and closed.

'Okay to stand up now?' Cy came out of the bathroom wiping his hands

'I'm fine now. Sorry I was such a wuss. I've been like it all my life.' She stood and walked across to him. 'See I'm fine. A wash and a Band-Aid and I'll get back to work.'

Cy raised his eyebrows and Tarni stood there watching as he opened a bottle of Dettol and measured a capful and poured it into the water.

She felt like an absolute fool. It was that damn rat's fault.

Chapter 16

McLaren Mango Farm - Sunday noon
Cy

Cy knew Tarni was in pain and was doing her best to hide it. Her usually fair skin held no colour at all and contrasted with her long dark hair more than it usually did. Yesterday morning when they'd sat in the sun and had their morning tea together, she'd closed her eyes and tilted her face up to the sun and he'd thought how pretty she was. When they'd first met, he'd found her closed down and uncommunicative, but she'd thawed over the past few days.

Then again, he hadn't exactly been friendly or welcoming on Monday. She'd opened up a little bit about her background over their cuppa, and he'd surprised himself when he'd been more talkative than usual too.

He had enjoyed the company. He'd enjoyed *her* company.

Tarni had insisted the cut was nothing and only needed a Band-Aid, but when he'd seen the blood running down her hand, he was pretty sure she was going to need stitches. Blood was still seeping from the laceration. It was lucky he'd come back to the shed when he had. He'd frozen when she'd screamed, and he'd raced into her mini laboratory to see what the problem was.

He'd deal with the rat later.

'Okay, you ready? This is going to sting to start with. Just pop your hand in that water for me. Give it a bit of a swish around, but gently. You don't want that heavy bleeding to start up again. I've got a clean dressing here to put on when it's out and dry. A bit of pressure to try to stop it.'

'Ouch,' she said as she did as he asked. 'Dettol always stings.'

'It'll get the germs out. What exactly did you do it with?' Cy tried to distract her as she screwed up her face in pain.

'Oh, now it's throbbing too.' She shrugged. 'I was putting the last box together and I jumped when I saw that damn rat. The box moved when I jumped and I drilled clean through that soft part between my fingers with a small drill bit.'

'We're going to have to take a trip to Emergency, you know.' Cy kept his voice even as her eyes widened.

Tarni shook her head. 'I can't. I have to get that final tray into the incubator in the next hour at most. And I'm sure you've got stuff to do. And you said that guy is coming for an interview today, didn't you?'

'Do you want to have a healing hand to be able to keep working? Or do you want to get an infection and end up in hospital?'

She looked up and held his gaze and Cy waited.

'I guess I'll have to.'

'Good, I didn't want to have to pull rank as manager. I'll do that drilling for you and you can talk me through whatever has to be done with your seeds.' She was still staring at him, and he grinned at her. 'Another skill to my new agricultural repertoire.'

'Thank you. I'll owe you,' she said.

Cy kept the conversation going as he lifted her hand from the now pink-stained water. 'Sounds good to me.' He examined the jagged tear in her soft skin. Holding her hand high to dry for a moment, he frowned as the blood began to drip down her wrist again. He tugged her towards him gently and put her hand palm up on the clean towel he'd left beside the sink.

The first aid kit was ready. They were both silent as Cy wiped the wound gently, and put some Betadine on it, followed by a dressing patch. He then placed a gauze dressing on it and firmly wrapped the bandage around her hand.

'Too tight?'

Tarni's face was white and she bit her lip. 'No, that's okay. Thank you. You're very good at that.'

'At what?'

'The first aid stuff. You're very gentle.'

'You have to know what you're doing when you're mustering a hundred kilometres out on a station. I've seen some nasty gores in my time. A rat peeking at you is nothing to a five-hundred-kilogram scrub bull staring you down from close range.'

'How did you know the rat was peeking at me? And it was more than peeking. It was downright looking daggers at me.'

Cy chuckled. 'Because it's done the same to me over the past few nights. But don't worry, the good news is I'll set a trap tonight.'

'And the bad news?' she asked. The colour was starting to come back into her face.

'The bad news is there are a lot more of them where that fellow came from. They come in under the eaves. Now follow me and I'll set up a chair for you near your bench and you can tell me exactly what to do.'

'Okay, and thank you. Like I said, I owe you.'

'One of those curries sounds good.'

'I was thinking of asking you up for dinner one night, so I definitely will now.'

'I'll look forward to it.'

Cy held Tarni's arm as they walked back through the shed. Her skin was smooth and cool beneath his fingers. He couldn't remember the last time he'd touched a woman. He'd kept himself well away from anyone after Joe went to jail. He'd felt as though he was tainted by association, and he didn't have the emotional energy to deal with that. His counsellor said he had to stop blocking, so he blocked her as well.

'You haven't got the shivers or anything from shock, have you?' He wanted to let go of her but the last thing he wanted was for Tarni to face plant the concrete floor. His voice was brisk, and he quickly pulled out the chair and let go of her. She settled in front of the workbench.

'No, I'm fine. I always feel cool in here.'

'Hang on.' Cy hurried back to the shed and grabbed his denim jacket. He came back and draped it over her shoulders.

'Thank you, again. I guess that's two meals I owe you now.'

'Or one with dessert. I love my dessert.' He looked at her as he lifted his hands and their eyes met again. It was the strangest feeling. He barely knew her, but suddenly he felt as though he knew her well.

Too well. It scared him right down to his boots, and Cy's voice was hard when he spoke again. 'Just wait here for a couple of minutes. I'll go and see what time it is and give that guy a call. Are you right there? Warm enough now? I'll bring some Panadol back for you too. I'd say it'll be throbbing by the time we get to Emergency.'

'How far away is the medical centre from here?' Tarni asked with a frown.

'Darwin.' Cy stood back and folded his arms. It was strange to see his jacket around her.

'What! What about the little towns in between here and Darwin? I'm sure I saw some on Google Maps when I was looking at the highway map before.'

'No funding for rural hospitals. We've had so many medical centres close down in the Territory in the last few years. Can't get doctors, plus COVID killed a lot of them. The medical centres, I mean, not the doctors. There is a medical centre at Humpty Doo, but we'd have to wait there for hours. They'd probably look at your hand and send you to the hospital anyway. So, we might as well go straight to Royal Darwin.'

'Listen. I'm fine to drive. I can find my way there. I feel really bad taking you away from your work. I was bloody careless.'

'Nah. We'll blame the rat. And I *am* taking you. You didn't see the colour of your face, Snow White. I don't want to have the responsibility of you passing out at the wheel and running into a road train. Besides, if you use that hand to hold the steering wheel and change gears it's sure to start bleeding again.'

Tarni reached out and touched Cy's forearm. His skin zinged when she touched it, even though her touch was as light as a butterfly's. 'Okay, dinner and dessert for a week.'

'I was only joking before. It's not a chore to drive you in. I'm happy to do it. I haven't got much on this afternoon. I got everything finished down there this morning. That's why I came up early. I was going to have a shower, have lunch, and wait for that guy to come about the labouring job.'

'Oh, I forgot about him. You don't have to take me.'

He shook his head at her. 'You're a slow learner, Tarni Morgan. I'll give him a call and put him off. I've been starting to think I'm slack to hire someone anyway. There's no reason why I can't dig those trenches myself. I'm getting soft in my old age. I'll be back in a minute. Don't move, and don't touch anything.'

'Yes, Cy.'

He was pleased to see a smile tilt her lips. His phone was in the ute and he stood in the warm sun as he turned it on. There were a couple of missed calls from a number he didn't recognise and a voicemail message. He called the voicemail number and listened; he thought it might have been Jerry White cancelling. That would save him a call.

Cy closed his eyes and put his hand to his face as he listened to the message from the hospital.

'Mr Prescott, it would be good if you could come into the hospital today. Your father has taken a turn for the worse.'

For a moment he considered returning the call, but that wasn't going to do Joe any good.

He quickly called the number on the card that Tarni had left on the bench. It picked up straightaway.

'Yo, bro,' a man's voice answered, and for a moment, Cy thought he must have called the wrong number.

'Is that Jerry?' he asked.

'No, it's De—' there was a chuckle and the guy continued. 'Sure is. I'm Jerry. Who's that?'

'It's Cy from the McLaren's Mango Farm. Sorry for the late notice, but we have to head into town. We'll have to reschedule if you're still interested. No matter if you're not.'

'Oh, I am. I am. I was just getting ready to come over from the pub. But I can do that another day.'

'Okay,' Cy said slowly. 'What suits you.'

'Tomorrow any good?'

'Yep, that suits me fine. Say around the same time? About two?'

'That's good, Mr McLaren. I'll see you at two tomorrow.'

Before Cy could correct his name, the guy kept talking. 'I'm super-duper keen to do this for you. It's just the sort of thing I love to do. My father had a mango tree farm when I was a kid. I'm so looking forward to it. See you tomoz!' He disconnected and Cy shook his head.

Tomoz? He didn't need someone working alongside him who couldn't shut up.

Anyway, he'd suss this Jerry guy out tomorrow, and if he wasn't impressed, he'd dig the irrigation trenches himself.

Tarni wouldn't be able to work for a few days. Maybe she'd like to come down and keep him company in the trees tomorrow if she felt up to it.

Chapter 17

Hotel Playa Feliz, Mexico - Sunday
Ellie

The smell of coconut oil wafting over from the occupied sun lounges surrounding Ellie took her back to the days when she, Emma, and Dru used to sunbake on the old wooden pier of the dam when the mango farm had belonged to Mum and Dad. So much had happened since those days, so much sadness and tragedy, but also there had been much to be thankful for.

Sometimes she wondered where their lives would have taken them if Dad hadn't been murdered, but soon realised it was a waste of emotion.

Contentment filled her as she lay back on the padded lounge and soaked up the sun in the northern hemisphere. The three children were in the crèche not far from the pool, and Ellie was absolutely relaxed. An appointment for a facial and a massage was waiting for her in half an hour. Again, it was close to the crèche, and she'd call in and check on the kids before she went in.

Yesterday, when she'd checked on them, James and Verity had barely wanted to talk to her, and Matilda had been sound asleep. Ever since the issue with their friends, David and Gina's children at Makowa Resort, Ellie had been nervous about leaving their children in anyone else's care.

A ripple of excitement added to her contentment. When they'd been waiting for their flight in LA, Kane had suggested that they go to Italy this Christmas and visit the Johnson family at their villa in Chianti. Since Ellie had rescued Gina when she'd been kidnapped by Russell Fairweather's henchman when she was pregnant with their third child, she and Ellie had grown very close. Even though David had quit as Chief Minister of the Territory, and the Johnsons had moved to Italy where Gina had grown up, Gina and Ellie had stayed in touch. They Facetimed most weeks.

'Now that Cy has shown he's interested in learning about the farm, we could leave him to look after things,' Kane had said.

Ellie had thrown her arms around his neck and kissed her husband, not caring who was watching; they'd been planning on taking that trip for over five years, and now it was looking like a possibility.

She jumped as a shadow fell over her. Opening her eyes, she came out of her daydream and tilted her sun visor back. A tall man in a white tuxedo, with a black bowtie, stood next to her holding a silver tray. 'I have your drink, Mrs McLaren.'

'*Gracias*, Juan,' she said after she glanced at his discreet name tag.

'Would you like to refresh?' he asked. She looked up at him quizzically, and he put the drink on the table next to her, then he lifted a pair of silver tongs from the tray and passed her a hot towel.

'Yes, *muchas gracias*.'

'It is entirely my pleasure, *senora*.' Juan clicked his heels and turned and walked away.

Ellie couldn't wait to tell her sisters about this place Her happiness clouded for a moment. She hadn't heard from Dru since they'd arrived in Mexico almost a week ago; she'd texted a couple of times, but even though the Wi-Fi in the hotel was good Kane reminded her that maybe her texts weren't sending. She sipped from her fruit cocktail and then sat up straight, digging into her beach bag for her phone. She would call home now; that way she could stop worrying and enjoy her beauty appointment.

And while the children weren't around, she might have time to have a good chat. Once she'd called Dru, she'd try Emma too. Ellie quickly did the time difference calculation in her head; it was just after ten thirty in the morning here, so that would make it around teatime, Monday, at home.

She'd set the international call numbers in her contacts to dial out from Mexico as soon as they arrived. Mr Google had certainly been a good help, but she hadn't tried any of them yet. Maybe it would be like her texts and not work.

Pressing the contact for Dru from Mexico, she pressed her phone to her ear as several long clicks, and then two shorts sounded. Then a series of beeps and Ellie crossed her fingers. She waited, and then to her delight, the phone rang.

Her face fell when the call dropped to voicemail. 'Hello. this is Dru Kirk. Please call me later. I'm unavailable right now.'

Not one to give up easily, Ellie decided to try Emma. Her number was also in the international folder she'd set up.

Again, the beeps and clicks, then the last drawn-out beep and the phone rang this time without going to voicemail. After it rang half a dozen times, Ellie waited for it to go to a message, but was pleasantly surprised when Emma picked it up.

'Hello,' she said. 'Dr Emma Langford speaking.'

'Em, can you hear me? It's Ellie. Have I got the time right or have I woken you up? Can you hear me, okay?'

'Clear as a bell all the way from Mexico. How are you?'

'We're all good. I tried to call Dru first because I was worried about her, but it went to voicemail so I thought I'd ring my big sister and have a nice long chat. Is it a good time?'

'Sort of. I'm still at the hospital, but I'm not working.'

Ellie frowned. 'Is everything okay?'

'Yes, everyone's okay. Hang on a minute.' Ellie could hear Emma calling out. 'Ruby, just wait here with Aunty Em, sweetie. We'll be with Mummy in a minute.'

'Oh my God, Em. Is Dru in hospital?' Ellie put a hand on her chest. 'Is she okay? what's wrong? Did she have an accident or is it the baby?'

'Yes, it's the baby but don't stress. She's fine. Dru had an early labour scare last week, and she's on total bedrest here until the baby's born. She's fine, the baby's fine, and we've got Ruby. We're just going to visit her now, so I'll call you when we're there if you want to talk to her.'

'Hang on, what about Connor? Why have you got Ruby?' Ellie had a bad feeling about that.

'Connor's working away this week. Now tell me quickly. How are you?'

'We're great. Having the best time, plus Kane is over the moon with what he's seeing and learning. Between him and Tarni when we go home, he thinks we'll have a "super" farm, or as James says, a "super-duper" farm. I'll take a picture and send it to you. I'm lying around the pool sipping on a non-alcoholic fruit cocktail delivered to me by a gorgeous man in a tuxedo, who then proceeded to pass me hot towels with silver tongs from a silver tray.'

'Stop it. I've been at work all day. I went home to collect Ruby from Jeremy. It's his day off, and then I drove back to the hospital.' Emma chuckled. 'And it sounds like you're doing it tough, kiddo.'

'I'm having a good rest. Okay, so tell me more about Dru.'

'She overdid things and her waters broke, but the obstetrician is confident that they can keep an eye on her. All the tests are indicating everything is fine. Her blood pressure is a little bit high, but not in the danger zone, but they're keeping a very close eye on pre-eclampsia.'

'Oh, poor Dru.' Ellie persisted with her questions. 'How did she overdo it? That's not like her, she's usually careful.'

'She got herself a bit upset, and ran to the apartment.'

'What! Where from?'

'Connor's office. But Ellie, she's fine.'

'Oh shit.' Ellie couldn't help the expletive falling from her lips. 'I knew it. I just had a bad feeling. What about little Ruby? Is she okay?'

'She's fine. She and Akasha are wearing Jeremy out.'

Ellie's voice was hesitant. 'And Connor?'

All was quiet at the other end of the phone and Ellie prompted her. 'Emma, what's going on?'

'Nothing. Connor's working away at the moment and we've got Ruby.'

'He's not at the hospital with Dru?'

'No,' Emma said slowly. 'The day she had her episode she called me because she couldn't get onto him. He was already away so he hasn't seen her yet.'

'But what about them?' Ellie asked carefully. 'Are they fine?'

'I honestly can't answer that, Els. It's not our place to ask. It's between them. Had Dru spoken to you before you went away? She hadn't said anything to me before.'

'Yes, she had, and I knew what she was worried about so please tell me what's happening.'

'Okay, I've told her not to jump to any conclusions until she speaks to Connor.'

'But Connor's not there?' Ellie said.

'No, that's the problem. Connor is not there. He's at work and we've only been able to text him. I've only spoken to him once.'

'What about Greg? Surely, he can take over? Dru is more important than any case!'

'I'm not sure what case Connor's working on at the moment but he's kept Greg out of the loop with this one too. He's as much in the dark as Dru is. All Connor will say is that it's top secret and he can't tell anybody what's happening.'

'For God's sake,' Ellie said. 'I just can't believe it. His wife's in hospital and he can't see her and he can't talk to her?'

'I know,' Emma said. 'Calm down, bub. It's okay, Dru's fine. I'm almost to her room now. Would you like to speak to her?'

Ellie smiled as her nickname of many years ago came out of Emma's mouth automatically. It was the first time Emma had called her bub for a long time. Dad had christened Ellie "Bub" before Dru was born and it stuck until Ellie went to school.

'What do you think, Em? Do you think I should?'

'On second thought, maybe not. When she talks about what happened, her blood pressure does go up a bit.'

'What happened?'

'She thought she saw Connor getting into a car with another woman and that he reached for her hand as soon as he got into the car.'

'Not Connor. It has to be innocent,' Ellie insisted. 'He adores Dru and Ruby.'

'That's what I keep telling Dru, but until she and Connor sit down and talk, she is stressed. She tries to hide it, but you know what she's like.'

'I do. Ever since that bastard, Zayed, in Dubai. He did such a number on her.' Ellie lightened her grip on the phone. She was holding it so tightly her hand was pins and needles. 'Surely Connor can come and see her. Or is he overseas?'

'That's the problem. He won't say where he is.'

'Does Mum know what's going on?'

'No, Dru's fine, so I decided not to bother either of you.'

'I'm glad I called,' Ellie said.

'I am too, but Ellie, you let go of it too. Dru's in the right place, she's got me close by, they're keeping double tabs on her, her obstetrician's great and the nursing staff here have been fabulous. There was talk of moving her to a private hospital, but the neonatal unit's here so she's made the wise decision to stay in the Royal.'

'That's good. Please stay in touch with me. Send me a text every day and keep me in the loop.' Ellie sighed. 'It's so out of character for Connor. What's he playing at?'

'I honestly don't know,' Emma said. 'Jeremy and I have discussed it endlessly at night after the girls have gone to bed and we can't figure out what's happening either.'

'Well, I hope he shows his bloody face shortly,' Ellie said as anger rose. 'How can he do that!'

'I'll send you a text or ring you tomorrow. I have to work out the time difference.'

'Tea time for you is good for me,' Ellie said.

'Okay, that sounds easy. And if I don't call or contact you, don't panic. It will just mean I've been called into work. We're so short at the moment.'

'I won't worry. Thanks, Em, and take good care of our little sis. Love you.'

'Love you too, bub.'

Ellie disconnected the call and slipped her phone back into the bag. She quickly finished her drink, stood and slipped her sarong over her bikini.

After talking to Emma, she wanted to be with her kids.

Chapter 18

Arnhem Highway - Sunday afternoon.
Tarni

It didn't take Cy long under her instruction to make the box that she'd been making when she drilled through her hand and fill it up with the soil that she told him to take from the specially made mix. He used the tiny hand rake to smooth the soil.

'It's really important that the depth is consistent,' she said.

She nodded once Cy had the soil at an even depth in the shallow tray. 'Now there's a pair of new gloves up on that shelf.' Tarni pulled a face as she lifted her injured hand to point to the box of gloves. 'Oh, I keep forgetting about it,' she said as she pointed with her other hand. 'Find a pair that's marked large and put them on.'

Cy's grin was wide as he did as Tarni directed, snapping the gloves as he pulled them up over his wrists.

'I feel like a doctor, about to perform surgery.'

She shook her head. 'That comes after the incubation period.'

'Surgery?' His eyes were disbelieving.

'Yes, on the seeds. It's a very fine process. Now see that round green tray on the second shelf'—he touched it— 'Yes, that's the one.' Tarni nodded as he lifted it down. 'How many seeds are in it?'

'I can see five,' Cy said.

'Good. Right, now really gently pick up the seeds one at a time. Put each seed between the tip of your thumb and your forefinger and while you're holding it, use your left hand to dig a little dent. About one centimetre deep. Now drop the seed in, and don't touch it again once it's in the warm soil. Use your other hand to lightly brush the soil over it, just enough so you can't see it, but just put enough of the soil over it so that you might just see a hint of colour through it.'

Tarni smiled, stood up and used her good hand to wipe the perspiration from his brow with a tissue. 'You've worked up a sweat.'

***

Cy

'Can't let sweat drip into the trays.'

Cy was surprised when Tarni reached over and mopped the perspiration off his brow. Once she was standing, she moved behind him and she was so close he could feel the warmth of her body through his denim jacket.

He turned around and was surprised to see her face only centimetres from his. She coloured and a strange feeling jerked through him.

'You're doing well,' she said.

'Don't trust me to do the right thing, Tarni. 'As soon as he spoke, he realised the double meaning of his words. 'The seeds I mean.'

Her face went a deeper pink and Cy realised it would have been better if he'd kept his mouth shut. His thoughts scattered when Tarni stood so close to him; he felt like a gawky teenager.

She nodded. 'Perfect, you've done well.'

Cy's second and biggest surprise came when Tarni stood on her toes and brushed her lips across his cheek. He held her eyes, and the silence was electric. Her cheeks were heading towards red now and she was the first to look away. 'Sorry, I shouldn't have done that.'

'It was nice. I must have done okay with the seeds.' Cy forced a laugh. 'I was terrified if I stuffed up, you wouldn't talk to me again. And it would be very quiet in the car for our long drive to the hospital. Are you ready to go?'

'I'll just change my shoes and get my purse. Will I need a coat?'

'Might be wise. It could be late when we get back if we have a long wait.'

Cy locked up the shed and waited at the bottom of the house steps for Tarni; he was still worried about her being a bit fragile from the wound. She wasn't long, and she carried a small bag. 'I put some fruit in case we need a snack, and I filled two water bottles from the water filter,' she said as she joined him at the bottom of the steps. 'Oh shoot, I meant to top it up, it's almost empty.'

'The tap water should be okay. It comes straight from the water tanks.'

Tarni shook her head. 'It still needs filtering or boiling. You'd be surprised what can get into water tanks. Plus, up here in the tropics, I would say the water would be quite warm. An ideal temperature for breeding microbiological organisms.'

Cy nodded as they walked across to his ute. 'You sound like Dee. I must get them to call in one day. You'd have a lot in common.'

'Dee?'

'Dee is my cousin's wife on the other side of the family. My cousin Ryan is Ellie's half-brother. That was how I got the job here, although I had met Ellie's family at Dee and Ryan's wedding.'

'What would we have in common?'

'Dee managed her family's macadamia nut farm in New South Wales before she came to the Territory. She's been very interested in what Kane is doing here.'

'It would be nice to meet her.'

Cy locked the shed and then opened the door of his ute for Tarni. 'Sorry, hang on a minute. I'll make some room for you. I don't usually have a passenger.' He picked up a couple of empty KFC cartons, a milkshake container, and three empty Coke cans.

'Sorry,' he said again as he held the door open for her after he'd put them in the bin outside the shed. 'It's always a bit grotty in there. A bloke's ute.'

Her eyes were full of laughter. 'I can see now why you were so keen to wangle a dinner invitation.'

'Chicken is good for you,' he said defensively, but he couldn't help his grin.

Chapter 19

Arnhem Highway - Sunday afternoon.
Dean

About half a kilometre from the McLaren Mango Farm on the road towards Darwin, a black ute sat in the truck parking bay. He'd pulled in there and leaned back in his seat with his cap half over his face so he could keep an eye on the front gate of the farm.

He imagined that the McLarens would be coming this way because he had said they were going to town, and to Dean, that meant Darwin.

Strange bloke, that McLaren guy. He always sounded posh on the phone calling himself "I" all the time. He never even said "me" as a normal person would. His wife was a looker though. A bit tall for Dean's taste, but he'd got a really good look at her so he could describe her to Russell when he went back to the jail next week.

If they were going to Darwin, they'd be gone more than two hours, even if they turned around and came straight back. He could have a good look around the place and set his traps.

Dean sat there with the air conditioning running until the ute cooled down, and then he lowered the windows to let some fresh air in; it was still strange being out in the fresh air and being able to go where ever he wanted to when he wanted. He hadn't got used to the heat having been in that air-conditioned shit box for seven years. He loved the ute so much that he'd already used three tanks of diesel driving around.

The freedom to go where he wanted, whenever he bloody wanted. To eat what he wanted when he wanted, and to eat real takeaway, not prison shit.

His parents were at the Gold Coast, so he hadn't had to explain anything to them. His old man had been bloody rude when he'd called to say he was getting out, so not seeing them suited him just fine.

The feeling of freedom when he stepped out of the jail a couple of weeks ago had been fucking awesome. He kept waiting for someone to pull him up. If someone yelled near him, he cringed, waiting for a baton to come down on his shoulder. It was a full week before the tension left his body, and to be honest, he was a bit worried about going back there to report to Russell. He knew his mate didn't expect it, but Dean knew he owed him for the great new start Russell had set up for him. As long as they treated him like a visitor and not an inmate.

Russell was a bloody magician; he'd organised the ute and his new identity from the inside. The only thing Dean couldn't figure out was if he could do that, why couldn't he have got the same person to take care of the McLaren woman?

Anyway, it was none of his business, but he did want to go back and thank Russell and let him know once he'd done the job. And once she was dead, the money would hit his new bank account. With a bit of luck, he could get it all set up this afternoon. If he did the big doses in one hit, she'd cark it pretty quickly. He'd have to be very smart and try to figure out where to put it. He didn't want to spend time checking out what she drank like Russell had told him to.

How the bloody hell could a worker on a property do that? He'd figure it out himself and cover all bases.

And then he'd tell Russell, say goodbye, and head off to the west. Easiest damn job he'd ever done. Just a shame that the woman wasn't here by herself; he could have had a bit of fun with her. But Russell stressed it had to look like a natural death.

Life was bloody good. His first night on the outside as Jerry White had been spent at the pub and he'd got absolutely shitfaced. The second night he'd stayed half-sober and found himself a woman. Jerry White had the same tastes as Dean did. She had been the first trophy of his new life, and with his new name and fake ID, they'd never connect Jerry White to the recently released Dean Drummond. If he travelled around, he could take his fun wherever he wanted. They could look for Dean Drummond as long as they wanted, and they'd have no fucking luck. He didn't exist anymore.

The problem was, he had to remember he *was* Jerry White these days. He'd stumbled over his name a couple of times when he was talking to blokes in the pub, but hey, it was cool. They'd been as pissed as he was so they wouldn't remember anything either.

A flash of light glinted off a car turning out of the farm gate. Dean pulled his cap a little lower, slunk down in the seat and watched through narrowed eyes.

Good, they were turning this way which meant they were heading to Darwin. By the time the ute passed the parking bay, it was travelling at speed and he couldn't turn his head so he couldn't see how many people were in the vehicle.

He'd wait for a while and then drive to the farm, and suss out if there was anyone else working there. He had answers ready in case there was someone there.

Fifteen minutes later, he pulled out on the highway and turned his right indicator on. The front gate of the farm was open and the timber sign saying it was the McLaren Mango Farm swung in the light breeze.

He'd driven past here most days this week because the Marrakai pub wasn't far away. The locals had been happy to talk about Kane McLaren when Dean said he was going to work there. One stupid bastard who seemed like a know-all reckoned McLaren and his missus were overseas, but he'd got howled down by a couple of other blokes.

'Bloody McLaren won't leave his precious farm. He's making a motza.'

Dean got the impression that McLaren was an arrogant bastard. The old bloke in the corner who reckoned he was away just shook his head.

Sounded like McLaren was a jerk. Russell hated them and Dean would do his best to get Russell's approval. The man was a king; he'd made Dean's time inside bearable. He'd never find another mate like Russell, and he had no intention of getting caught again. Maybe when Russ got out, he'd come back to Darwin and they could hang together.

Dean drove into the farm, and all looked quiet. The shed was locked up and there was no sign of any vehicles.

Here he was out in the wild blue yonder in the fresh air earning money, with a brand-new ute and a brand-new name.

Life was bloody damn good.

##

An hour later Dean drove out of the gate satisfied with his afternoon's work. On second thoughts he'd decided to do what Russell had told him to. Everything had been enhanced with a first dose of ten mls from his bottle of orange magic, and he'd made sure that he'd missed nothing. He grinned to himself, feeling very clever. He reckoned Russell should hear a result within a week.

Now his biggest dilemma was which pub to go to tonight. He weighed up his options and headed for Darwin. As he drove past the Marrakai pub, he wondered if he should have quizzed the locals about Kane McLaren. If the cops ever went there, those blokes might remember him asking about the McLarens.

Maybe he wouldn't mention that to Russell.

Chapter 20

Arnhem Highway - Sunday afternoon.
Cy

As they drove west along the Arnhem Highway, Tarni put her head back on the headrest. Cy glanced over at her; her eyes were closed, and a frown marred her usually smooth forehead.

'Hurting again?" he asked quietly.

'A bit. The painkillers haven't done much.'

'Hopefully you won't have to wait too long. It's only about forty-five minutes from here.'

'You were right. I couldn't have driven myself. What do you do if there's a medical emergency out here? I haven't seen an ambulance station yet. Is there any help at all? A doctor's surgery? Or a small health centre?'

Cy shook his head. 'You're in the bush now, even though we're so close to Darwin. We're lucky it's only an hour for us. Most of the outlying stations have to depend on the Royal Flying Doctor service. And there is a medical air service with helicopters operating out of the international airport in Darwin.'

'I don't think a cut hand would warrant calling one of them,' Tarni said.

'No, but it's reassuring to know it's there in emergencies. Ryan and Dee have twins and they're about two and a half hours out. You need to have good first aid skills and a well-stocked medical kit when you're that far out.'

Cy stared ahead remembering the situation the night that Joe had blown up the donga thinking that Dee was inside. She would have had no chance if she had been. And the afternoon that Ryan had set the trap for Joe out at Hidden Valley, and Dee had needed stitches in her head.

'We could have gone to Jabiru, but being Sunday, I doubt if the clinic will be open. There's a new health centre under construction; since the Ranger Uranium mine closed there's been a lot of changes there. Once the health centre is open, it will make a difference to the stations around here. But many will still have to rely on the RFDS.'

She pulled a face. 'I feel like a fraud even going to emergency.'

'No, it's a nasty cut and it needs attention. And you did plan to go to Darwin today, but this wasn't what you expected. I know you said you had a bit of shopping to do. If you like, once you're stitched up and have had some painkillers, I'm happy to take you to the shopping centre.'

'That's very kind of you. I'll see how I feel, although I do need a couple of things.'

'I'll be honest. I do have an ulterior motive,' Cy said. 'There's somebody in another hospital which isn't far from the Casuarina shopping centre. I should call in. If you're up to it, I'll drop you at the shopping centre and make a quick visit. Maybe.'

'I'll be fine. So, take the opportunity.'

Cy shook his head. 'To be honest, I don't have to go there. I'm still thinking about it.'

Joe might be his father, but he had done some dreadful things and Cy wondered why he should go and see his father.

He appreciated that Tarni didn't dig with more questions. The longer he spent with her, the more he respected her. He glanced across; her head was back again and her eyes were closed. The colour had left her face again; he wouldn't go to the palliative care place to see Joe. It wouldn't be fair to drop Tarni off and leave her.

Cy looked ahead as she dozed quietly beside him; the smoke haze from the woodland burn-off was getting thicker and he focused on his driving rather than letting his chaotic thoughts take over. Half an hour later, they approached the small settlement of Humpty Doo, and Tarni opened her eyes and sat forward. 'Is this the beginning of Darwin?'

'No, this is Humpty Doo. There are a lot of mango farms around here too. It's known locally as "the Doo".'

'I thought South Australia had some strange place names, but that's a classic. Is this near where you worked on the cattle stations? It's a lot greener here than I thought it would be. South Australia is a lot drier.'

'No, I worked further southwest, close to the Western Australia border. You have to remember this is the tropics. This lush green environment soon changes to red dust and dirt.'

'Do you miss being on a cattle station?'

'If anyone had asked me that a few months ago I would've said I'd be back in the cattle industry like a shot. But since I've been working on Kane's farm, I'm not so sure. I hated being in the city. I was working with cattle but not out in the open spaces. I was laid off and was about to head back west when Kane offered me the management of the farm while they were away. I've been really surprised at how much I've enjoyed working on the agricultural side of things.'

'They say a change is as good as a holiday,' Tarni said.

'True. What about you? How are you enjoying it up here so far?'

'I am, even though it's only been a week or so, it's been really good for me. I love my work, but doing it in this environment is wonderful. I feel calm and settled. It happened before I got here actually. I spent a couple of nights at the Makowa Resort and I had the best sleep I'd had for months.'

'Maybe you're not a city girl.'

'Maybe not.' Tarni looked down at her bandaged hand. 'Maybe I do need a new start somewhere, a new me.'

Cy couldn't imagine Tarni being any different. 'Kane's turned the property into a showpiece, but it does have a good feel to it,' he said.

'It has. Hard to say why. I know the climate is different, but just sitting out on the veranda in the early morning, watching the sun rise and seeing that beautiful dawn as it steals over the green mango trees as far as you can see to the horizon, I feel calmer in myself.'

'Did you live right in the city with your job?'

'I did. I sat at my window and watched the sun rise above the rooftops. The closest I got to a big sky like the one here was a couple of puffs of cloud occasionally drifting across. The land and the air here are so natural and so clean. It's funny you know, but I was even thinking about staying up here once I finish up with Kane. I thought I might be able to do some more work up here. There's a university in town and some agricultural institutes. And there's a lot of different crops up here; I've read in the paper about research over at Kununurra on the Ord River.'

'Might be worth a try.'

'I'm due for a change,' she said.

Cy looked at her curiously, but he respected her privacy, as she had with him. He didn't ask any more questions. If she wanted to talk, he would listen.

Chapter 21

McLaren Mango Farm - Sunday night
Tarni.

Tarni slept most of the way home. Cy glanced over at her every so often, but she didn't stir until he slowed at the gate to the farm just after seven. The headlights illuminated the gate and he hit the brakes hard.

He'd left the gate open and now it was closed. Someone had been at the farm; maybe one of the family had called in. Cy jumped out and opened the gate. When he got back in the car, Tarni was stirring. He reached over and touched her arm lightly.

'We're home, Tarni.'

She stretched, put her head back and then turned to face him with a smile. 'I feel so much better after a good sleep. Sorry, I wasn't much company.'

'That's fine. You needed the sleep. Did they give you some tablets to bring home?' Cy drove through the gate and jumped out and shut it behind them. Tarni nodded when he was back in.

'Yes, a card of Panadeine Forte and a script in case I need more, but I only need to take them and get it filled if the pain is bad again. It's not hurting at all now.' She moved her fingers a little. 'It only feels a little tight, and the tablets would be wearing off by now.' Cy hadn't been surprised when they'd stitched it.

After they'd left Emergency, he had driven them to the shopping centre and stayed with Tarni while she did a little bit of shopping. She insisted she was feeling fine, so he'd left her in a coffee shop with her new book and headed off quickly to the private hospital to visit Joe. He'd felt strange all the way home after spending time with him. The visit that he knew would be the last time he saw his father.

They reached the house and Cy parked close to the steps before he turned the engine off. For a moment they sat there quietly, and then Tarni reached to open her door.

'Hang on, I'll get it. Watch that hand.' Cy quickly opened his door. 'I'll open the door for you and help you out.'

He hurried around the front of the ute and paused briefly as he heard the dogs barking.

He'd fed them before they'd left this afternoon, but the sound of his ute had probably stirred them up. He'd check on them once he had Tarni inside.

Cy opened the passenger door and held his hand out. Tarni lifted her bag over her shoulder and reached out and took his hand.

'Thank you,' she said, once she was standing beside him next to the car.

'You're not getting woozy at all?' The security light above the front steps had come on when they parked there and he could see that Tarni's cheeks had some colour in them again.

'No, I feel as good as new,' she said. 'I might even be able to get back to work tomorrow.'

'One-handed.' Cy nodded.

'Yes, one-handed. I can't afford to get this infected. I can type with my left hand. I can record the results without touching anything. It's only a few minutes of checking. I will spend some time down in the shed and just have a look at everything, and type up the results from the first twenty-four hours.'

'Come on and I'll get you up to the steps and unlock the door for you. Then I'll come back for your shopping.'

'You've got a house key, haven't you?' She started walking up the steps in front of him. 'That's right, you used it the other day to get that guy's card. When's he coming?'

'Tomorrow afternoon, I think.' Cy kept a step behind her.

They reached the veranda and as they walked across to the front door, the security light above the door came on.

'What the—?' Tarni stopped suddenly. 'Look, Cy, the screen door's open. Somebody must've been here.'

'Did you close it when we left? Maybe it didn't latch and the wind caught it.'

'I closed it and I locked it with the key too.' She reached into her bag and held her keys p.. 'I've got a key to the security door on the set of keys Kane gave me. I locked the deadlock on the front door with the key too, and the bottom lock.'

'You're sure?' Cy frowned and opened the screen door wide.

'I'm one hundred percent sure. I was a little bit woozy, but I locked—' She stopped as Cy reached past her and turned the door knob of the front door.

'Hang on. The front door's open too.'

Tarni stepped back and stared at the open door. 'I locked them both,' she whispered. 'Do you think there's someone inside?'

'Wait here,' he said quietly. Cy pushed the door open slowly. 'Just be watchful.'

Tarni touched his arm. 'I'd rather be behind you than out here by myself. They could be on the other end of the veranda.'

'They would've heard the car pull up. There's no sign of another car around here, so I'd say whoever it was has been and gone.'

'Maybe someone walked down from the highway.'

Cy stood there quietly for a moment, but there was no sound apart from the dogs barking down the back.

'That's the first time I've heard the dogs barking since I arrived,' Tarni whispered. 'Do you think whoever it is might be there around the dog pen now?'

'I don't know, but I'm certainly not going to leave you here by yourself. Come on, we'll go inside and turn all the lights on and take care as we check each room.' He held his hand out to her and she took it willingly and followed him across the foyer and into the kitchen.

'Everything looks okay,' she whispered.

They walked quietly down the hall, checking each room thoroughly. After turning the lights on, Cy checked under each bed, in each cupboard and behind the curtains in each room.

'I feel like I'm intruding, looking into their rooms.'

'I know what you mean,' Tarni said. 'I've only been in the kitchen and laundry, and the living room and guest accommodation.'

Cy nodded. Tarni respected the McLaren's privacy as he would have if he'd been staying in the house.

'What about the back door and the side verandas?' she said. 'We should check those too.'

They walked through the laundry and to the back door that opened onto the veranda. Unlike the front door, it was locked.

'That's strange. Please don't doubt me.' Her eyes were wide. 'I really did lock the doors.'

'I don't doubt you, Tarni. I'm sure someone's been here but, strangely, there's no sign of forced entry.'

'Who else would have keys? she wondered aloud. 'Maybe some of the family called in, but if they had, I'm sure they would've locked the door when they left.'

'Someone shut the gate,' Cy said. 'I left it open. Come on, we'll lock the door and go down and have a look down at the shed and check the dogs. Or would you rather stay here now we know it's clear?' He was still holding Tarni's hand.

'No, I'm not staying here by myself. Not now, maybe in the morning when it's light. I don't want to be here by myself in the dark.'

Cy thought long and hard trying to figure out who it might have been. The more he thought about it, the more suspicious he found the situation. He'd give Ryan a call later. All he could think of was the McLaren's emphasis on security.

The roller door and the side door of the shed were locked securely.

Cy let go of Tarni's hand and walked over to the ute and switched the headlights on, lighting up the space between the shed and the dog pen. When he walked back to Tarni, she slipped her hand into his again.

It felt good.

Molly and Max ran around barking. 'Calm down, guys. Are you hungry?'

Max, the blue heeler, let out a yelp and nudged over to his food bowl.

'Do you think it's food they want? Or are they trying to tell us something?' Tarni asked. 'I don't know much about dogs. I've never had one.'

'No, they only get fed once a day, and I did feed them both this afternoon before we left. It was a little bit out of their routine. Plus, they haven't been out for a run today.'

'They seem unsettled, don't they? They should be used to us by now.' Tarni looked around as if expecting an intruder to jump out of the shadows.

'They should.' She was still holding Cy's hand tightly and he stopped and faced her. 'I don't want you to take this the wrong way, but what would you say about me sleeping in the house tonight?'

'Why? Because of my hand or the intruder?'

'Both. Until I'm sure there's no one around, I'd feel better being close by. It's a long way from the shed up to the house if you called out for help—'

'Of course, it's fine. There's a spare bedroom just down from mine.'

'Yeah, Kane wanted a lot of bedrooms when he designed the house. I remember Ryan paying out on him for planning to have half a dozen kids.'

'Kane and Ellie seem lucky. Sounds like they have a big extended family too.' Tarni sounded wistful.

'They are a very large and close family and yes, they are very happy. Mind you, they've done it tough. They've had their share of tragedy.'

'Haven't we all?' Tarni whispered. She lifted her head and looked at him. 'That's one of the reasons why I think I might stay up this way when I finish my research here at the end of my PhD studies. A new start in a good place.'

'Sounds like a good plan.' Cy held her eyes with his and was dismayed to see tears welling in Tarni's.

'One of the reasons I want to move is to get away from my past. I think we've established a bit of a friendship today where we can talk freely.'

'A problem shared is a problem halved,' he said surprising himself. 'My dad used to say that.'

'I lost my partner almost two years ago,' she said. 'Jonty was killed in an industrial accident. I guess I haven't really let myself get over it and coming here and this change has been very therapeutic for me. I even wonder if that's why I think I should stay up here, but I guess it's because I moved away and I've let go. I didn't think I'd ever be happy again but I've enjoyed spending time with you this week, Cy.' She shook her head. 'Please don't get me wrong. I'm not saying I've fallen for you or anything as heavy as that; it's just been really good to spend time with another human being and talk. To be honest, I haven't done that in the last two years. So, thanks for being kind to me.'

Cy cleared his throat and his voice was gruff. 'Ditto. I've enjoyed your company too. And we've all got our demons.'

'We do.'

'Come on, let's go make a cuppa.' Cy held Tarni's hand all the way back to the house.

Chapter 22

McLaren Mango Farm - Sunday night
Tarni.

Tarni yawned as she stood at the kitchen window, looking out into the dark. The moon was just rising and the tops of the mango trees were touched with golden light. The shadows beneath were more sinister, but she knew if there was anyone about, the dogs would be barking. Cy had assured her that whoever had been here was long gone.

She turned as he came in from the hallway. His hair was damp and he was wearing a white T-shirt and a pair of shorts.

Tarni looked away from the well-defined muscles of his chest. 'Did you find everything you needed?'

'Yes, I grabbed a towel from the hall cupboard. Listen, I don't think I'll have that cuppa now. I put some cans of Coke in the fridge. I'll have a cold drink.'

'Very healthy,' she said. 'Coke would keep me awake.'

'Nothing will keep me awake tonight. A drink and off to bed.'

Tarni got the impression that Cy wasn't feeling very talkative. He'd been quiet since he'd come back to the shopping centre where she'd sat reading in a coffee shop while he visited the hospital. He still hadn't been forthcoming about who he had visited, but she had noticed the definite change in his demeanour afterwards. When he came back, he'd barely spoken before she went to sleep on the trip back to the farm. Even though she'd known him for a short time, it was clear something was bothering him. It probably was none of her business, but she found the courage to ask; he'd looked out for her. She could do the same for him.

'Are you okay, Cy?'

He nodded and then looked away. 'Yep.'

'Okay, I don't think I'll have a hot drink either. I'll take a glass of water to bed with me, in case I need to take more painkillers through the night.' Tarni walked over and stood beside him. It was very much out of character but she put her uninjured hand on his forearm. His skin was warm and still slightly damp. 'Thank you, Cy. It was very kind of you to look after me today. I appreciate it.'

'Not a problem. How's the hand?'

'Not hurting too much. It's been a long time since anyone has looked after me, so thank you. I know you had a lot of work planned.'

'It waited. Back to work for a normal day for me tomorrow. I hope you're going to take some time out.'

'I might have a bit of a lie-in and I'll just go down later in the morning and look at the seeds. Write up some figures if I can.'

'If your hand can take it.' He smiled slightly but still looked distracted.

'Yes. Would it be all right with you if I came down to the dam and watched you work for a while? It would be nice sitting in the sun down there. I'd like to take a walk through the trees and have a good look at the orchard.'

He nodded slightly but didn't reply and she wondered if he would prefer to be alone.

'Anyway, I'll see what the morning brings,' she said briskly. 'I might have a fair bit to write up depending on what happens with the seeds overnight.'

'Okay. Sleep well.' Cy disappeared up the hallway without looking back and soon she heard the bedroom door close.

Tarni went back to the window and looked out over the orchard. The moon had cleared the tops of the mango trees now, and a peaceful scene met her. Full and heavy, the light of the moon made the shadowy corners under the trees seem less sinister. The fear that had gripped her when she knew someone had been in the house eased a little.

The unlocked front doors had thrown her; now she scanned the darkness looking for any sign of anyone still out there. She still felt uncomfortable, because she knew she *had* locked both the doors before they left.

A movement near the shed caught her attention; she tensed and then relaxed as a small wallaby hopped across to the trees. Another yawn reminded her she should go to bed as did the slight throbbing of her hand.

On the way to the guest bedroom, she double-checked the doors that Cy had locked when they had come inside. Then she checked the windows in each room, except for the bedroom Cy was in.

After Tarni was sure the house was secure, she went back to the kitchen and found a Ziplock bag. She covered her hand and clipped as much of the bag together as she could one-handed and had the best wash she could manage without getting the bandage wet.

Dressing in her pyjamas, she folded the bed back before she went back to the kitchen to refill her glass from the water purifier. Her mouth was very dry; it must be from the strong painkillers she'd taken this afternoon. She opened the pantry cupboard to take out the plastic jug she'd been using to refill the water purifier all week. Lifting the lid of the stone urn, she frowned. Water lapped the rim of the porcelain insert.

She must be losing the plot. She could have sworn it was almost empty this morning and didn't remember refilling it. With a shrug, she hoped the same memory lapse didn't apply to the front doors. Maybe she hadn't locked them.

Tarni was still frowning as she filled her water glass and took the box of painkillers from her handbag on the kitchen bench. Once she was back in her room, she shut the door, climbed into bed and was asleep within seconds of her head hitting the pillow.

***

Cy lay in bed for a long time before he went to sleep. Tarni came down the hall and he listened as she pottered around the house checking the doors and windows he'd already checked. If it hadn't been for the gate being open, he might not have believed that she had locked the doors, but someone had been there.

Nothing appeared to be missing; it was strange.

He rolled over and thumped the pillow. Seeing Joe this afternoon for what he knew would be the last time had rattled him. The gaunt, sallow man lying in the bed was not the loud, argumentative father he remembered. Joe had been half-lucid and had slept for over half the time Cy had been with him.

Cy's emotions were in chaos. As much as he hated his father for what he done during his life, Joe's greeting had thrown him. As he walked into the room, he'd struggled to sit up, but failed and flopped back onto the pillow, breathing heavily, his words slurred.

'I'm sorry, son. So sorry. Please forgive me.'

Cy had sat in the chair beside him as Joe drifted in and out of sleep. His speech rambled, but the gist of it was easy to follow.

'I messed up my life, and yours.' Once he'd called him Colin, and then Suzanne. His dreams and his reality were mixed up. 'I paid the price, son.'

'You started to pay the price anyway, getting caught.' Cy couldn't help himself. 'I wonder if you'd be sorry if you hadn't been caught?'

'No, the cancer is my punishment.'

'Nuh. Lots of good people get cancer and die.' Cy's voice was husky.

'I made mistakes.' Joe's breath wheezed as he tried to sit up, but Cy pushed his shoulder gently so that Joe's head was back on the pillow. 'Bad father. Bridget screwed me up. I was vindicative.'

Cy leaned forward and put his head in his hands. He didn't need to revisit all this. He tensed at Joe's next words.

'I told Colin I killed her when he had his heart attack out in the bush.' Joe closed his eyes and fought for breath. 'Told him I would have killed those kids too, after he left her, that Dee girl, half the bloody station. But he got what he deserved, the bastard. He hurt my sister but he could never acknowledge his daughter.' His eyes glazed when Cy looked at him. 'She should have been mine, Colin. You took Bridget off me.' His eyelids dropped again. When he opened his eyes again, they were clearer. 'Cy? Come closer.'

Cy moved the plastic chair closer to the bed. His chest was tight and his throat ached, but still, he didn't regret coming.

'I know I haven't got long, son, but it would ease me greatly if you would forgive me. I will get what I deserve when I go.'

Cy's eyes blurred with tears. He had to remember the good times, the jokes, watching football games with Joe, travelling around with him; all the good things before he'd discovered his father was a murderer.

'I forgive you, Dad.' He stood and walked to the door, and when he looked back, his father's face was peaceful.

Chapter 23

McLaren Mango Farm - Monday
Cy

Cy woke early the next morning. He'd had very little sleep; he'd been listening for Tarni for most of the night and worrying about who'd broken in. His senses had been on high alert and at least it took his mind off Joe.

He drifted into a restless sleep at dawn and was woken up soon after by his phone buzzing.

'Cy Prescott,' he said sleepily.

He closed his eyes as the doctor at the palliative care ward told him that Joe had passed through the night. He disconnected and got straight in the shower, allowing himself a few tears and then tipped his head up for the hot water to wash the tears away. His chest ached and he felt empty but, in a way, cleansed. The only person he had to ring was Ryan, but that could wait until a decent hour. Once dressed in the work clothes he'd brought over to the house last night, Cy opened his door quietly and walked to the kitchen in his socks. All was quiet at the end of the hall in Tarni's room.

Cy considered making a cup of tea in the kitchen but thought he might wake Tarni, so he took his keys out and unlocked the doors. He crouched down and examined the lock on the screen door and noted a deep scratch beside the silver lever that locked the door manually. He hadn't seen that in the dim light last night. Someone had broken in.

He crouched and examined it more closely.

Maybe the scratch was new, maybe it had always been there. The wooden door looked fairly new, with not a mark on it. If anyone had come inside yesterday, they had either had keys or were a master lockpicker.

Cy's thoughts were churning as he closed both doors, key-locked them and walked quietly down the steps. He'd keep a close eye on the house until Tarni appeared for the day. He hesitated, wondering if he should check on her, and then decided to let her sleep.

He looked around as he walked down to the shed. There were tyre tracks in the dust on the road from the gate. The road that the paved circular driveway came off. Crouching, Cy examined the tracks closely and decided that it was not the tread of his tyres. And Tarni's Jeep hadn't been out of the shed since she'd arrived.

He was thoughtful as he walked down to the shed. The morning was crisp and mist still lingered over the trees. The night had been cool; his ute was covered with condensation. He unlocked the shed and took a jacket from his bag. He hoped Tarni was feeling better; he should have been more receptive when she'd asked about coming down to the dam. If she hadn't come down by smoko, he'd come back up and make her a cuppa and invite her down.

He felt unsettled. He couldn't stop thinking about Joe since he'd had the call. Putting his jacket on, he checked the shed but everything looked okay. He walked into Tarni's section to check it as well.

Who knew? Maybe it was someone from another mango farm trying to sabotage Kane's work. Cy didn't think the best of anyone these days. He'd had too many experiences with people you couldn't trust. But thinking about a neighbour coming in with intent to sabotage was a bit far-fetched. He'd been watching too many Netflix shows in Darwin; television had filled the lonely nights.

Cy boiled the kettle, dunked a teabag in the cup, and headed outside. He sat in the chair by the fire pit and put his feet up on the log. He pulled his phone out and glanced at the time; it wasn't too early to call Ryan.

His cousin picked up straight away. 'Cy, I was going to call you later. How goes it?'

'It's good here. Making progress and looking after the place. I think the trees'll survive until Kane and Ellie get home.'

Ryan chuckled. 'They'd better.'

'Before you tell me what you were going to call me about, you need to know I had a call from the hospice earlier. Joe passed away through the night.'

There was a long silence before Ryan spoke. 'You okay?'

'Yeah, I guess.'

'I'm sorry for your loss, mate.'

'Thanks.'

'Funeral?'

'Haven't thought about it. Prison's organising it all.'

'Are you gonna go to the service?'

'No. I went to see him yesterday afternoon.'

'Fair enough. I'll have a beer for Joe tonight.'

'So, what were you going to call me about?' Cy stood and walked around the side of the shed. He thought he'd heard a car drive in but there was no one there.

'I wanted to know if you could spare me a day or even half a day over the weekend. My crew have gone to a rodeo and I've got a mob to drench.'

'I should be able to come. A bloke's coming to see me later about digging the last of the irrigation trenches. If he suits,

I'll hire him for a few days. I'll give you a call and let you know after I talk to him.'

'Be good to catch up for a few hours even if you haven't got time to help me.'

'Yep, we're long overdue for a catch-up. Listen, would you mind if I brought someone with me for the day? Would it bother Dee if she had a visitor?'

'Sounds interesting. You finally got yourself a lady friend?'

'No, not a "lady friend", just a lady and a friend. Tarni's the researcher working here on Kane's hybrid program. She's good company, and she's never been to the Territory before. She's keen to see a cattle station.'

'Yeah, no problem. I'll check that Dee will be here, but I don't think she's got any plans to go to town.' Ryan chuckled. 'It all depends if we need nappies.'

'Okay, I'll let you know. Talk later. See ya, mate.'

Cy loaded the pick and the crowbar into the ute and headed down to the trees. After the first half hour, he'd shed his jacket; the mist burned away quickly as the sun climbed. The perspiration rolled off him and when he reached the end of the second trench, Cy headed for the ute to get his water. The noise of an engine caught his attention and he looked up. A black ute was heading down the track. The driver parked about twenty metres away from where Cy was standing, jumped out and sauntered over.

Cy frowned, wondering who it was. That Jerry guy wasn't supposed to come until this afternoon.

'Can I help you?' he called out as the short stocky guy approached.

'Gidday, mate.' He held his hand out to Cy. 'I'm sorry I'm early. I'm Jerry. I stuffed up. I have somewhere else to go this afternoon to see about another job so I called in on the off chance you might be here.'

'Yeah, that's fine.' Cy gestured to the trees. 'I've been working here for a couple of hours. I'm Cy.'

He was taken aback when the guy chuckled. 'Gotta love it,' Jerry said. 'Anyway, I drove down when I couldn't raise anyone at the house.'

Cy frowned, wondering where Tarni was. She should be up by now. 'Right, so you're after a few days' work?'

'I am, mate. I'm heading over to Camooweal in a couple of weeks. Going back to Queensland. My old man had some mango farms there, so I'm pretty experienced working with the trees.'

Cy shook his head. 'I'm after someone to do some trench digging, I thought I said that on the phone.'

'Look, mate, I've talked to so many people over the last few days, I can't remember what the job here was. I don't know if I'm coming or going half the time. Seems like there's a big shortage of labourers around here.'

'Yeah, you could say that.' Cy stood back and checked him out. He was short but well-muscled. He'd either developed his muscles working out or by hard manual work. The ute was a bit clean for a work ute though. He nodded towards the vehicle. 'New rig?'

'Yeah, only had it a couple of weeks. Hasn't got a scratch on it yet, but that won't take long.' Jerry laughed. 'I got it to impress my old man.'

Cy was fast taking a dislike to Jerry, but he reminded himself he didn't have to like him. As long as he could dig, it didn't matter if he was a smart arse. He'd worked with all types on cattle stations out west. Seemed to be a thing with short guys. They always had to big-note themselves. He'd found that out more times than he could remember.

Jerry walked past him and looked at where Cy had been digging. 'You're not digging with a machine, hey?'

'No, is that a problem?'

'Nah, just wondered. With a spread like this, I thought you might have had all the bells and whistles.'

Cy bit back a smart reply. 'The trenches are too close to the trees so I prefer to do it with a crowbar and a shovel.'

'Yeah, I can do that. How many you got left?'

'These two avenues are done.' Cy walked through the trees and Jerry followed. 'I've done that avenue up to the sixth tree and then I'm almost done with the next one. I'll finish that today. If you're happy to come tomorrow, that leaves trenches to be dug in three avenues as far as six trees in.'

'Why only six trees in?' Jerry asked.

Cy didn't need to tell him about the hybrid program. 'Because there are irrigation pipes that far already. What do you think? Interested in three days' work?'

'Not a problem if you're happy to have me, I charge thirty-five bucks an hour, cash in hand. Half up front. Been caught too many times not getting paid.'

'Sounds fair. I want someone who can finish the work and do it quickly.'

'Well, Sir I—' the smart arse drew out Cy's name '—you got the right person here.'

'When can you start?'

'I can start this afternoon if you want.'

'I thought you said you had to go and see about a job this afternoon.'

Jerry mimed hitting his forehead with the heel of his hand. 'Fuckin' oath. I told you I didn't know what I was doing half the time. Yeah, I gotta go and see a bloke, so I better see him because he can give me a couple of days' work before I start here, so when do you want me to work? I reckon three days will get it done. How about Friday, Saturday and Sunday?'

'You're happy to work on the weekend?' Cy asked.

'Bloody oath. One day's the same as another to me.'

'I mightn't be here on Saturday and Sunday. Do you reckon you'll be okay by yourself?'

'Mate, give me a shovel and a pick and I can do whatever. I'll bring some tucker with me. Nowhere to get a feed around here anyway, is there? I think I can go for a piss down the back of the dam and if I need a crap I can dig a hole.' He laughed again and for the first time, Cy noticed his blackened teeth.

Jerry was certainly a charmer, but as long as he could dig, Cy didn't care.

'Friday?'

'Eight o'clock do?'

'That'll be fine. See ya then, Sir I. Don't forget half the dosh up front.'

Cy expelled a deep breath as Jerry climbed into his ute and gunned the engine. He walked up to the top of the rise and checked that he drove straight out the gate.

He waited until the black ute disappeared up the highway, and he went back to his digging. Another hour and he'd go up and check on Tarni.

Chapter 24

McLaren Mango Farm - Monday morning
Tarni

Tarni spent a restless night. She woke up a couple of times to go to the toilet and when she got up the second time, she realised she must have had a massive sweat. The sheets were tangled around her legs and damp.

She was too tired to stay up and go looking for fresh sheets so she moved across to the other side of the queen-sized bed, where the sheets were dry. She went back to sleep instantly, and her sleep was filled with strange dreams. She dreamed about Jonty working down on the mango trees, and she dreamed about her parents. Her grandfather appeared at one point, telling her to go home. 'It's too hot up here for a lass like you,' he said.

When she woke the next time, sunlight was streaming through the open blinds, and she put her hand to her eyes. Her head was pounding. She'd rolled on her hand through the night, and it was tender, but it wasn't as sore as she had expected it would be. It was her head that was hurting the most.

Tarni lay back for a moment and closed her eyes, intending to get up soon. When she woke again the room was darker, the sun had moved off the window. She glanced at the clock, surprised to see it was after nine.

Swinging her legs over the side of the bed she cooled her feet on the smooth white tiles. She loved the tiled floors that were right through the house. Even though it was late autumn, the house stayed warm all day. There was no carpet and it would be so easy to keep clean. If there was one thing that Tarni was, it was a clean freak and it had been hard living in rented apartments in the city.

One day, she thought, I'll have a home like this.

She cradled her sore hand in front of her as she stood, and she swayed on her feet as her head pounded.

Making her way slowly to the guest bathroom she picked up the plastic bag, she'd used last night and put it over her bandaged hand. Her shower was quick, and she washed her hair one-handed, managing not to get the dressing on her injured hand wet.

Drying herself with one hand was a little bit more difficult, and she dropped the towel a couple of times, her head pounding as she bent to pick it up.

She rubbed her wet hair with the towel and then struggled to pull it back into a scrunchie. Once it was back, she stood in front of the mirror.

Her face was pale, but she had twin spots of colour high on each cheek, and that concerned her. Using the back of her hand to feel her forehead, it didn't appear she had a temperature. Tarni was tempted to take the dressing off her wound and have a look at it but instead, she moved her thumb gingerly. It didn't hurt and it wasn't throbbing like it had been yesterday afternoon, so she assumed there was no infection there. She was just run down and headachy from yesterday.

There was no sign of Cy when she walked out to the kitchen. He would have gone down to the trees at dawn. The coffeemaker was still on and she decided to sit out in the sun with a real coffee. She removed the clear plastic water container from the back and filled it with water from the water purifier. After clipping it on and plugging the machine in, she turned to the small container beside the coffee maker and looked at the selection of coffee pods. Using the pods worried her because they created such environmental waste.

One wouldn't hurt; hopefully, it would help ease her headache. She chose a strong espresso coffee, opened the hatch and put the pod inside. As it heated, she found a cup in the drawer beneath the cupboard and put it under the spout. Seconds after she pushed the button the enticing aroma of fresh-brewed coffee tickled her nose.

She looked in the pantry for the granola she usually ate, but her head was pounding, and she decided to have the coffee and some painkillers first; she'd think about breakfast later when she felt better. Then she'd go down to the shed and have a look at the seeds, log the temperatures, and hopefully be able to measure the overnight growth, even if she was one-handed.

Taking her coffee Tarni wandered out to the veranda. Placing it on the small coffee table, she went back to the bathroom and took two of the strong painkillers with the remaining water in the glass by the bed. She went to refill the glass in the bathroom sink and then decided to go back to the kitchen and use the purified water. On top of her sore hand and headache, she certainly wasn't going to risk a tummy bug from microorganisms in the tank, no matter what Cy said.

Five minutes later, she was sitting in a comfortable papasan chair, looking out over the lush green trees. There was a slight breeze and the leaves rippled as the wind blew through the plantation. She really should go down and start work, but her headache was gradually easing. Resting her head against the soft back of the comfortable chair, Tarni put her head back and closed her eyes.

##

Cy put the tools in the back of the ute and reached for the towel he always carried in the cabin. He wiped the dirt-streaked sweat from his face, neck and shoulders. As much as Jerry whatever his name was, seemed like an absolute tool, it would be good to have a break from digging. He knew that Kane hadn't expected the trenches all to be done at once, but if he got it out of the way, he could go over and help Ryan with the cattle.

Cy stretched and pulled his T-shirt over his head. Hopefully, Tarni and Dee would hit it off; it would get Tarni away from the shed for a bit. He sensed that her work was her life, and he understood why since she'd revealed her sad past to him.

He drove back to the shed; he'd spend the day up here. He was surprised to see the shed was still locked up. Maybe Tarni had gone back up to the house for a break, or maybe she wasn't well enough to work.

He opened the door and called out.

'Are you in here, Tarni?'

No reply. Concern tugged at Cy. He should have checked on her before he left this morning. Hurrying up to the house, he took the front steps two at a time. The front door was open and he walked inside. She wasn't in the kitchen. He walked down to her bedroom, and looked through the open door; a wet towel lay on the floor, and the bedsheets were in a tangle, half on the floor and half on the bed, but there was no sign of Tarni.

His worry grew. He went back to the kitchen and noticed the coffeemaker was switched on, so she must be around somewhere. He leaned over the sink and looked out the kitchen window. Relief filled him as he spied her feet hanging over the chair on the back veranda.

##

'Good morning, sleepyhead.'

Tarni jumped as Cy's voice woke her. 'Damn, I must have drifted off again. I can't seem to stay awake.'

'How's the hand?' He came over and sat in the other papasan chair.

'Not too bad actually, but I had a stinker of a headache when I woke up so I took some more painkillers and they knocked me out. What time is it?'

'It's closer to lunchtime than morning tea. I got held up. That Jerry bloke turned up early.'

Tarni sat up and stretched. 'I've wasted the whole morning. I haven't even been down to the shed yet.'

'You needed the rest. I set the hotplate on the fire pit and got the fire going before I went down to the trees this morning. Feel like sausage sangers for lunch?'

'Sounds good. I haven't eaten yet.'

'Okay, how about I throw an egg on for you as well?'

'As long as you put tomato sauce on the egg.' Tarni stood and picked up her coffee cup.

'Gross,' Cy said. 'Eggs and tomato sauce do not go together.'

'Have you ever tried it?'

'Nope, and I'm not about to.'

'I'll bring the sauce down,' Tarni said.

'Okay. I'll go and get the snags on.'

'Would you like me to bring you a coffee down? I've figured out the intricacies of the coffee maker.'

'No, I'm good thanks. I'll have a Coke.'

Tarni shook her head. 'You're addicted to the stuff.'

'What? No worse than the caffeine in coffee.' Cy grinned at her and then went down the stairs and started back to the shed.

Tarni watched until he disappeared around the corner. The relationship between them now was very comfortable but she had wondered about him last night. She'd told him a bit about her life and he'd shut down.

She wondered if it was what she'd told him, or whoever it was he'd been to visit that had made him go quiet.

Tarni stood up. Her head spun and her legs were shaking, so she sat back on the chair for a moment. Her eyes were heavy and she jerked herself out of it.

What the hell is wrong with me? As she pushed herself up, her vision blurred and she grabbed the side of the chair.

That's all I need. To be too dizzy to focus on the measurements.

Tarni went to the bathroom, took the rubber band out of her hair and brushed her now-dry hair and pulled it back again. By the time she changed into a cooler T-shirt and headed down to the shed she was feeling a bit better.

Brunch and work, in that order.

Chapter 25

Darwin Royal Hospital - Tuesday morning
Emma

Emma frowned as she left Dru's private room. So far, she'd been able to persuade Dru that staying in the hospital was the wisest course of action, but she knew how strong-willed Dru was. She was getting restless and was sure to insist on going home soon. When Emma had come into the room earlier, she noticed traces of tears on her sister's cheeks when she took her blood pressure. It was gradually getting higher. Emma made a mental note to talk to Dr Rickard about it.

'Are you worrying too much, Dru?'

Her little sister rolled her eyes. 'What do you think, Emma? I've been stuck in a bed here using a bedpan, not allowed to get out and walk, only seeing my darling Ruby once every day or so if I'm lucky, depending on your shifts and Jeremy's schedule, and worrying about where my husband is. Yes, everything is just hunky dory.'

'Have you heard from Connor again?' Emma put her fingers on Dru's wrist. Her pulse was racing.

'No, he texted and said he was going out of service for a while.'

'I'm sure he'll be back in town soon and he'll come straight to the hospital, and you can talk and sort out all this misunderstanding.'

'If it *is* a misunderstanding,' Dru said. 'I think your Pollyanna-ness is showing.'

'Please be positive, Dru.'

'I'm being positive. I have courses of action planned for whatever happens when he comes back. *If* he comes back. If he has found someone else, I'll cope.'

'Don't even put that into words. Jeremy and I've talked about this every night and we think you're way off base. You've seen a situation and you've misconstrued it.'

'Well, if you want to live in fairyland, then go ahead. You always have, Emma. I face reality. I'm prepared.'

Emma sighed. No matter how hard she tried to persuade Dru she was wrong, she couldn't shift her. Dru had been stubborn since the day she was born into the Porter family. Dad had always said she was like his mother, Grandma Tilly, who Ellie had named Matilda after. 'Okay, I'll see you tomorrow. It's my day off. I'll bring Ruby in for the day.'

'Thank you.' Dru looked away from her towards the window. Emma patted her sister's hand and walked out of the ward to start her shift. She'd been seconded to oncology today because Mary Butler had called in sick.

She stopped at the nurses' station, and read the clinical notes that had been left. As usual, it was going to be busy as outpatients came into the ward for their chemotherapy. Some patients in the wards had completed their treatment regime and were waiting for the doctor to discuss options before discharge.

Emma consulted with the three nurses on duty and once she was sure the day had started with no problems, she made her way to the tearoom and made a quick cup of tea before commencing her ward round.

If she'd specialised, and Jeremy and Akasha hadn't been the focus of her life, this was the area she'd been particularly interested in. Emma still did a lot of professional reading and kept up to date with the literature. One day, when Akasha was older, she'd probably go back and do some more study. Emptying the dregs of her tea in the sink and putting the disposable cup in the bin, Emma tried to focus on the day ahead, and not on Dru and her unhappiness.

It was such a strange situation, and so out of character for the Connor who, Emma knew, adored his wife and daughter.

Emma put a smile on her face as she walked into the first ward. With cheery comments and a couple of longer chats with patients who had questions, she worked her way through the wards, checking observations and notes. There were six wards with four beds in each of the chemotherapy wards, and most of the patients were upbeat today.

Two of the beds were empty and she knew those patients would be in having their treatment. She glanced at her watch as voices came from the waiting room. The inpatients should be finished shortly; it sounded as though the outpatients for the morning had already arrived. The cancer care outpatient facility across town had been overwhelmed with patients this month and the oncology ward in the hospital had taken the overflow.

Emma decided to wait until the final two patients came back to the ward. It could be an emotional time and she liked to be there to reassure the patients after they came back. Occasionally stress levels increased because they had time to think about the treatment and their prognosis while the chemicals were being infused.

She made her way to the nurses' station. 'Did the last two patients go in on time?'

'Yes, Dr Langford.' The young male nurse looked up from the computer. 'They should be back in the wards shortly. It's the last treatment for one of them today and he can be discharged if you're happy with them. Or if you'd rather wait,

Dr Mulholland is due in at ten. She's Mr Kirk's attending physician.'

'Okay, I'll go down there in a minute. I'll take the papers with me, to save coming back.'

He flicked through the files and retrieved the forms she needed and handed two sets of paperwork to her

'Thank you, Brett.' Emma glanced up and saw another nurse pushing a wheelchair into the ward. 'There's the first patient back now.'

Emma's flat shoes squeaked on the polished lino floor as she walked along the corridor. Entering the last ward, she was surprised to see both patients had returned.

A young man with a shiny bald head sat up in the bed to the left, and she smiled at him. She glanced across to the bed on the right next to the door, and Emma stared in disbelief. Her heart beat hard and fast, as the discharge papers slipped from her hand and for a moment she felt as though she was going to faint.

Connor Kirk lifted his eyes and met hers as she stood in the doorway, one hand over her mouth. 'Hello Emma, I thought it would only be a matter of time before I bumped into you or Jeremy here.'

'Connor?' Emma couldn't keep the shock out of her voice. 'What on earth . . . I mean, what are you doing here? I mean . . . Crumbs!' She grabbed his hand. 'This is where you've been all this time. You've been calling and texting from the hospital!'

The young man across the ward was following their conversation with interest. Emma shot him an apologetic smile and reached up and closed the curtains around Connor's bed.

'No one knows you're in here? Dru doesn't even know? I can't believe it.' Emma dropped into the chair beside the bed and stared at her brother-in-law.

Connor shook his head. 'I'm sorry, Emma. This is the way I wanted it to be. Nobody knows except my GP, my oncologist, and the staff in this unit.'

'But what about Dru?' Emma said. 'I don't understand.'

'I had to do this by myself. I wanted to do it by myself.'

'But why? You needed support. How long have you been going through chemo?'

'Six weeks, this is my last round. I hope.'

'And what is—' Emma cut her question off. If Connor wanted to tell her, he would. It wasn't her place to ask. Being the duty doctor, she could simply look at his files to see the prognosis, but being a relative that would be wrong. If Connor wanted her to know, she would let him tell her.

'The prognosis is good. I just had to go through the treatment and I didn't think Dru or Ruby or the family needed that worry.'

'My God, Connor, you can't go through something like this yourself.'

'It's all right, Dru thinks I'm working on a very heavy case.'

Emma raised her eyebrows and let that go for the time being. 'How's your mental health?' She was back in doctor mode.

'Fine. I'm coping with this and staying positive. Dr Mulholland has been a great support. She's kept me informed at every step. Told me what would be happening and how long it would take. I'm expecting her shortly for the final results. And then I can go and see Dru. If it's good, I don't need to tell her anything about the past few weeks.'

'Do you think that's the right thing to do, Connor? I'm speaking now both as a doctor and as your sister-in-law.'

'Yes, I think it's the right thing to do. It's my decision.'

'It is, but I always thought you were a man of intelligence and compassion. I'm speaking out of turn here, but I cannot stand to see Dru the way she is for a minute longer than necessary. I think she will accept the fact that you have—?'

'Stage one testicular cancer,' Connor filled in. 'And what do you mean the way she is?'

'I think she will deal with that much better than she is dealing with her fear that you're leaving her for another woman, Connor.' Emma's voice broke. 'Dru has refused to talk to you when you called because she thinks you're going to tell her you're leaving her. She thinks you've found someone else.'

'What! Why?'

'How could you think she hasn't noticed something was very different? She's breaking her heart; she thinks you're having an affair and it's not doing her or the baby any good.'

'What the hell? Where on earth would she get that from?'

'Just think about your behaviour over the past six weeks. What does it look like? Leaving early, not talking to her, coming home late, and having days away?'

'I stayed in a hotel in town after each chemo session until I felt better and then I went home.'

'For God's sake, Connor. Dru is your wife! What were the vows you made? In sickness and in health, for better for worse, and all those promises.'

'Yeah, I know but—'

Emma interrupted. 'No buts. You are going to have to handle this so carefully. If you don't know your wife and how she'll take this, you haven't been paying attention. She is in the same hospital as you are. Do you know she's likely to have the baby early? You haven't even been to see her.'

'I don't want her to know I'm sick.' His voice was flat, but Emma could sense he was having second thoughts.

She pursed her lips, stood, and moved to the end of the bed. 'As the doctor on duty I should look at your clinical notes but you tell me if you'd prefer I didn't?' She pointed to the chart at the end of the bed. 'I'm supposed to take your obs and check your chart after the session you've just had. I'm checking each patient as they come back from the chemo room.'

Connor looked at her. 'Go ahead.'

She quickly scanned down through the clinical notes, and his observations, and didn't say a word as she wheeled the blood pressure machine over and slipped the cuff on his arm.

'Perfect, thank you.' She picked up the digital thermometer and put it against his forehead, and when it beeped, she nodded.

'All good. How have your neutrophils been between treatments?'

'No problems and I didn't need injections.'

'And you've been keeping well?'

'I'm fine, just tired.'

'And you've lost weight. We all commented on that.'

'I'm being positive, Emma. I'm hoping this is over. Why does Dru have to know?'

Emma narrowed her eyes. 'It's called honesty. What if she finds out another way? Will she ever trust you again? She already thinks you're having an affair because she saw you leave your office in another woman's car the other day.'

Connor frowned and then nodded. 'Why was Dru there? That was Dr Mulholland. I'd just left her surgery. She was going to the hospital that morning, and she followed me and picked me up so I could leave my car in the basement car park at the office.'

'And that was a reason to take her hand?'

'I was showing my gratitude. I owe Vera a lot. She made the diagnosis very quickly. She's a good doctor.'

'She is. And very happily married with three children.'

'Are you doubting me, Emma?'

'No, I'm playing devil's advocate so you're prepared for Dru's questions, because believe me, Connor, she's going to take some convincing.'

'Okay. I guess I can take on board what you're saying. Although I'd prefer to just go back to normal.'

'Good. She's been so worried about you that the baby has been at risk.'

'I'll reassure her. I'll tell her I'm not having an affair.'

'You have to let her raise that.' Emma was adamant. 'She is not to know that I told you. Right?'

'I'll go and see her and apologise for how I've been lately and I'll let her tell me.' For the first time, concern was etched into Connor's expression. 'Is she really upset?'

'I'll leave you to judge that for yourself. It's between you and Dru, Connor. All I can do is give you the advice that I think is right. When are you going to see her?'

'As soon as Dr Mulholland comes with the results and discharges me.'

'Good.' Emma slipped the clipboard over the end of the bed and opened the curtains. 'I have another patient to check. I wish you well, Connor.' She blinked tears away as she left the ward.

Chapter 26

Darwin Royal Hospital - Tuesday morning
Connor

Connor looked up at Dr Vera Mulholland, his oncologist, as relief coursed through his veins, just as the chemo had for the last two months. He was still unsettled from talking to Emma.

'So, it's looking very good, Connor. We are very pleased with your response to the chemo and the prognosis is excellent. There's no need for surgery; we got it early enough.'

'Thank you, doctor. What do I do now?'

'I'll sign the discharge papers and once the nurse removes the cannula you're right to go. I'll write a prescription for some tablets that I'd like you to keep taking for the next month, but apart from that life goes back to normal for you. I'll get you to come in for some blood tests in three months, but I'm expecting those results will be good.'

'Thank you. And thank you for looking after me so well. I truly appreciate it.'

'I don't want you to worry, Connor. Your blood results are really good. I'm quite confident that we won't have to do any more treatment.'

Connor's hand shook, as he held it out to the doctor, and her hand closed firmly over his.

'This is one of the best parts of being in oncology when we have a response like yours,' Dr Mulholland said.

'I'm sure it does,' Connor said. 'It makes me want to rethink my career choice.'

'What do you do, Connor?'

'I have a security firm. My partner and I specialise in industrial espionage.'

'I'm sure you sometimes get results that make a difference in people's lives.'

Connor grinned. 'It's how I met my wife.'

'Well, there you go. Worthwhile.'

'Yes, but I'll be having a look at what I do. This has been a huge wake-up call for me. It's made me rethink several aspects of my life.'

Dr Mulholland raised her eyebrows. 'You've been given a great chance to make any changes that you think will make a difference.'

'As soon as this drip's out, I'll be making the first one, doctor. My wife is down in the maternity ward and I have some things I need to tell her.'

Before she moved across to the other patient Dr Mulholland smiled at him. 'All the best, Connor. See you in three months. My office will contact you with an appointment time.'

Connor waited patiently for the nurse to come and remove the cannula; the half-hour felt like three hours before the male nurse came from the nurses' station.

'Time for you to go home.' He deftly removed the cannula and put a circular Band-Aid on his wrist. 'Are you right to walk? Do you need us to call the wardsman with the wheelchair or have you got someone coming to get you?'

'I'm fine, thank you, Brett. I have to go and visit my wife in maternity.'

'Oh, are congratulations in order? A new bub?'

'On the way,' Connor said with a smile. He hadn't allowed himself to think of the new baby while he'd been going through the treatment. And no matter what Emma's thoughts were, he'd saved Dru from that same worry. He'd had some pretty dark days wondering if he'd be around to see Ruby and the new baby grow up.

'You feeling good?' Brett stood back and removed the gloves with a snap and dropped them in the bin.

Connor couldn't help the smile on his face. 'You've got no idea how good I'm feeling. I don't think I've ever felt this good in my entire life.'

Once Brett had gone, Connor opened the small cabinet next to his bed and removed his clothes and went into the bathroom. Once he was dressed, he leaned over the basin, sluiced his face, patted it dry and then flicked some water through his hair in the absence of a comb.

He needed a shave, but he wasn't going to waste time. He wanted to get to Dru and stop her worrying. He only hoped she'd be pleased to see him.

His hand shook a little as he picked up his bag, but Connor knew the shakes had nothing to do with the treatment; he was feeling strong physically. The news that the doctor had given him made him feel as though he could face the world.

His smile widened. He could even face Dru; he knew how scary she could be when she was worked up. The three nurses said goodbye as he walked past the nurses' station. 'No offence, but I hope I don't see you guys for a long time,' he said.

'All the best, Mr Kirk. Great news.'

The maternity ward was two floors above oncology, and Connor stood patiently in front of the lift. He was in such a hurry to get to Dru, everything seemed to be in slow motion.

Finally, he stepped out of the lift on the maternity floor. Emma had told him that Dru was in the first room on the left and his nerves kicked in as he walked to the room.

It was a private room and although the door was closed, he could look in through the glass panel at the top. He stood there, and as he looked in, a surge of love filled his heart. He had missed Dru so much, and the thought that he had caused her so much worry sat heavily in him.

She was lying on her back, staring out the window. Connor pushed open the door, but she didn't turn; she was probably used to people coming and going all day. He put his bag on the floor inside the door and walked slowly over to the bed.

And waited.

Finally, Dru became aware that someone was standing next to her and turned her head slowly.

Her eyes were wide and a soft gasp puffed out. Her hand lifted to cover her mouth. 'What are you doing here?' Her voice was cold.

'I've come to see my wife. I need to talk to you, Dru. To explain my behaviour to you.'

Her bottom lip quivered as she turned away. Guilt rose in Connor knowing he was responsible. Dru rarely cried.

'Is this the right place to talk?' she said, still looking away from him.

Connor was taken aback at the hardness in his wife's voice and he knew he had to handle this carefully. He sent a silent thank you to Emma for preparing him.

He sat on the chair beside the bed. 'I know I've been aloof with you lately, Dru, and I'm sorry I had to be like that. I've made a wrong choice in how I've handled something.'

'Why did you have to make a choice? How did we get to that?' Her voice rose, and still, she wouldn't look at him.

Connor didn't answer her question. 'I was so caught up in what was happening to me, I shut down, and I didn't realise that you were hurting too. Today, when everything worked out, I realised what you must be feeling.' He focused on not mentioning Emma. 'I'm sorry, Dru. I never meant to hurt you, but I know I have. I knew you wanted to talk to me at dinner last week, and I was deliberately obtuse. I knew if we started talking, I'd tell you what was wrong and I didn't want you to know. I didn't want you to worry. That's why I snuck out of the apartment like a coward the next morning.'

'I'm strong, Connor.' Dru's gaze was steely. 'You know that. I survived my father's murder, I survived Zayed's treatment, and I survived being accused of stealing diamonds, not to mention being kidnapped and left in the outback. So, *I* can cope with whatever you throw at me. Yes, *I* can, but what are we going to do about the children? Ruby's been missing you already. How is she going to deal with this? We'll have to plan very carefully. I will not have my child—my children hurt.'

'They don't need to know, Dru. It's over now.'

Her laugh was bitter. 'And how do I know it won't happen again?'

'Life is uncertain. We just take what we're given. How did you know what was wrong?' Connor was disappointed. Emma must have rushed straight back to Dru. He could understand it though, they were sisters and he knew what the Porter sisters' loyalty was like.

'No, I figured it out myself.'

Connor frowned. 'How?'

'I went to your office I saw you with her.'

Connor shook his head. 'No, you misunderstood.'

'I didn't imagine you getting into a car with another woman.' Dru's voice shook as she finally looked at him. Connor tried to take her hand but she took it away. 'Don't touch me, Connor.'

'What do you mean about the children? What do we need to tell them?' He needed to go into his explanation carefully; he knew exactly what she meant but Connor wasn't going to break Emma's confidence.

'When you leave.'

'Leave for where? I'm not going anywhere, Dru. And this experience has made me rethink my job. I'm going to hand a lot more over to Greg. I'm going to be at home a lot more. I'm going to be more of a hands-on dad this time.'

She stared at him, her mouth still straight, but he could see the emotion in Dru's eyes. Knowing that he had hurt her so much twisted his gut.

'What? You're going to spend some time with us? Pretend to be a happy family? I don't know if I could accept that.'

Connor put a perplexed look on his face. 'Dru, I have no idea what you're talking about. Will you listen to me without interrupting while I tell you what's been happening? What you saw is not what you imagined. I do not have another woman. I've been in hospital and I made the choice not to tell you as soon as I knew I was unwell.'

'Unwell? What do you mean?' As she lifted her head to meet his eyes, Dru's welled with tears. Her face was swollen and puffy and he knew she'd been crying. His heart broke again.

'Oh, sweetheart, don't cry. Trust me when I tell you that everything is going to be fine. More than fine. Everything is going to be wonderful. Please let me start at the beginning and listen to me. Okay?'

She nodded, and he gently brushed the hair from her forehead. This time, she turned her face into his hand and her tears dripped onto his fingers.

Connor felt like an absolute louse. He had decided the day that he had first received the news of his cancer that he was not going to tell Dru. It was something he had to deal with himself. He didn't want to make her unhappy. He didn't want to make her worry, especially as she was pregnant.

Their eyes met and held. 'Dru, you are my world. If I'd known what I was doing to you, maybe I would have told you at the outset. I should have told you the truth.'

'What is the truth? I don't understand what you're telling me. Have we lost all our money? Has the business gone bad? Greg's worried too.'

Connor stood and then sat on the bed beside his wife. She held his eyes as he took both of her hands in his. Before he started his explanation, he leaned over and put his lips on hers. Dru's lips were soft beneath his and her lashes brushed his cheeks. The dampness of her cheeks clenched his heart. He had hurt her so much.

'Before I start, I want you to know that I'm better. I've fully recovered.'

He felt her stiffen against him as she noticed the circular plaster on his wrist. Her eyes travelled up his arm, from the Band-Aid on his wrist to the bruising inside his elbow.

'What's all that? Better from what?'

'I couldn't come and see you, because I've been in hospital since you were admitted last week. Every time I told you I was going away over the past couple of months, I was in and out of the hospital. When I was recovering, I bunkered down in a hotel until I looked well enough to come home. I was in the study and the office so much between treatments because I fell way behind on work. I know it looked bad, sweetheart, but I didn't want you to know. I didn't tell Greg and I know he thinks I've lost the plot. I was fighting for my life. For our life.'

'Why?' she whispered. 'What's the matter with you?' Connor could tell by her expression that she had twigged already.

'About three months ago I wasn't feeling well and I'd felt a lump down below. I went to my GP one morning and he sent me off for some tests and the results were unexpected.'

'What was it, Connor?'

'Dr Mulholland has just been to see me. I've been discharged with the all-clear. The lump was a non-aggressive form of testicular cancer—'

Dru gasped and he held her hands more tightly.

'Dru, it's gone. The tests are clear.'

'But you had to have chemotherapy, it must have been bad.'

'I had the choice because it hadn't spread to my lymph nodes, and I chose to have it as a double guarantee after surgery.'

'Surgery?' Her face screwed in confusion.

'I had one testicle removed at the outset. That was the time I was away for eight days. But it's okay. Dr Mulholland assures me there's no reason we can't have more children if we want. I'm well, Dru. It's over. She doesn't want to see me for another three months.'

Dru pulled her hands away from his. One shaking hand covered her mouth and she placed her other hand on her stomach.

'Why couldn't you tell me, Connor? I'm your wife, for God's sake.'

Chapter 27

Darwin Royal Hospital - Tuesday afternoon
Dru

Dru reached back and gripped Connor's hand tightly as he wheeled her out of the lift and into the hospital's foyer.

Emma and Jeremy were behind them, Emma carrying Ruby and Jeremy with Akasha. The two little girls were chattering happily. Dru closed her eyes for a moment; she was so pleased Ruby hadn't picked up on any of the unhappiness and sadness of the past few weeks.

Connor's fingers brushed hers as she left her hand on his.

When they reached the main door, she lifted her head and held his gaze, still not used to the gauntness of his face. How could she not have noticed that he had been losing weight? What sort of life had she been living not to realise that he was hiding something from her and wasn't well?

Emma had spoken to the nurses, and they'd let Connor stay at the hospital when visiting hours ended this morning. They talked for hours, and both shed tears, but when Connor put his arms around her and Dru buried her face into the familiar-smelling skin of his neck, she knew everything would be all right.

Connor *loved* her.

It took him an hour to convince her that he was well and truly in recovery from the cancer. He even offered to call Dr Mulholland's surgery and have her speak to Dru directly, but he finally convinced her that he was well and that there was nothing for her to worry about.

'I need to come home and cook and fatten you up,' she said as he sat on the bed with her. 'You're too thin.'

'You can when you get the all-clear to leave the hospital or when our bub arrives.' Connor dropped another kiss on her forehead.

Dru felt cherished and secure in his love; all her doubts and fears had disappeared, and all she wanted to do was go home with Connor and Ruby.

'I'm going to take a month off and let Greg run the business,' he said. 'Not because I'm recovering, but because I want to be with you. It'll be more than a month because I'll take another month off when our baby comes.'

'Have you rung him yet?'

'I will now,' Connor said.

Before he could ring, Dru's lunch and Dr Rickard arrived at the same time. She insisted that Connor eat half of her sandwiches. He declined but agreed to go to the coffee shop and buy lunch while her doctor examined her.

Dr Rickard had been pleased. 'Your blood pressure is down, Dru. Any more leakage?'

'No. Can I go home? Please?'

'It looks like your husband is back from his business trip.'

Dru nodded. 'Yes, Connor is home.'

'Well, as long as you keep to a sensible regime, with a lot of rest, and do nothing strenuous, I can't see a problem. Do you have a blood pressure monitor at home?'

'No, but we'll get one if it means going home.' Dru couldn't stop smiling. When she'd woken up this morning, she'd felt utterly miserable. Now her husband was back, and she was going home.

Dr Rickard had signed the discharge papers and was leaving the ward when Connor returned. 'I'll get the nurse to organise a wheelchair, and you're right to go, Mrs Kirk.'

Connor's smile was as wide as hers.

'Did you call Greg?' Dru asked.

'I did from the coffee shop,' he said. 'I had to turn the speakerphone off and go outside.'

'I can imagine,' Dru said. 'I know how I felt!'

'You know how Greg can swear?'

Dru nodded. 'Not so much now that Ruby's around.'

'Well, it's the worst I've *ever* heard him swear, but when he cooled down, he listened to what I had to say and was pleased to hear that everything was okay. He was worried about you too. I'm sorry I put you through so much, but I didn't want to worry you, sweetheart. I never dreamed you'd think I didn't love you anymore.'

'You've got some making up to do, Connor Kirk,' she said.

'And I'll enjoy every minute of it. I'll love you till I take my last breath.'

'Don't tempt fate.' Dru shivered. 'Now, are you going to take me home?'

Connor's forehead crumpled in a frown. 'Damn, I forgot.'

'Forgot what? What's wrong?'

'I don't have my car here.'

'It's okay. I'll ring Emma. She should still be here, and we can borrow hers.'

As it turned out, Jeremy had just arrived with Ruby and Akasha. Emma had finished her shift.

In the foyer, Connor held the two little girls' hands as Jeremy walked across the car park to get their Land Cruiser. Emma leaned forward and talked to Dru quietly. 'How are you feeling now, little sis?'

'A bit stupid,' Dru said.

'It's all good. Connor's well, and you're going home.'

Dru smiled. 'And Ruby's ecstatic. As much as she loves Aunty Em's house, she's excited about coming home.'

'And things going back to normal.'

'Yes. As soon as we get home, I'll call Ellie too. I know she was worried when they left on their trip. I hope she hasn't spent too much time worrying. I'm so glad I didn't share my fears with Mum.'

'Mum and Graysen will be home next week.'

'Wow, that went fast.'

Emma nodded. 'I think you've been preoccupied. Now, do you need any shopping done, Dru?'

'I have no idea. I didn't think when I left to go and see Connor the morning I ended up in the hospital, so we probably do.'

'Okay, well, once we get you back to the apartment, I'll have a look and do some shopping for you and bring us all some dinner home.' She smiled at Dru. 'Unless you and Connor would rather be alone?'

'We have the rest of our lives for that. I'd love you all to stay. We can have a celebration.'

Ruby looked up at her. 'Can we have balloons, Mummy?'

'We sure can, sweetie. I'll add them to Aunty Emma's shopping list.'

Chapter 28

McLaren Mango Farm - Friday
Cy

Jerry had started at the farm yesterday, and Cy had left him alone to dig the trenches. His instruction had been very specific; he was picking up quickly that Jerry needed to know exactly what to do. There didn't seem to be much common sense there.

Cy was patient, showing him exactly where to dig and what to watch out for. Yesterday afternoon he'd checked on his work at the end of the day and was pleasantly surprised that his instructions had been followed perfectly.

'Jerry's done a good job down there,' Cy told Tarni when he came into the shed after paying him on Thursday afternoon. 'He'll be back tomorrow. He even washed the tools down afterwards.'

'That's good. It'll save you some time.'

Cy pulled up the other stool and sat beside Tarni as she worked. 'How are you going?' He didn't like to say she looked pale and tired.

'I'm okay.'

'Really?' he asked. 'Only okay?'

Tarni put the thermometer on the bench and lifted her hand. 'My hand's not sore anymore, and it's stopped pulling. I can use my hand just fine.' She shook her head. 'I'm just tired all the time. Exhausted actually. 'I've taken too many Panadeine, I think. I can't shake this headache. The tablets don't ease it much.'

'You sleeping okay?'

'I am, but I find it hard to wake up in the morning. Maybe I picked up a bug in the hospital. I'm thirsty and drinking heaps of water too.'

She was constantly thirsty and emptied the water purifier after a couple of days. It needed filling this afternoon, and she'd put some water in the fridge to cool down before she filled it.

'Maybe you need to go back to the hospital.'

'I'll get over it. Let whatever it is run its course. Anyway, I'm finished here for the day. I was going to go up and have an early tea. Do you want to eat with me?'

'Salad?' Cy smiled.

'You're getting to know me well. Yes, salad.'

'You make a salad, and I'll cook the steaks I thawed today. Might give you a bit more energy.'

'Worth a try.'

Cy frowned as Tarni stood and then grabbed for the benchtop. 'Whoa, there,' he said as he steadied her, both hands on her waist. 'Don't go passing out on me.'

Her face coloured, and she moved away from him after a few seconds. 'I'm okay. Just got up too quickly.'

'Do you want me to cook and bring the steaks to the house?'

'No. let's sit around the fire pit. It's going to be a nice night, and I like being outside.'

They walked out of the shed together. Cy went to his ute and lifted the bonnet under the pretext of checking the oil, but he was more concerned with checking that Tarni got up to the house okay.

When she unlocked the front door and went inside, he closed the bonnet and went around the back of the shed to see to the fire and get the steaks cooking.

***

Tarni

Tarni had lost her appetite, and nothing made her feel much better. She'd enjoyed the sausage and egg sandwich that Cy had cooked for lunch on Monday, but since then, she had barely eaten. She berated herself, thinking that was probably the reason she was lightheaded—she needed to make herself eat and get some energy. She rubbed her back with her good hand; her lower back had been aching for several days.

As she chopped the last of the fresh salad vegetables she'd bought at the shopping centre on Sunday after they left the hospital, Cy's footsteps sounded on the front stairs. She waited for him to enter the kitchen, but there was a tap on the front door, and she frowned again. Wiping her hands, she walked to the door.

'Did I lock the screen door?' Her memory had been dreadful this week.

'No.'

'You don't have to knock.'

'I'm just being polite,' Cy said. 'My Aunty Suzanne taught me manners.'

It was the first information he volunteered about growing up, and she let it go. 'Well, I'm pleased to see you have good manners. Come in and don't knock again, silly. I grilled some leftover chicken breasts to put in the salad. Is that okay with you? Will it go with steak?'

'Does it taste like KFC chicken?' Cy asked with a grin.

'I can put some spices in there if you want.'

'Sounds good. Colonel Sanders' secret herbs and spices?'

She chuckled. 'You're a KFC tragic, Cy. I'm sure I can rustle up something similar.'

'You look a bit better than you did before.' Cy sat on the stool at the bench while she mixed the salad.

Tarni grinned. 'I pinched one of your Cokes from the fridge. That water is giving me an awful taste in my mouth.'

'Told you to drink the tank water. But you're welcome to my Coke.'

'Next thing I know, I'll be craving KFC.'

'That's not a bad thing. I've got a proposition for you,' he said. 'And we could get some KFC on the way.'

'On the way to where?'

'How would you like to visit a cattle station?'

Tarni's interest flared. 'A cattle station? When?'

'My cousin asked me to go out for the weekend to give him a bit of a hand with drenching.'

'What's drenching?' she asked.

'Are you a philistine? You don't even know what drenching is. Do you know anything about cattle?'

'I know they moo, and we get milk from them, and the steaks in the supermarket come from cattle,' she said.

Cy shook his head. 'Well, you're in for an education, girl. Drenching is used to balance their diet, plus it's like vaccination. Protects them from getting sick.'

'How do you do it?'

'We bring the cattle into the yards and put it in their mouths with a nozzle.'

'I've never seen a cattle yard.'

'If you'd like to come on the weekend, I can show you around the property. I spent a lot of time there when I was growing up. I can take you out to Hidden Valley and show you how spectacular it is. I need to go out there.' Cy's voice was quiet, and he stared past her.

'Is it a special place?' she asked.

'Sort of. I didn't tell you that my dad died a few days ago.'

'Oh no, I'm so sorry. You should have told me! What happened?'

'It was him I went to visit in the hospital on Sunday. It's okay; we had a pretty difficult relationship. I'll tell you about it around the fire later. Anyway, I'd like to go to Hidden Valley. To remember him.'

Sadness filled Tarni. How could Cy not even have mentioned it?

'I'd be honoured to come out with you. Thank you.' Tarni crossed to the fridge and stared at the interior.

She froze, and her eyes widened. 'Cy, this might sound silly, but have you been doing stuff in the fridge?'

'Doing stuff? I only took my Coke out the other day. Why? What's wrong?'

'Someone's been in here today. Look, three plastic water bottles lined up in the door, and each one was full to the brim this morning. Now two of them are half empty. I noticed that this morning because I left them here to get cold, ready to fill the water purifier this afternoon.'

'Did you fill it and forget, maybe?'

She put her hand to her head. 'No, I'm sure I didn't. I know I haven't been thinking straight with my hand hurting, but I didn't take them out.'

'Strange.'

'And look, the lid is off that two-litre milk container. I haven't touched it. Ellie left it there, and I haven't opened it because I drink my coffee black. I've got a bit of lactose intolerance. I have not opened it. I keep meaning to take it to the shed to see if you could use it.'

Cy walked over to the fridge and lifted the milk container out. 'There's no sign of the lid in the door, and some's been tipped out of it. Are you sure it wasn't already open?'

'I am one hundred per cent sure.'

'Were you in the shed when Jerry left?'

Tarni nodded. 'I think so. I did hear a car, but I didn't take much notice. I assumed it was you. I forgot he was down there today.'

'I'll have a chat with him tomorrow. He's the only person who's been on the place apart from us.'

Tarni shook her head. 'It couldn't have been him because both doors were locked just now when I came up.'

Cy looked at her strangely, and Tarni wondered if maybe he thought she was losing the plot. She was beginning to think she was.

Chapter 29

Darwin Correctional Centre - Friday morning
Russell Fairweather

Some days, Russell Fairweather didn't think he'd be able to take incarceration for much longer. He laid the wooden cutlery on his plastic plate and stared at the congealed egg stuck to it. His breakfast had been cold when he'd taken it from the *bain marie*, and he'd barely touched it. What would he give for a plate of smoked salmon and lightly poached eggs garnished with rocket on the side, seasoned with the black pepper grinder he'd ordered from a timber merchant in Tasmania a few years ago?

He closed his eyes as the more frequent rage began to build; he couldn't afford to lose his temper again. He'd already gotten the guards' attention in the last couple of weeks. Sitting and waiting restlessly, wanting to know if Ellie Porter had met the ghastly end she deserved, was doing his head in. The thought of her death was the only thing that kept him going. Once he knew Dean had been successful, he would settle down and endure the last years of his sentence.

Strangely, he missed Dean. He had been company—he didn't waste any breath talking to any other inmates—and it had given Russell focus, planning her demise and going through the method with Dean repeatedly.

Russell scanned the papers every day, reading the funeral notices first. Then he read the police reports, but there had yet to be anything so far. He pushed his plate away, stood, and as he turned to the door, the guard called to him.

'Fairweather, put your plate in the bin.'

With a tight smile, he returned to the table, picked up the sticky mess, and walked to the bin. He held it with two fingers and dropped it about a metre above the bin. It didn't even make a satisfying clatter.

The guard looked at him as he walked past. 'What's up your craw lately, mate?'

Russell composed his features into a bland expression. 'Nothing.'

The guard shrugged, and Russell walked along the corridor to the library. It was his morning to put the books back on the library selves. The "put", the stupid librarian called it. Russell glanced at the scrawny-looking man as he walked in and looked across to the newspaper rack; the papers should be in by now.

After he'd finished reading the print newspaper each day, Russell would read the little online news. He was given access to some sites on the library computer. What they were allowed to do on the computers in the library was extremely limited. Once upon a time, Russell would sit in his breakfast room and peruse the *Wall Street Journal*, the *New York Times*, the *London Times*, and a variety of European papers, informing him and allowing him to keep his finger on the pulse of the financial markets around the world.

Now the best he could do was the *Darwin Sun*, and most of that was full of garbage. Yesterday's lead article on the second page was "Why is Snot Different Colours?" He almost gagged with disgust. What happened to responsible journalism? What happened to good reporting?

The library held two more prisoners, and they sat at the two available computer screens. Russell walked across to the racks where three copies of the daily paper always sat, and as he passed the desk, he was pleased to see the books had already been shelved. It was beneath him to touch some of the trash in this library. Cowboy novels, for God's sake.

Russell nodded to the guard, collected a copy of the paper and walked across to a table near the window. He sat back and spread the newspaper on the table, and for a moment, he closed his eyes, imagining that he was sitting in his apartment. As he looked out at the harbour, the marble tiles would be cool beneath his feet. He could almost hear the soft classical music coming from the Sonus Faber freestanding speakers that had cost him a quarter of a million dollars.

His rage began to lick at the edges of his calm again; Russell let it build and leaned forward to open the paper. The front page was full of COVID reports and medical figures; he didn't care about that. So far, the jail had been isolated from it. Surprisingly, the last thing he wanted to do was get sick in this hellhole. But then again, if he did get sick enough, he could be moved to a hospital, and there could be a chance of escape.

He started to think. He could find a way to get out. He had enough money to disappear, a couple of forged passports and access to a super yacht. He had contacts on the outside waiting for him. He honestly didn't think he could survive any more time in this place. The more he thought about it, the more the plan took hold. His rage subsided a little, but not for long.

Russell turned to the newspaper's second page, wondering what absolute garbage would be reported today. He sat straight; raw physical pain pierced his chest as he read the headline.

'Local Mango Farmer on International Jaunt.'

The words themselves were innocuous, but the photo of Kane and Ellie McLaren beneath the image had white rage seething through him.

While Kane and Ellie McLaren and their three children are in Mexico on a research tour for three months, award-winning international researcher, Tarni Morgan, commenced work on improving the efficiency of the successful hybrid that Kane has developed.

Kane McClaren said that Ms Morgan's knowledge would be a considerable addition to their research program, and he and his wife, Ellie, a daughter of the original property owners, Peter (deceased) and Sandra Porter, are looking forward to hosting her on their property. Local cattleman Cy Prescott is managing the property in their absence. Local mango growers look forward to hearing about McLaren's experience in Mexico.

He quickly scanned the paper and read the rest of the article about the trip to Mexico.

'What the fuck?' Here he was, waiting to read of her death in the paper.

Why hadn't Dean got in touch with him? He gave Dean a mobile phone number in case of any problems. But typically, he imagined Dean had just taken the new identity and the new ute and pissed off.

Another mistake Russell wasn't happy he'd made. He refused to consider that he was losing his touch. It was this stinking hellhole that made achieving anything too hard.

'Fairweather!' The guard Russell had in his pocket called out from the doorway. The library guy put his finger to his lips and told him to be quiet.

'You've got a visitor. Get to the front now.'

Russell was intrigued. He returned the paper to the rack and followed the guard to the section where prisoners met their visitors. He sat and waited behind the glass wall in the visitors' area, aware of the correctional officer standing behind him, listening to every word exchanged. It was the guard who was always on his back. A few minutes later, Dean sat on the opposite side of the glass and picked up the phone to speak to him.

Good God. Could he trust him not to say anything? He nodded at Dean, holding his gaze to warn him, and then picked up the phone set.

'Hey, Russ, how's it going? How are they hanging?'

He glared at Dean and forced a smile between gritted teeth. 'Gidday, mate, what's it like on the outside? Nice of you to come and see me.'

Dean's eyes widened, and he finally picked up Russell's displeasure. 'Sorry you're still in here, mate. I've been thinking about you a lot. Got a lot going on already, travelling around. It's pretty good to be out.'

'What have you been doing?' Russell said, maintaining eye contact with Dean.

'I saw my old man, picked myself up a little ute. Bought it at the car yard. Cheap price, mate.'

Russell nodded. 'Sounds good. Lucky bugger.'

'I took myself out to Kakadu for a drive and took a gander at the waterfalls. Climbed that special rock, the one Paul Hogan stood on in *Crocodile Dundee* that time. Everyone raves about it, but all I could see was a bit of water and some green grass and a bit of rock. Didn't do anything for me, mate.'

'Did you find a job?' Russell asked, his gaze steely as he kept his voice casual.

'Yeah, I called into a few mango farms along the highway. My old man used to have a farm, and I thought my experience might get me a job. On my way back from Kakadu, I stopped overnight at the pub and saw an ad. Exactly what I wanted.' Dean raised his eyebrows at Russell. '*Exactly*. Bloke at a mango farm's got me digging some trenches for irrigation pipes. A little bit of extra money, and I'm thinking about going for a big trip.'

'Keeping busy, Dean.'

'Yeah, and I tell ya, Russ, his missus is pretty good to look at too. After being in here, it's like heaven on a stick. Tall, great body, long dark hair.'

Russell wondered what the hell he was trying to tell him. Who the fuck was he talking about? Ellie McLaren was supposed to be in Mexico, for Christ's sake.

'You want to watch yourself with your record, Deano,' he said. 'Don't want to upset the husband and find yourself back in here.' This time Russell raised his eyebrows. The guard couldn't see his face from where he was standing.

'Sure am. Might not be coming back into this joint again. The owner bloke, Kane's a bit of a jerk, but he pays well.'

'Pleased to hear that. Why is he a jerk?'

'Calls himself "Sir I"! Stupid bastard. Must think he's something special, and it took him half an hour to show me how to dig a fucking hole.'

Russell's hopes were lifting. Maybe they hadn't left yet. Perhaps the paper had jumped the gun.

'Be good when you get out, Russ. How much longer have you got?'

Russell stared at him. Dean knew he still had almost four years to go as long as he maintained good behaviour. And with

Dean coming in and trying to send him hidden messages in general conversation about jobs and things, he was jeopardising that. When Ellie McLaren died, he wanted no whiff of any contact linked to him through Dean.

'Be good to see you out on the other side. It'll go quick, mate.'

'Listen, Dean, it's hard for me to see someone going out there and listening to how good it is. I'd appreciate it if you never came here to see me again.'

'Fair enough, mate. Suppose that's what you want. It'll give me something to look forward to when you get out. Anyway, I thought I'd just come in and say gidday.' He beamed up at the correctional officer. 'It's good outside, hey mate?'

Russell stood and turned his back on the stupid idiot and gestured to the guard. He was ready to go back to his cell.

Rage filled Russell as he walked along the corridor.

Were they at the farm? Or were they in Mexico? He felt useless not being able to find out something so simple.

That fucking Porter family had won again, and he had to deal with it. He gagged, stopping the bile from filling his mouth. A sharp pain sliced down his chest from the temper he was holding in. That bitch had beaten him again. If they were out of town, who the fuck was Dean poisoning?

All he was doing was enjoying the proceeds of the money he'd been given. There was probably no one there. The stupid bastard had conned him and came to gloat.

Russell put his hand to his chest as he walked to the door. The guard looked at him, and Russell stared. 'I need to make a phone call now.'

'Yes, I'll get it organised.' Five minutes later, he dialled his contact outside.

'Russell, how are you?'

'Get rid of him. Now. He's gone. He screwed up.'

He disconnected and walked back along the corridor with the guard behind him. The pain in Russell's chest pressed down hard, and he struggled to breathe. He had never felt such anger before.

His eyes widened, and suddenly it became clear. This wasn't his temper; he put his hand to his chest and turned to speak to the guard. 'Help me, help me.'

His legs crumpled beneath him, and his world went black.

Chapter 30

Wilderness Station - Friday afternoon
Cy

Cy and Tarni had chatted for the first fifteen minutes of the trip, and then she'd put her head back, pulled her hat over her face, and was soon sound asleep. He knew he'd shocked her with his honesty, but she had listened, and Cy sensed she hadn't judged him as he'd feared she would. Tarni's opinion of him was starting to matter a lot. He filed that away to take out and examine later.

She had started the conversation when they turned off the Arnhem Highway onto the back road to Wilderness Station.

'I'm keen on looking for a job in the local region,' she said, looking at the landscape that flashed by.

'What sort of work would you look for once you finish your PhD?' Cy asked, keeping his eyes on the road. He was impressed. He didn't know anyone who'd done a doctorate before he'd met Tarni, but strangely, it didn't make him feel inadequate. Once upon a time, it would have, but he'd toughened up over the years.

'Something in agriculture. I'm sure there are quite a few government departments and maybe some institutes in Darwin. I haven't had a look yet, but once I finish here, I might take some time to travel around the place and decide if I like it up here. One thing I do like is the warmth. I can't imagine going back to winter down south now.'

'I love it here,' he said quietly. 'The place gets into your blood.'

'Sitting out on the back veranda at dawn every morning and watching the new day come to life has been good for me. It's given me hope for the future, and I feel I can continue. Please tell me if I sound silly. Maybe it's the painkillers. They tend to loosen my tongue.'

'No, Tarni, I know exactly what you mean. I haven't experienced the same tragedy you have, losing someone you loved, but I did lose the life I loved. It was my father's fault. I shouldn't say it, but his death has released me.'

Tarni's eyes widened in shock. 'In what way?'

'It was a difficult situation, Tarni. My father was in the palliative care unit attached to the private hospital because it was more secure.'

'What do you mean secure?'

'He was in the Darwin Correctional Centre. My father is a murderer. And don't feel bad if that shocks you and you feel like you don't want to be my friend anymore. I have enough trouble living in my own skin, knowing I'm the son of a murderer.'

'Tell me more, Cy. And no, I don't judge you. You know what they say about the sins of the father.'

His laugh was bitter. 'Yeah, I've read it all. And I went to therapy for a while.'

'Anyway, enough about that. Let me tell you a bit about Ryan and Dee. It was Dee's mother who Joe killed long ago, but it's not talked about much these days. Dee didn't ever know her; her aunt adopted her. Ryan is Ellie McLaren's half-brother, and when I look at how happy they all are, I know I can overcome this fear that Joe's actions make me what I am.'

'A good way to be. I feel for your pain, though, Cy. It must be tough.'

'Sometimes. Anyway, Dee and Ryan have twin boys. Dee's the one I told you about who used to manage the macadamia farm, so you both will have a lot to talk about.'

'I look forward to meeting them, and yes, thank you for asking me. I might try and have a bit of sleep now if you don't mind. I wish I could kick this tiredness.'

'You do look a bit pale.'

'I'm over it.'

'How about we go in to get your stitches out on Monday, and you can make an appointment with the doctor?'

'I'll see how I feel. Hopefully, some sleep will make me good company over the weekend.'

As Tarni dozed off almost immediately, Cy frowned. She had obviously picked up a bug or some infection, perhaps from the soil she had been working with. He would make sure she saw the doctor on Monday. He hummed under his breath as they approached the station, feeling content. Jerry had made good progress this morning. He was a good worker, keeping to himself. Cy had checked that he was okay to work there by himself over the weekend, and when Jerry had agreed, Cy had paid him in advance, although he'd wondered if he was being gullible. He'd offered to check on the dogs too, and top their dry food up.

'I'll be right, mate,' Jerry said. 'If I work Saturday and Sunday, it'll be finished when you get back. I'm heading off after that. I'm gonna drive across to Camooweal. I got some work on a cattle station over in Queensland.'

He was a funny little guy and always seemed to want approval. Jerry kept asking if Cy was happy with the trenches he'd dug.

'It's fine, exactly what I wanted,' Cy reassured him. And he had done well.

'A cattle station in Queensland, huh? Haven't worked there. I've worked in the west most of my life,' Cy said.

Jerry looked at him quizzically. 'I didn't know you worked on stations too. Anyway, I'm really looking forward to it. Got my new ute. Heading off when I'm done here.'

'Sounds good. Okay, we'll leave this afternoon. We'll be home late Sunday. So dig those two areas on the third and fourth avenues on Saturday and Sunday, and that's everything done, mate.'

'Thanks for giving me the work.'

'You've done well. It saved me a heck of a lot of time.'

'I aim to please,' Jerry said, beaming. 'See ya around sometime.' He turned and walked away to his ute.

'Jerry!' Cy called him, but Jerry ignored him. 'Jerry! Hey, mate!'

Jerry finally turned, and there was a strange look on his face. 'Sorry, sorry. I didn't mean... okay, yeah, what's wrong?'

'When you finish, I'll get you to leave the shovels and the crowbar outside the shed. I'll be locking it up when we go out tomorrow.'

'No wuckers.' He looked strangely relieved.

Cy had shaken his head. He was a strange one, but it took all types.

Half an hour later, as they approached the homestead, Cy glanced at Tarni; she was sound asleep. He reached over and gently touched her hand, but she didn't stir.

'Tarni, wake up. We're almost there.'

She opened her eyes and looked at him in confusion. 'Where are we? What are we doing in the bush?'

Cy waited until she woke and stretched. 'We're almost to *Wilderness Station*,' he said.

'Sorry, for a minute, I forgot where we were going. I was sound asleep.'

'How did you sleep last night?' he asked.

'Not too bad, but I kept having crazy dreams. It must be the residue of the pain medication in my system.'

'Side effect, huh? You said you hadn't taken painkillers for a few days.'

'I haven't. I forgot.'

Cy frowned; Tarni seemed confused, but she sat straight, removed her hat, and pulled the rubber band from her hair.

'Okay, we're only about three kilometres out. See those mountains over there? That's where Hidden Valley is.'

'I hope that cheesecake hasn't bounced about too much,' she said. 'I left it in Pyrex dish before I put it in your camp fridge,' she said. 'With a cover over it.'

Tarni had packed the cheesecake she made last night and put it in the camp fridge on the back of his ute. She managed to find the ingredients in Ellie's fridge and cupboard, and borrowed a touch of Baileys liqueur from the bar in the dining room. She'd buy new bottle and leave it here when they came home.

'Thoughtful of you to make it.'

'Was it?' she said. 'I'm not up with visiting people. I thought the given thing was to take something with you.' She yawned and covered her hand over her mouth. 'Did you pack that thermos of coffee I made?'

'You didn't give me one.'

'I must have left it in the kitchen,' she said. 'Talk about forgetful!'

Cy glanced at Tarni as they approached the homestead; she leaned forward and exclaimed.

'Oh, how pretty. I didn't expect such a beautiful house and garden way out here.'

Cy smiled; he'd always loved the homestead that Aunty Suzanne had made into a beautiful showpiece. The sprawling house was built from large sand-coloured bricks. The red iron roof rose to a peak high above a single-story building, fronted by a veranda held up by rough-hewn posts. The lawn had always been lush and green, and it looked like Dee had restored the colourful gardens he remembered from his childhood. 'Here we are.' Cy smiled as they turned into the driveway of *Wilderness Station*. Dee and Ryan were waiting on the front veranda. It was like coming home.

Chapter 31

Wilderness Station
Tarni

Tarni tipped her head back to the morning sun and enjoyed the warmth bathing her face. The air was redolent with the sweet fragrance winter roses as she sat with Cy, Dee and Ryan under the pergola at the back of the homestead.

'We could almost be in an English country garden,' she said. 'It's every bit as beautiful as Cy described. I noticed that Ellie's planted roses at the end of each row of the mango trees at their place too. Neither place is anything like I'd imagined.'

'I did the same at our macadamia planation at Byron Bay,' Dee said. 'I'd really love to come out to Kane and Ellie's place and see what you're doing. It seems ages since I was on the east coast working with macadamias.'

'I'd love to show you the process with the seeds,' Tarni said. 'We'll set a date.'

Tarni had slept well and felt well for the first time in a week or more. Angus and Wyatt, Dee and Ryan's adorable twins, had gone down for their morning sleep. Ryan and Cy were having coffee before heading out to drench at the yards. Dee and Tarni were going to take lunch down later in the morning, and Tarni would get to witness the workings of a cattle station firsthand.

Tarni and Dee had hit it off the moment they met. Tarni couldn't believe how much they had chatted and shared already; it seemed she had known Dee for ages. They had a lot in common, and Dee had asked pertinent questions about what Tarni was doing at the farm.

'I started experimenting with hybrids when I was over at our farm,' Dee said. 'My life changed suddenly when Ryan's dad left half of *Wilderness Station* to me. I pretty much packed up and left the farm, and came here. We clashed at first, and the requirement that I stay for a set length of time looked pretty unlikely at first. Now that's a long story for one night over a couple of bottles of wine.'

'I'll look forward to it. Have you studied biology?' Tarni asked.

'No, would you believe my degree is in business management? I was managing our nut farm—'

Ryan interrupted. 'And from all accounts, doing a very good job,' he said.

Dee bumped her husband with her shoulder. 'He's my biggest fan club,' she said. 'But it's only because I took over the books for the station, and he gets to watch TV at night.'

'Aw, that's not fair,' Ryan protested.

'I'm just winding you up, sweetie.' Dee reached out and held Ryan's hand. The love between them was plain to see. Tarni was envious, but grief didn't wash over her for a change.

'How did you cope moving here?' she asked Dee. 'Was it hard to adjust to the remote location?'

Cy sat back with a smile on his face. Tarni couldn't believe how much more relaxed he was here. He was definitely in his element. He chuckled. 'Tarni, if you settle up here after the job at Kane's place is done, I'll take you for a drive to a remote station. It's only a couple of hours to Darwin from here.'

'I only get there about every two to three months,' Dee said. 'It's a huge production getting the twins packed up for the trip, plus the gear we have to take, not to mention trying to juggle feeding both of them between shopping. I was sorry we didn't get to Dru's barbeque for Kane and Ellie before they left. The family haven't seen the twins since we were in hospital. Fortunately, I love being a stay-at-home mum.'

Ryan stood and leaned down and kissed Dee. 'Okay, we're going to head down to the yards now. Lunch about one, love?'

Cy stood and nodded. 'See you both down there. Don't you overdo it, Tarni.'

Tarni frowned, and Dee looked at her curiously as they walked back inside with the tray of mugs and the leftover cake.

Dee crossed to the coffee machine. 'I could go another coffee, how about you?'

'That would be great,' Tarni said. 'Thank you.'

'Since I stopped breastfeeding the twins, I'm almost addicted to coffee again. I was one of those good mums who didn't drink coffee, drink alcohol, eat peas, all that stuff. But the little loves still had colic and sleepless nights.'

'It's all a mystery to me.'

'Tarni? What did Cy mean about overdoing it? Tell me if it's none of my business.'

'It's fine. I've been a bit off-colour this week. I had to go to the hospital and get some stitches. Now there's a story for you. Being stared at by a giant rat and putting a drill through my hand. I've been off-colour ever since, and Cy's been great. I feel good today, though.'

Dee's cheeks held a pink flush. 'Just as well I didn't say what I was thinking.'

'What was that?'

'That's what Ryan used to say to me when I was pregnant. "Don't overdo it", that is.' Dee filled another mug from the coffee machine and brought it to Tarni. 'You pair suit each other, and I saw how Cy looked at you. I haven't ever seen him like that before.'

This time Tarni coloured up. 'He's a kind guy.'

The silence was slightly awkward until Tarni broke it. 'This coffee is divine. I'm enjoying it.'

'I love my coffee. Only the best here. Do you mind if I ask you a personal question?'

Tarni tensed a little bit. 'Depends what it is.'

'Do you think Cy is okay?' Dee looked concerned.

Tarni didn't want to reveal the conversation Cy had with her on the way in. He'd opened up, and she sensed that he'd told her some pretty personal stuff. She looked up at Dee, seated opposite her.

'I suppose being family, you know that his dad passed away recently,' Tarni said.

Dee's face set in a blank expression. 'Yes, Ryan told me that Joe died last weekend.'

'Well, I guess he's a bit upset about that. He was a bit quiet over the last couple of days.'

'How long have you been seeing each other?' Dee asked.

Tarni lifted her head in surprise. 'Seeing each other?'

'Oh, sorry, I just assumed you were a couple. You seem so easy together,' Dee said. 'I guess it's wishful thinking. I love Cy like a brother, and I'd love to see him happy. He's had a very tough run the last few years.'

'We've only known each other just over a week.'

Dee's eyebrows rose. 'A week? Wow, you're really comfortable with each other.'

'We are. To be honest, I enjoy his company, and like I said, he's been more than kind to me.'

'Tell me a little bit about yourself, Tarni,' Dee said.

'Well, I'm pretty boring. I worked at the university for the last six years, immersed in my work, but sadly, my partner was killed in an industrial accident. I've been slow to move on. When the opportunity was offered to work on Kane's farm, I saw it as a new start.' She smiled. 'And, do you know what? I love it so much I'm even thinking about staying up this way for a little while.'

'That would be so good. I'm sorry to hear of your loss. I do hope you think about staying on. It would be nice to have a little bit more company around here. Although it is a fair way out here from the mango farm. You'll have to come out and stay a whole week rather than just a weekend,' Dee said.

'I'd like that,' Tarni said. 'I'm only working at the farm until Kane and Ellie come back.'

'Ryan's family is lovely. I'm sure you've met Ellie and Kane.'

Tarni chuckled. 'Would you believe I was late getting there, and they were actually in the car ready to go to the airport? I felt so bad.'

'Kane and Ellie would take it in their stride. Have you met the rest of the family? But I guess you haven't in a couple of weeks.'

'No, I really don't know a lot about them. Cy did mention Ellie has a couple of sisters and Ryan is their half-brother.'

'They're the most incredible family. They've been through so much. One day, over a coffee, I'll fill you in on the details. I don't want to overwhelm you now, but just let me say that when Ryan discovered he was a half-brother to those three girls, it completed him. We were together by then, and I will never ever forget the look on Sandra's face when she realised that Ryan was her deceased husband's son.'

'Sounds like something out of *Days of Our Lives*,' Tarni said.

'Just about. I won't tell you my story yet. It's even more complicated. Did Cy tell you Joe was in prison?'

Tarni nodded slowly. 'Yes, he did.'

'He's been struggling with that for quite a few years now, ever since Joe went to jail. And I think Joe passing might be a relief for him. For all of us. It really changed Cy when his father went to jail. I hope I'm not speaking out of turn or that you don't want to hear this.'

Tarni picked up her coffee and looked at Dee over the rim of the mug. 'No, Cy and I have established a good friendship since we've been working together. He took me to the hospital when I hurt my hand last week, and he went to visit Joe before he passed away.'

'Oh, that's good. He did go and see him. We wondered.'

Tarni didn't comment. Cy's personal business had nothing to do with her. 'To be honest, when I first came to the farm, I didn't want to share the house with anybody. We had a cold start.'

A small smile played around Dee's lips. 'He's not bad-looking, is he?'

Tarni blushed, and then she smiled. 'Okay, I'll give you that. He's very good-looking.'

'So, you've noticed.'

'Maybe.'

The sound of a crying child came down the hall, soon followed by a second. Dee put her coffee down and stood up.

'Well, there goes my rest time. Come along and meet the terrible twins.'

Tarni rinsed her cup before putting it in the sink.

'How old are they?'

'Almost three. They are the lights of our life,' Dee replied.

'You don't mind living this far out?'

'No, I enjoy it. It is nice to go to Darwin occasionally, and I love catching up with Ryan's family. I hope you meet them before you leave the farm. Sandra and her husband—her second husband—are overseas in Africa. Graysen is a famous photographer. Their youngest sister, Dru, is about to have another bub. Emma and Jeremy, Ryan's oldest sister and her husband, are both doctors at the hospital.'

'Wow, what a family.'

They walked along the hall to the loud cries of two children.

'What about you, Tarni? What's your family situation?'

'I don't want to sound like Little Orphan Annie, but it's just me these days,' Tarni said. 'So, if I do decide to stay up here, I don't have to tell anyone.'

'Oh, that's so sad. You need a friend.' Dee linked her arm through Tarni's. 'Come and meet the boys and prepare yourself for chaos.'

Chapter 32

McLaren Mango Farm - Saturday morning
Dean

Dean was confused when he left the correctional centre. Russell had treated him as though he wasn't even a mate, and telling him not to come back again had left him a little bit pissed off. Russell had organised the ute and some decent cash, but who was doing a damn big favour for the bastard, and he'd been treated like shit?

Dean stewed over yesterday's visit as he drove down the highway to the mango farm. He should turn around and head west like he'd always planned. But as he thought about it, he remembered what Russell had done for him in jail.

Russ's problem yesterday must have been jealousy. Dean knew how good he felt since he'd been outside. Russell was probably jealous of his freedom, and that's why he'd acted strange yesterday.

He'd accepted the money, had a ute, and, best of all, he had a new identity and no fucking record. He might be a criminal, and he might not be honest a lot of the time, but he'd do what Russell had organised.

But stuff this gradual doctoring of a few mls here and a few mls there, he'd use what was left in the bottle today and take off. He'd dump all the coolant into the water filter. If she drank it and died, he'd done his job. If she didn't, he'd done his best, and who would know anyway? It would have been easier to strangle the bitch.

Dean glanced in the rearview mirror and saw the same bloody truck that had followed him to the Marrakai pub yesterday afternoon. He'd given the driver the finger as he'd turned into the pub. The bastard had tailgated him most of the way from Darwin.

Now it looked like the same bloody truck. The guy must do the run to Jabiru a few times a day. The bastard was on his tail again. Dean indicated well before he turned into the farm, but that didn't help much; the truck almost hit his ute as it roared past.

As he drove into the farm, Dean wondered if they'd gone away like McLaren had said they were. They didn't seem to spend a lot of time together, so maybe they weren't happy. None of his business.

He looked around as he drove in; the place was quiet, and it did look like they'd gone. He grinned, suited him. He had no intention of digging any bloody trenches.

The dogs were yapping down the back, and he was tempted to go down and deal with them, but he wouldn't waste time; all he wanted to do was get the job done and get out of there. They could starve for all he cared.

He parked behind the shed, just in case they did come home. He didn't want to be caught in the house. The dogs kept barking as he walked towards the homestead. It wasn't a bad place. He wouldn't mind having a house like this one day, but he didn't want to work in the boondocks like this. He might move to Fremantle. He had a mate who lived there, a guy he'd done time with in WA a few years ago. He'd look him up when he got over there.

Dean pulled out his tools and put the coolant on the floor as he picked the locks. The screen and front doors were open within seconds. To make sure there was no one in there, he knocked on the front door and yelled, 'Hello, anyone home?' All was quiet.

He strolled into the kitchen and opened the fridge. There was nothing decent to eat there—just healthy crap. The water bottles were full again, so he tipped a little out of each one and then topped it up a few mls of the coolant. The milk was a quarter empty, so he took the container out, put a few more mls in there, and gave it a good shake after he screwed the lid back on. The water thing on the bench was only half full. He'd topped it up the other day and wondered if she noticed it had been full. This time she wouldn't notice anything; the stuff would probably kill her in a couple of hours.

The coolant bottle still had about a third left, so he took the lid off the water container and tipped the blue coolant into the water. It swirled and coloured the surface.

Dean opened a couple of drawers before finding a spoon. He gave it a good stir, and the water cleared almost instantly. He turned, and his elbow knocked the bottle.

'Shit!'

The bottle tipped over, and some blue liquid ran down the front of the white cupboards. He found a sponge in the sink and wiped it off, then chucked the spoon and the sponge into the sink, put the lid on the empty coolant bottle, and dropped it in the kitchen bin. By the time they found it, he would be long gone. If they found his fingerprints, they would be looking for Dean Drummond, not Jerry White, the cool man about town in the black ute.

This time, Dean locked the doors as he left. He wondered if McLaren had blamed her for it last time. From what Russell said about the symptoms when he had been planning it, there would be confusion and shit like that. So, he got away with it. This time, he would lock the doors to be on the safe side.

He climbed into the ute, started the engine, listened to the throaty purr with satisfaction, and gunned it along the dirt driveway that led to the gate.

When he reached the highway, Dean tapped the steering wheel. 'Right to Queensland? Or left to WA?' he muttered.

The west won, and he roared to the left and sped up the highway, turning the stereo on full blast. He sang along with the country and western channel, glancing in the rearview mirror occasionally.

Looked like that fat bastard truck was behind him again.

'Fuckin' hell,' he yelled. But it couldn't be because the truck was going in the opposite direction to the way it had been going on his way in.

Dean grew more nervous as he drove. He turned the music off as the truck roared up behind him. What was the bastard doing? Had he waited for him? Or was it another mad truckie? He looked ahead; there was another truck coming towards him. The truck behind him accelerated, closing in on the back of his ute. His ute began to slide across the road towards the oncoming truck. Dean yelled and swore as he fought with the steering wheel, but the truck behind kept pushing harder and harder.

'What the fuck!' he yelled as his ute headed too close to the truck heading east. He gripped the wheel and tried to swerve left, but the momentum from behind forced him across the road.

Pain jarred through his entire body as his ute went under the front of the truck. The sound of screaming, grating metal filled the cabin as excruciating pain tore up his legs, through his stomach and into his chest before black descended.

Chapter 33

McLaren Mango Farm - Sunday afternoon
Cy

Cy watched as Dee and Tarni said goodbye to each other. It had been a fantastic weekend, and he'd enjoyed both Ryan and Dee's company. He'd seen a totally different side to Tarni; she'd blossomed in a social situation. Watching her build cubby houses with the twins and crawl around the living room floor with them had been hilarious. He'd been surprised by how well she interacted with the two little boys, and by the end of the weekend they were calling her Aunty Tarni.

Dee hugged Tarni one more time. 'Don't forget to email me the recipe for that cheesecake,' she said. 'And thank you so much for bringing it. It was yummy. I love Baileys.'

Ryan hugged Tarni too. 'Make sure you come back and see us again soon.' Cy didn't miss the significant glance his cousin sent his way. 'You make sure you bring Tarni back, won't you, bro?'

'I'd love too,' Tarni said. 'Honestly, I had the best time. I feel so refreshed.'

'For sure,' Cy said. 'We'll see you soon. Don't forget to call me if you need a hand with the mustering.'

'We'll miss Ellie this time. It's hard to find a pilot as good as she is.'

Tarni's eyes widened as she stood by the car. 'Ellie does the helicopter mustering?'

'She sure does and she's the best around,' Ryan said.

'And Fallon Malone moved to south Queensland, I heard,' Cy said.

'Yeah. She settled at a place called Augathella. Got a partner and a bub now,' Dee said.

'I'm still looking for a pilot,' Ryan said as they stood at the ute. 'I'll let you know how I go, Cy.'

'Okay, Tarni, let's hit the road.' Cy opened the passenger door for her, and she smiled at him as she climbed in. She really looked great.

Cy felt good; they still had weeks together at the farm before Kane and Ellie got back. Then he had to decide where he was going to work. If Tarni decided to stay up north, he intended seeing more of her.

'Drive carefully,' Ryan added. 'Apparently there was a bad smash on the Arnhem Highway yesterday afternoon, not far from Kane's place. The highway was closed for a while. One fatality.'

'Not good.' Cy frowned. 'I wonder what happened.'

'It was on the ABC news. A truck and a ute head-on.'

'It's a shit of a road there with the smoke, so we'll take care.' Cy got in beside Tarni and started the engine.

Tarni waved to Dee and Ryan until they were out of sight. Cy hadn't seen her animated like this since he'd met her.

'Thank you so much for bringing me this weekend. I've had the best time,' she said.

'You look much better. You've got colour in your cheeks, and you look great.'

The pink in Tarni's cheeks deepened 'I slept well. I didn't have any dreams. My headache's gone, and I'm not dreading going back to work,' she said.

'That's good, but don't overdo it, Tarni.'

She smiled.

'What are you grinning at?' he asked.

'Nothing, just a girls' joke,' she said.

Cy grinned back at her. He had seen a totally different side of Tarni this weekend and enjoyed every minute of her company. 'I'm sorry we didn't find time to get to Hidden Valley.'

'You'll have to bring me back here again,' she said.

'We'll come back, for sure. So, back to normal for us now.'

'Yep, I've got a lot to do this week. I fell behind last week when I was feeling so crappy.'

'Me too, now that you mention it. Not fallen behind, I mean. I've got a lot to do now that the trenches are dug.'

'I hope Jerry got them done for you.'

'He'd better have. I paid him in advance.'

'Was that wise?'

'Time will tell,' Cy said. 'He was a strange bloke. He thought I was Kane, even though I told him my name.'

'He must have got mixed up that first day when I said my husband was down at the dam.'

'Probably. I don't think he's the sharpest tool on the shelf.'

'As long as he can dig and follow instructions.'

The silence was companionable, and Tarni stayed awake the whole way home.

They both frowned when they passed the site of the yesterday's accident. The vehicles must have been towed away, and all that remained was police tape and white markings on the road.

'So sad,' Tarni said.

'I guess we'll hear more about it through the week,' Cy commented. They were both lost in their thoughts for a while.

'I think whatever bug I had has finally gone, thank goodness,' Tarni said as they turned into the farm gate.

'That's good. I'm pleased you came along. I wouldn't have left you at home by yourself, and Ryan needed a hand. Did you enjoy the cattle side of things?'

'Um, I did.' Tarni hesitated. 'But it was different.'

'In what way?'

'I'm going to sound like a city slicker now, but it was smelly and dirty at the yards. And noisy. I nearly died when Angus and Wyatt were playing in that wet dirt and there was cow manure all around them. Don't get me wrong, though. Dee's a great mum, and I did enjoy watching you and Ryan drench the cattle. Puts a whole different take on buying meat in plastic trays at the supermarket.'

Cy chuckled as he parked the ute in the driveway. 'Wait there. I'll help you out.' Tarni had nursed Ellie's Pyrex dish on her lap all the way home; she'd been worried about it getting broken in the back of the ute. He walked around the front and opened her door. Holding his hand out, he took the dish she passed to him and carefully placed it on the tray of the ute. He turned and held out his hand to Tarni. She grasped his fingers and jumped down.

Cy could have moved back to give her more room, but when her feet landed on the paved drive, she was chest-to-chest with him. He let go of her hand and put his arms around her.

Tarni's eyes were wide as she looked up at him, but she didn't move away.

'Before we say goodnight, I just wanted to thank you for a fabulous weekend,' he said quietly.

'It was great,' she said. 'I feel better, and you look less stressed. Thank you for taking me.' Before Cy could make a move, Tarni reached up, her lips touched his and stayed there.

Cy deepened the kiss and a pleasant shiver ran down his spine as Tarni's mouth opened beneath his. The tentative kiss lingered, and held promise. When Tarni pulled back, Cy's heart was beating hard, and the blood thrummed though his body. She rested her cheek on his shoulder and happiness settled as he held her close.

Chapter 34

McLaren Mango Farm - Sunday afternoon
Tarni

Tarni finally lifted her head from Cy's shoulder. It felt so good, she could have stayed there for longer. His hands were pressed gently across her lower back, and being held close made her feel secure.

'I guess we need to get unpacked,' she said moving away.

'We should.' His smile sent a ripple of pleasure through her. 'And I want to go down and see if Jerry finished what I paid him to do. Do you want to come down to the dam with me?'

'How about I get a meal going for us? Just something light? Dee fed us well.'

'Sounds good. A toasted sandwich would do me.'

'Shame there's no KFC close by.' She couldn't help teasing him.

Cy grinned back. 'Don't laugh. I did think about driving via Darwin on the way home to pick some up.'

Tarni nudged him with her shoulder. 'If we're going to hang around together, I'm going to teach you some good eating habits.'

Cy nodded and held her gaze. 'I like the sound of that.'

'Good eating habits?' she teased some more.

'No, the hanging around together bit. Sounds very good to me.'

Tarni held his gaze for a few more seconds. 'Now I'm going to head up to the house.'

'I'll just check the doors are locked first.' Cy took her hand and held it as they walked up the steps together. The security light came on outside the front door, and he nodded with satisfaction when he reached the screen door. 'All good.' He put his key in the lock and unlocked the security door, then the front door, before he reached in and turned the hall light on for her. 'I won't be long. I'll just check the trenches and come straight back up.' He leaned down and kissed her briefly, and Tarni resisted putting her arms around his neck.

Just.

'See you soon.'

'I'll bring your bag up when I come back.'

'Okay. And Ellie's dish. I forgot it.' Tarni pressed her fingers against her lips as Cy ran down the stairs. She was almost gliding on air as she walked into the kitchen. Crossing straight to the pantry, she took out the sandwich toaster. There wasn't much in the fridge until they went back to Darwin to shop. Cheese and tomato toasties would have to do.

Tarni smiled. She was thinking of them as a pair now.

Softly, softly, she warned herself.

Take it lightly; you don't want to get hurt, girl.

After plugging the sandwich toaster in and lining it with baking paper, Tarni walked to the sink and turned the tap on. She reached for the hand sanitiser and soaped up her hands. When she rinsed the soap off, she glanced down at the spoon that was in the sink and frowned. She thought she put everything in the dishwasher before they left, but maybe not. She picked the spoon up, opened the dishwasher, and put it on the top shelf with the rest of the cutlery.

As she straightened up, she noticed a streak of blue liquid staining the side of the dishwasher. It was strange. She hadn't used anything blue. The only thing she'd used near the sink before they left had been the Baileys for the cheesecake. With a shrug, she got the dishcloth from the side of the sink and wiped it off. Maybe it had always been there and she hadn't noticed it before.

As she looked along the bench at the water purifier, she couldn't resist lifting the lid. Relief filled her as she saw that it was still half-full, just as she remembered before they left. She'd really worried she was losing the plot last week. Whatever that virus was, it had played havoc with her memory and her feelings.

Tarni went to the fridge and took out the cheese and tomato, and quickly made three sandwiches. She was sure Cy would be able to eat two.

She stood at the window and waited for his headlights to appear, but there was no sign of him yet, so she didn't put the sandwiches in the toaster. Instead, she went to the cupboard, took out a glass and some ice cubes from the freezer, and poured a glass of water from the purifier. There was still a lemon on the fruit bowl, so she cut it in half and squeezed some lemon juice into her glass. She took out a second glass, filled it with ice, and with a smile, added Coke from the fridge. She was learning Cy's preferences very well.

He was taking ages, and she wondered what was holding him up. Eventually, after she'd finished her water and was pouring another glass for herself, his lights lit up the trees as he drove back from the dam.

The blinkers flashed quickly, and the lights wavered, and another headache began to target her temples. 'Oh bugger,' she thought. She'd been feeling so much better.

Tarni went back to the sandwich toaster and slid the three sandwiches onto the large surface, and closed the lid.

She was sitting on the veranda with her glass of water and Cy's Coke when he came up the stairs with her bag.

'Everything okay?' she asked, going into the house.

'That rotten little turd took his money and hasn't done any more since we were here down there on Friday morning.'

'Oh no.' Tarni shook her head. 'What a lowlife.'

'Yep, I should have known better. I thought he was a bit strange. I should have known better than to trust him. Anyway, no matter. I put your bag down the hall outside your room. I left mine in the car.' Cy looked at her intently as he put the Pyrex dish on the bench. 'I'll move back down to the shed tonight.'

Disappointment filtered through Tarni, but she pushed it away. It was too soon. If their relationship did go that way, there was plenty of time to get to know each other before they slept together. It was weeks before Kane and Ellie came back.

'The sandwiches are ready, and there's a glass of Coke on the veranda for you. I thought we'd eat out there. It's such a lovely night,' Tarni suggested. 'It's hard to believe we're into June, and we can sit out there without a jumper on at night. I love this climate.'

'So, you're thinking you still might stay around?' Cy asked.

'I'm thinking I might.' Tarni nodded and smiled at him.

She brought the toasted sandwiches out to the veranda and put them on the table between them. Leaning back, she took a deep breath and looked out over the dam. 'Hard to believe that someone can do that, isn't it. Jerry, I mean. Maybe he got sidetracked for the weekend. Maybe he'll turn up tomorrow.'

'I don't think so. I think I made a poor call,' Cy said. 'Anyway, I'll get down there digging tomorrow. I should've done that in the first place, and not been lazy. Only puts me two days behind where I wanted to be.'

'Yeah, I better get back to the shed tomorrow too. I really should go down and check the incubators tonight, but I'm feeling tired again.' Tarni put her head back and yawned before she reached for the sandwich, but her hands were shaking.

'You okay?' Cy asked.

'I guess I'm just tired from the trip home. Maybe I didn't get over that bug as quickly as I thought.'

She noticed Cy looking at her as she ate only half her sandwich and left the rest on the plate. He'd eaten both of his and finished the glass of Coke.

'It's nearly eight o'clock. It's probably not too early to go to bed,' he suggested.

'That sounds good. I'll have a quick shower, then go to bed. I'll get up early tomorrow and start work.' Tarni stood and took Cy's plate, and reached for his glass, but her hand was shaking too much, and she pulled it back.

'I'll bring the glasses in, and then leave you in peace,' Cy said.

Tarni put the plates in the sink; she didn't even have the energy to open the dishwasher. Her head was really pounding, and she was feeling quite nauseous. 'Okay, I'll see you in the morning. Thanks again for the weekend.' She could barely get the words out.

Cy walked to the door. 'Sleep well.'

As soon as the front door closed, Tarni bolted down the hall. She only just made it to the toilet before she vomited violently. When there was nothing left to bring up, she went to the bathroom and laid her hand on the sink, looking at her pale face, tears streaming from her eyes. If there was one thing she hated, it was vomiting, and she gagged as the nausea rose to her throat again.

Half an hour later, after being sick a dozen times, Tarni managed to wash her face and hands and put clean pyjamas on. She climbed into bed, feeling strange and a wave of dizziness hit her as she put her head on the pillow.

Chapter 35

McLaren Mango Farm - Sunday night
Tarni.

Some time through the night, Tarni's legs jerked and cramped, and she woke with a start. It was pitch dark in her room, and the blinds were down. She'd put them up to let the moonlight in before she went to sleep.

Her mouth was dry, and she reached for the glass of water and drained it. Suddenly, strange red lights flickered around the wall of her room, and she looked at the window. The blind was up again; had a car come into the driveway?

She must've got out of bed and opened it when she woke up a minute ago.

Tarni lay there, her head aching; the ache went down her neck and into her back and down around her kidneys, and she knew she had to go to the bathroom soon.

She closed her eyes and drifted back to sleep again, and then woke a short while later. There were noises in her room and banging in the hall. Buzzing noises came from outside the door, there was somebody out there.

Maybe it was Cy.

She really needed to go to the toilet. She sat up and pushed her hand on the side of the bed as she swung her legs over, and it was her sore hand; excruciating pain shot up her arm, and for a moment, she wondered if it was infected.

She felt along the wall for the light switch, but it wouldn't come on when her fingers pushed it. Feeling her way around the room with her uninjured hand, she tried to find the door to the ensuite, but it had gone. There was no door in the wall now.

Tears rolled down her face, and she slid to the floor. Crawling across the room, the door to the ensuite appeared in front of her. The pain in her kidneys was getting worse, and anxiety filled her chest as she wondered if she was going to die tonight.

Poor Cy. She couldn't die, his father died this week.

Tarni pulled herself up onto the toilet and sat there, her feet cool on the bare tiles. Had she taken more painkillers? She couldn't remember. Her eyelids started to droop, and she pushed herself up and flushed the toilet. She walked across to the basin but couldn't find the taps, so she stumbled back to bed. She fell across it, and the world went black.

***

Cy

Cy was up at dawn; he'd had a restless night but forced himself to get up as soon as it was light. There were trenches to be dug. He glanced across at the house, half-expecting to see a light on in the kitchen, but it was in darkness. For a moment he considered going up there but he shook his head. He'd let Tarni sleep. She hadn't looked well again last night. As much as he'd wanted to stay in the house, he'd done the gentlemanly thing last night and moved back to the shed. And it had been the right choice, Tarni had seemed keen for him to leave.

After three hours of digging, his muscles ached and he drove back up the shed, surprised to see it locked. Tarni must have gone up for morning tea. He glanced at his watch; it was almost ten.

Maybe she was sitting on the veranda upstairs. He checked that his keys were still in his pocket and hurried up the steps to the screen door, it was locked. He knocked, but there was no answer. Taking out his keys, he unlocked both doors, stepped inside, and called out.

'Tarni? Are you there?' He looked through the kitchen window to the veranda where they had tea last night, but it was empty.

He stood in the hall and listened. There was no sound of a shower running, and there was no movement. He walked quietly down the hall. He had left his door open, but Tarni's bedroom door was still shut. He tapped on it gently. 'Tarni, are you in there?'

There was no response, and his concern kicked in. He turned the door handle quietly and opened the door a fraction, just enough to put his head in and look around. The room was in darkness. The blind was down, but a small glimmer of sunlight illuminated the room enough for him to see that Tarni was still in bed.

He walked over and looked down at her, and his heart jumped. Her face was white, and she was wet with perspiration. He wrinkled his nose and noticed she had been sick beside the bed.

He touched her shoulder gently and gave her a little shake. 'Tarni, wake up. Are you sick?'

Her eyes opened and she looked at him without recognition before her head lolled to the side and they fell shut again. He felt her forehead; her skin was icy cold. He tried to sit her up, but her limbs flopped. Cy lay her in the recovery position and pulled his phone out of his shirt pocket and dialled triple zero.

Chapter 36

Hotel Playa Feliz, Mexico - early June
Ellie

Kane had been very quiet for the last two nights, and Ellie wondered what was wrong. They had gone down to breakfast early this morning because he wanted to get to the farm, and she didn't understand why he had to be there so early. The kids had woken up early too, so they decided to have breakfast at the restaurant together before he headed off.

'Now tell me again why you had to go so early,' she said as she reached for the bowl of fresh fruit and chopped some into small pieces for Matilda.

Kane hesitated, and Ellie looked at him. 'What's going on?' she asked.

'Nothing. What would be going on?' he replied, looking innocent.

'I know you, Kane McLaren. You're up to something. You've been a bit vague the last couple of days.'

'I just . . . my head is full of everything that's happening. I'm seeing and learning so much, I need to keep on top of it. Tarni is going to be really interested. I'll give her a call tonight.'

Matilda was sitting on Kane's knee and she reached out and took his spoon from the table. 'Look, Mum,' James yelled. 'Tilly wants to feed herself.'

'She does, but it might be a bit messy on that white cloth.' Ellie took the spoon and passed Tilly a small piece of mango.

'I can feed myself, Mommy,' Verity said, 'but can I have some fruit for Adora?'

Ellie and Kane exchanged an affectionate glance. Adora, Verity's doll, had been everywhere with them on this trip. She'd fallen in the pool, and there had been a near tragedy when the doll had fallen off the merry-go-round at a fun fair they'd stumbled upon in the next town last weekend.

Kane picked up his napkin and dabbed his mouth, and then wiped Tilly's fingers before he stood and passed her over to Ellie. 'Anyway, love, I'm going to have to go now. What are you planning for the day?'

'The usual.' Ellie smiled. 'Lazing around the pool.'

'They'll be bringing you your hot towels? Should I be worried about these guys who deliver cocktails?'

'Non-alcoholic cocktails, and no. None of the barmen are as good-looking as you, my love.'

'That's all right then.' Kane leaned down to kiss her goodbye. 'Listen, don't go far away today. I'll come home for lunch and we'll have it at the pool restaurant. How does that sound?'

'Good. I'm planning on taking the kids down for a swim as soon as we get changed. We'll go to the waterpark at the far end. It'll be warm enough to go for a swim in about half an hour, and it won't be so crowded this early. You have a good morning and we'll see you for lunch.'

Kane dropped a kiss on top of Verity's head, gave James a hug on the way past, and tickled Matilda.

'You guys have a great day too,' he said. 'I'll see you later. You've got your security card to the room, right, Els?'

'Yes, darling, I have.' Ellie's eyes narrowed as Kane hurried out. She knew him well enough to know he had a surprise up his sleeve. They'd had the most wonderful holiday, even with Kane working a few hours each day. He was keen to get home, and they'd discussed going back soon. Kane had seen all he'd wanted already.

'Can we have a big long swim today, Mum?' James asked as they took the lift back up to their suite. 'Gareth from the creche said they were going to be at the pool today too.'

'That'll be nice. You'll have somebody to play with. Slow down, guys. Tilly's getting heavy.' Ellie walked behind her two oldest children as they ran from the lift. 'Now, Tilly, my darling. You are going to miss your morning sleep, and then you can have a long one this afternoon. How does that sound?'

Tilly gurgled as they walked to the door.

'Can Adora come to the pool?' Verity asked.

'Mummy already said no, remember? She might get sunburned,' Ellie said, trying to think of a better excuse. The doll had been the bane of their trip, lost at the fun fair, and left at the train station. It was a miracle that they still had Adora.

'Okay, Mummy, that sounds like a very good idea,' Verity said.

Ellie dug in her pocket for the security card to get into the room.

Half an hour later, they were dressed in their swimmers. Ellie picked up a couple of beach towels and the bag she'd packed for Matilda, and called Verity and James from the television.

When Ellie saw there were three lifeguards on duty at the water park, she took Matilda to the creche, and came back via the bar. After ordering herself a mimosa she felt decadent. Sitting in the shade, sipping her drink, Ellie laughed as she watched her children.

The pool that James and Verity were in was only about half a metre deep, with lots of water play and fountains and wheelbarrows of water, and a big bucket of water that tipped on them every ten minutes or so.

Verity and James played so well together, laughing and giggling. A surge of contentment consumed Ellie; she was blessed. She had a wonderful husband who loved her, who had taken over the family farm and was so excited and enthusiastic about what he was doing. James hadn't missed being at school at all, and he had done his schoolwork every afternoon. Matilda had eased into a new routine, given up the morning sleep, and was sleeping three hours in the afternoon, plus going to bed at a reasonable hour at night. Ellie looked at her middle child as she jumped under the water bucket and smiled. Verity was just Verity. She was the sweetest little thing.

The gate behind her opened with a squeak and Ellie looked up, expecting to see James' friend coming in with his family. It was a couple with three children, and strangely Kane was in front of them. He was back early.

Kane reached her first and took her in his arms. 'Helo, sweetheart. I came to tell you about your surprise. Would you like to meet someone?'

Ellie nodded and then squealed as she looked at the couple smiling at her. 'Oh my God, Kane McLaren, you knew about all this. How long have you known?'

'A while,' he said with a huge grin as Ellie ran over to the couple who were standing at the gate, her arms flung wide.

'Gina, oh my God, Gina, how long has it been? David, it is so good to see you! And who are these big children? Oh, my goodness, look at you all!'

Gina, Ellie's friend from a long time ago, flung her arms wide open and embraced Ellie. '*Bella*, it is so wonderful to see you.'

'I can't believe it,' Ellie said. 'What are you doing in Mexico? It's a long way from Italy!'

'Well, we had to go to the States for business for David, and we knew you were here, and we wanted to make it the surprise.' Gina's accent had thickened since they moved to Italy. 'Kane has just collected us from the airport.'

'Well, it certainly is a surprise,' Ellie said. 'How long are you staying?'

'A whole week,' David said. Ellie stepped out of Gina's arms and David folded her in a close hug. 'So good to see you, Ellie McLaren. You don't look any different than what you did nine years ago. I still remember you in that baseball cap.'

'Let me see these children,' Gina said. She flung her arms around James and he looked embarrassed as she smothered his cheek with kisses. 'Oh, I cannot believe that you have three children, the same as us.'

'And this is Verity.' Verity looked down, a little bit shy, and Gina sensed it. 'Hello, Verity, it is lovely to meet you too.' She dropped a gentle kiss on her cheek, and David patted her shoulder.

'Tilly is in the creche. Kane, will you go and get her, sweetie? I don't think my legs will get me there. I'm in shock.'

Ellie and Gina hugged again and then Ellie spoke to Andrew and Binny. 'I haven't seen you guys for such a long time, but look how big you are.'

The little girl with dark curly hair looked up at Ellie. 'And this must be my namesake. Hello, Ellie, it's lovely to see you.'

Kane walked back carrying Tilly. 'And this little terror is Matilda.' He held Matilda out to Gina.

Gina looked at the smiling baby. 'She's gorgeous, Ellie. She's the image of you. Verity, you look like your dad, and James, who do you look like?'

'I look like me,' James said seriously.

##

After dinner that night, Ellie sat back and sipped her wine. It had been a day of love and laughter.

The McLaren children had gone to bed after playing with the Johnson children all afternoon. Seeing Gina and David again was wonderful, and Ellie and Gina had not stopped talking. She caught Kane looking at her across the coffee table.

'A nice surprise, my dear?' His grin was lazy. David and Gina were sitting in the double sofa at the end of the table, and Gina's head was on David's shoulder, her eyes heavy.

'A very nice surprise, but I think Gina is tired. I think you need to go to bed too, *bella*,' Ellie said.

'Yes, I think the jet lag is catching up with me,' Gina agreed. 'Not to mention catching up with you all again today and talking non-stop. It has been so very good.'

Kane's phone buzzed with a message, and he looked at it in surprise as they watched.

'It's Connor,' he said.

'Oh, maybe Dru's had her baby,' Ellie said. 'I hope everything is okay.'

'You worry too much, babe,' Kane said.

Gina sat up straight. 'Come on, Ellie we'll go and make a coffee while Kane makes the call.'

'Call me if I need to talk to them,' Ellie said.

Kane nodded and headed out to the balcony.

Ellie listened for Kane's call as they made coffee. Gina picked up a glass bowl and tipped in the chocolates they'd bought at the airport. 'I don't think I could eat another thing, Gina,' Ellie said.

'Chocolate, my dear, we can always eat chocolate.' They carried the tray back into the lounge just as Kane stepped in from the balcony. His face was set.

Ellie walked over to him, her heart pounding. 'I knew it. What's wrong?'

'It's okay, darling. Family is fine, but there is a bit of news. Russell Fairweather died this afternoon.'

Ellie sat down on the lounge as confusion filled her. 'Russell Fairweather is dead?' She put a hand to her chest.

'Yes, a heart attack in prison,' Kane said. He was dead before the paramedics got there.'

Gina reached out and took Ellie's hand. 'It is a relief, Ellie. It's over. I know you've always worried about what would happen when he got out of jail.'

'I did. Oh my God, Kane, I can't believe it. He's gone.'

'Yes, Connor thought he should tell us before we saw it online.' Kane hesitated and Ellie tensed.

'What? What else?' she asked quickly.

'There's been a bit of trouble at the farm. Tarni is in hospital.'

Chapter 37

Darwin Royal Hospital - Wednesday afternoon
Cy

Cy paced the floor of the waiting room in the hospital. Tarni had finally been moved from intensive care, and he was allowed to see her for the first time since the helicopter had brought her in on Monday morning. He hadn't shaved and had only been back to the farm twice to feed the dogs, shower quickly, and change his clothes.

The last three days had been horrendous. Tarni's condition had been touch and go for a while until the tests had detected the poison in her system and the appropriate treatment had started.

Emma Langford, Ellie McLaren's sister, and Emma's husband, Jeremy, had stayed with him on and off so that he hadn't been alone. Being doctors at the hospital, they were privy to more information than he was. Because as it was, he was only seen as her work colleague and the person who had called triple zero when he'd found her unresponsive on Monday morning. If Tarni had died, he would never have forgiven himself for not checking on her sooner.

He wasn't allowed to know what was happening for the first day, and he hadn't been allowed to see her in intensive care. He couldn't very well say, 'Well, we kissed each other on Sunday night, so I'm her partner.'

Emma knew how worried he was, and when Dee and Ryan came into the hospital this morning, leaving the twins with a friend, Cy broke down.

'She's a wonderful person, Ryan,' he said.

'I could tell by the way you looked at her over the weekend that you were falling hard, mate,' Ryan said.

'I can't believe that bastard was the one doing it all the time, and I fucking employed him. I hope he rots in hell.'

Once it had been established that Tarni had been poisoned, the police arrived at the hospital and insisted Cy accompany them to the farm. They put him in the police car and took him back to the house, where two detectives were waiting to interview him.

He was interviewed at length, and he told them about Tarni's arrival at the farm after him, about her research work and explained why he was looking after the farm. He told them about her cutting her hand and their trip to the hospital almost two weeks ago. The detectives had been distant; Cy worried he was being blamed for her condition.

'Who else has been here?' the older detective asked.

'I hired a bloke to dig some trenches, and he pulled the dirty on us.'

'Yes, we know that he was on the place. His name was Dean Drummond.'

Cy had shaken his head. 'No, his name was Jerry White. He turned up here one day looking for work. Hang on; I've got his card somewhere. It's down in the shed. Can I get it?'

The detective nodded, and Cy returned to the shed and found it on top of his camp fridge. He hurried back up to the house. He walked in, surprised to see they had removed the contents of the kitchen bin and were bagging it.

'What is it?' he asked, handing Jerry's card over. 'What have you found?'

'Have you been using coolant in your vehicle?' the younger detective asked.

'Coolant?' Cy frowned. 'What sort of coolant? Coolant for a car?'

'Yes.'

The other policeman held the bag up, and Cy saw a blue bottle with a label on it.

'I've never used it. Why would anyone need it up here in the heat? No, I've never seen it before, and I don't think Tarni would have used it either. Her Jeep's been in the shed since she arrived.'

'We'll be fingerprinting the bottle and the kitchen, but we have our suspicions,' the detective said.

Cy told them more about the suspected break-in when they'd been at the hospital.

'Why didn't you report it?'

'We couldn't see any need. To be honest, I wasn't sure that Tarni had locked the doors like she said. There was no sign that anyone had been inside. Nothing was missing. The only thing that Tarni noticed, and again I thought she was confused because of the painkillers she took after cutting her hand, she was worried about the water purifier being refilled. She also said there had been different water and milk levels in the fridge the other day.'

'Forensics are on their way.'

Cy shook his head. 'What do you think happened? I mean, why would Jerry or whatever his name is, have done that?' he asked.

'There have been quite a few connections today. Have you ever heard of Russell Fairweather?'

'No.' Cy frowned. 'The name sounds familiar, but I can't say I have.

'He was a prisoner in Darwin Correctional Centre and died last weekend. A heart attack.'

Cy stared. 'So was my father, and so did he. Die, I mean.'

The detective quizzed him and took some notes as Cy explained the situation.

'A coincidence, I think,' he said. 'A contact and a phone number were found in Fairweather's belongings, and then when I contacted the person, he told us one of the guards at the correctional centre was on Fairweather's payroll.'

Cy interrupted. 'How can a prisoner in jail be paying someone?'

'You'd be surprised what happens. The guard denied everything at first. As soon as being an accessory to murder was mentioned, he told us everything. Fairweather was responsible for the truck accident out on the Arnhem Highway last week.'

Cy nodded. 'On the weekend. We passed the crash site on our way back on Sunday.'

'Did you see the cars?'

'No, there was only police tape there. No cars or truck.'

'The fatality was the young bloke who was working on your farm here.'

Cy's mouth dropped open. 'What!'

'Dean Drummond, also known as your Jerry White, a fake ID provided with the help of Russell Fairweather, was identified by his fingerprints.'

'Why the hell would he break in and try to poison Tarni? He didn't know her,' Cy said. 'He turned up looking for work, and she took his card. That was their only contact.'

'It was under Fairweather's instruction. Is it possible that Drummond could have thought she was somebody else?' the detective asked.

'Yes. He was under the impression that we were the McLarens. We saw no reason to disillusion him.'

A look of satisfaction crossed the detective's face as he nodded. 'Why was that?'

'Tarni didn't want him to know that she was alone in the house. He did seem a bit of a strange guy.'

'That was wise, but what you didn't know that Drummond had just been released from jail. He was jailed for seven years after being found guilty of the violent rape of a young girl at Dundee Beach. He almost strangled her and left her for dead.'

Cy put his hands over his face. 'Holy hell, and we had him here.' He removed his hands and stared at the detective. 'And you're saying he poisoned Tarni? He put that stuff in the water and she drank it. Holy hell.'

'We believe that's how it happened. We'll be examining the contents of the fridge and cupboards when forensics arrive.'

'But why?'

'It was a contract killing organised by Russell Fairweather with outside help, as was the truck "accident". We are yet to find the truck that allegedly pushed Drummond's ute into the other truck.'

'But why Tarni?' Cy thought for a moment. 'Hang on. You mean he thought she was Ellie? Was he after Ellie all the time?'

'That's correct. Mrs McLaren was a significant witness in Fairweather's trial. He was responsible for the murders of her father and Mr McLaren's stepfather a few years ago.'

'No wonder Kane and Ellie are so careful about security here. I didn't know any of that.' Cy shook his head in disbelief. 'Do they know what's happened?'

'Yes, they've been informed and they are apparently cutting their trip short.'

Cy was keen to get back to the hospital; even though he'd been told that Tarni was out of danger, he wanted to see her for himself. 'Am I free to go back to the hospital now?'

'Yes, Mr Prescott. Thank you for your co-operation. Your information has been very helpful and tied up a few loose ends. Constable Baker will take you back in now.'

Cy worried about Tarni all the way to Darwin. He didn't know how she was going to react when she found out what happened. For God's sake, she'd almost died.

Emma had kept him in the loop about Tarni's treatment and recovery over the past two days. She'd been given an IV antidote to reverse the effects of the poison within half an hour of her arrival at the hospital in Darwin. A doctor from the UK who happened to be in emergency had recognised her symptoms from a case he'd had recently seen overseas. Emma had assured Cy that the fast administration of the antidote would prevent permanent organ damage.

'Your quick response probably saved Tarni's life,' she said.

Cy paced as he waited, and just as he sat in the chair again, the nurse came out to the waiting room and smiled at him. 'Ms Morgan is back in the room now, and she'd like to see you.'

Cy smoothed his hair back, regretting that he hadn't shaved, and followed the nurse across the hall to the private room.

Tarni was sitting up in bed, her face pale, her eyes circled with black. Cy's heart lifted when she smiled at him.

'Hello, Cy. I believe I owe you for saving my life.'

Cy walked over to the bed and stood beside her 'You don't owe me anything. It's enough to see you smile.'

Tarni reached out to him with both hands. 'Please sit down with me. I've missed you.'

Cy took her hands in his and sat on the side of the bed. 'I've missed you too.'

'Emma said you've been at the hospital since I came in.'

'It's where I wanted to be. Dee and Ryan came this morning too.' He couldn't take his eyes off her face. 'Tarni, I have to tell you one thing before I tell you everything that's happened.' He held her hands tightly, and then remembered her injury. 'Sorry.'

'It's fine. It's almost healed. She reached for his hand again. 'What did you want to tell me?'

Cy leaned closer to her. 'I thought I was going to lose you. You've made me happier than I've been for a long time, and then I thought you would be taken from me before you knew how I felt. I need you to know how much I care about you.'

Tarni's eyes held his and her smile was sweet. 'I know you do. And I feel the same way about you, Cy. I'm looking forward to getting out of here and showing you how much.'

Cy lifted one hand and gently held the back of her head. He lightly brushed his lips over hers. 'I'm looking forward to that very much too.'

Chapter 38

Hotel Playa Feliz, Mexico – a week later
Ellie

Kane and Ellie had talked and talked of the situation at home when the police had called a few days after Fairweather had died. Concern for Tarni had been their first reaction, and then disbelief that Russell Fairweather had been able to organise her poisoning, and then a truck crash from prison.

'It was lucky for you we were away, Ellie.' Kane had held her tightly.

'Imagine what he could have done once he was released.' Ellie shivered. 'But not so lucky for Tarni. I'm just so grateful Cy was there with her and saved her life.'

It had taken a few days for them to get back to normal, and Kane had finished up at the farms. They'd made the decision to go home early, but when Kane had suggested another week at the resort with him not going to the farms, and spending each day with Ellie and the children Ellie had jumped at the chance.

On the last night before they flew home, Ellie lay on top of the crisp, fresh-smelling sheets as Kane took a shower in the ensuite. The gentle sea breeze blowing through the garden outside their balcony filled the room with a sweet fragrance. She jumped off the bed and grabbed her phone. She had been meaning to do a plant search on the ginger plant that smelled so wonderful and see if she could plant it at home.

'That's a nice view,' Kane said with a chuckle as he stepped out of the bathroom. 'What are you doing, Ellie?'

'I'm taking photos of the plants.'

'I hope no one's looking in.'

'At a naked photographer?' she replied with a cheeky grin.

Their last night at the resort was bittersweet. It had almost become a second home to Ellie over the past weeks, and the kids had had an absolute ball.

She looked at her husband and thought how lucky she was. 'It's going to be good to go home, but sad in some ways. It's been a wonderful two months.'

'There's no reason why we can't have a holiday like this every year,' Kane said.

'That would be great, but the kids have grown so much Mum is not going to recognise Matilda,' Ellie said.

'I'm sure she will.'

'Mum and Graysen had a wonderful time in Africa. I am so excited about getting home and seeing everyone.'

The bed tipped. Kane sat on the other side and then stretched out and rolled over next to her. 'Have you had a good time, Els?'

'It's been wonderful, Kane. It's been like a second honeymoon.'

He waggled his eyebrows. 'Maybe we should make the most of our last night.'

She looked at her gorgeous husband and smiled. 'Maybe we should. I've been thinking perhaps we should have another baby. Three is such an uneven number.'

A broad smile crossed Kane's face. 'Would you believe I was going to suggest that when we got home?'

'Excellent. Decision made.' Ellie chuckled as Kane rolled over and put his arms around her. 'The trip's been worthwhile for you, hasn't it?' she asked.

'I can't wait to get back and put all of what I've learned to work in our orchard. And I'm looking forward to talking to Tarni some more. Since she's recovered, she's made some great developments with the hybrid program, and it's going to be great to combine what she's been doing and what I've learned over here. I have a feeling she's going to stay close by.'

'Yes, I feel so bad about what happened, but now that *he's* gone, we don't have to worry anymore. Do we?' Ellie said, snuggling closer to her husband.

'No, sweetheart, we don't. Anyway, forget about all of that. Let's make the most of our last night here in Mexico.' The faint moonlight coming through the window disappeared as Kane's head lowered to hers, and he gently kissed her lips.

'I do love you, Kane McLaren,' Ellie said.

'And I love you too, Ellie McLaren. It's going to be good to get home, isn't it, babe?'

'Sure is,' she replied, smiling.

Chapter 39

Darwin Airport - two days later

Excitement bubbled up as the pilot called the cabin crew to prepare for landing. They were only about fifteen minutes out of Darwin, and Ellie was sure there would be a welcoming committee there for them. Mum wouldn't miss seeing the kids come home.

Dru had gone to hospital last night; she'd managed to last until her due date, and her pains had started when Ellie and Kane had stopped in Honolulu for one night. Ellie really hoped the baby would arrive safely in the next little while.

Emma and Jeremy had emailed and said that they were both off for the weekend and they would be at the airport too. Emma had called Ellie to tell her she was four months pregnant when Gina and David were with them.

'I knew, Em. I guessed at Dru's apartment the weekend before we left.'

'Clever clogs,' Emma had laughed and then told them that Cy and Tarni, and Dee and Ryan were going to meet them at the airport too.

Ellie grinned to herself. It might be overwhelming with the whole family there, but it was going to be so good to see everyone. Kane leaned over and looked out the window. 'Look, there's land ahead. We're nearly there.'

'We're home, babe,' Ellie said. Matilda was asleep on her lap, and Verity and James were sitting at the end of the middle row. James told her last night that he was now a cosmopolitan traveller, and Ellie hid a smile. 'Where on earth did you get that term from?'

'That's what Juan in the restaurant told me on our last night.' James was a social child and had made friends with so many of the staff at the resort. There had been a big farewell and a few tears when they left. But the best part of the whole trip has been seeing Gina and David.

Ellie sat up as the plane landed smoothly on the tarmac and taxied to the arrival's terminal. She could feel the anticipation building up inside her. Gently nudging Matilda, she whispered, 'Wake up, sweetheart. We're home.'

Verity and James were jumping with excitement.

As they disembarked and reached the arrival lounge, Ellie scanned the crowd and spotted her family near the viewing window. A wide smile spread across her face as she saw her mother's familiar figure. Sandra was holding Ruby's hand. Ellie quickly made her way across to them, Matilda in her arms, and Kane and the children following closely behind.

'Mum!' Ellie exclaimed as she embraced her mother tightly. 'Oh Mum, I've missed you so much.'

Her mother hugged them back, her smile wide. 'Welcome home, darling. I've been counting the days until you all returned.'

'Dru?' Ellie ventured.

'A bouncing baby boy, three hours ago. Xander Peter Kirk.' Mum's eyes were shining with tears, and Ellie blinked hers away.

Emma and Jeremy approached, and Akasha jumped with excitement between them. Dee and Ryan stood beside them, each holding a twin. Ellie smiled as she saw Cy and Tarni standing a little bit away. Cy's arm was around her shoulder.

Ellie drew a deep breath and looked at her family. The airport was bustling with activity, but they were surrounded by family who loved and supported them. Her eyes welled with tears, and Kane pulled her close.

'We're home, Els.'

Epilogue

McLaren Mango Farm - six months later.

Ellie stood on the veranda of their homestead. Conversations swept around her, but she focused on the land that stretched to the horizon. In the distance, sunlight glinted off the dam Dad had put in many, many years ago. In front of the dam, avenues of lush green mango trees were heavy with fruit ready for harvest.

The children ran around the bushes that edged the circular driveway, playing and squealing. The children of the Porter sisters, and the one brother they had found later in life. The children were playing hide and seek, just as she, and Dru, and Emma had played on this farm many years ago. Ellie smiled as her Verity dropped to the ground and hid behind a bush. Ruby and Akasha, her sisters' little girls were holding Ryan's boys' hands as they searched for Verity. Angus and Wyatt had grown so much this year, they were fast catching their cousins.

'I see her!' James came running past them and pointing. 'She's behind that bush!'

Behind Ellie, a little voice giggled, 'Mumma, Mumma.' She turned to smile and saw her mother, jiggling Tilly on her lap. Dru was beside her, holding Xander. His blonde curls and blue eyes made him the image of Dru.

Ellie placed a hand on her stomach. It was going to be interesting with only eighteen months between Tilly and the new baby. She was going to have her hands full, but James and Verity were so excited, she knew they would help.

Kane still walked around with his chest puffed out. 'Four kids, Els. Whoever would have thought it?'

'Certainly not that cranky engineer I met at Makowa Resort,' she teased.

Behind Mum, Graysen stood with his hand on Sandra's shoulder, looking down at Tilly with a wide smile. Behind them, Connor and Jeremy stood head-to-head in conversation, and as Ellie watched, Connor reached down and twisted one of Dru's blonde curls around his fingers. She looked up at him with a smile and Connor leaned down and kissed her cheek.

Ryan and Dee were sitting with Cy and Tarni, and their laughter reached Ellie on the veranda. This farm had seen so much happiness over the years.

Cy and Tarni were living together now, and Kane had told her only yesterday that Cy had purchased fifty acres of trees a few kilometres up the road from them. Tarni looked totally different from the withdrawn young woman who had turned up at their property in May the day they left for Mexico. She had gained a little bit of weight. Her cheeks were rosy, and her features were softer. Amazing what love could do.

As Ellie watched, Cy turned to Tarni with a wide smile; he was much easier company these days. Ellie had watched him walk in beside Tarni when they arrived. His fluid grace reflected his now-calm demeanor. He wasn't as watchful as he had been as a young man, and she could see how much he and Tarni loved each other.

A warm hand slipped around Ellie's back.

'I know exactly what you're thinking, my love.' Kane's breath was warm on her cheek as he dipped his head.

'And what's that, my dear husband?'

'You're thinking the same as me. What a wonderful family we have. How lucky we are.'

She shook her head. 'It's not luck, Kane. It's knowing and embracing the power of love. Ellie turned her head and pressed her lips against her husband's. His mouth tilted against hers. She loved the way he always smiled when he was kissing her.

'You're spot on as usual. It is love,' he murmured against her.

Her heart swelled with love for this man, her husband and the father of her children.

'Dad, stop smooching with Mum,' James yelled from the steps. 'Are you ever going to turn that barbeque on? We're starving.'

Ellie pushed Kane away gently. 'You'd better go cook.'

The sun shot its golden rays into the sky before it dropped below the horizon in one of the most spectacular sunsets of the summer, and as Ellie's gaze shifted to the north, Mum, Emma, and Dru came over and stood beside her. Towering pillars of white cloud were edged with gold as the sun crept to the horizon. Ellie kissed her fingers and raised them to the sky. 'Thank you, Dad.'

She wondered if he was looking down on them now. If he was, she knew he would be smiling.

THE END

ABOUT ANNIE

Annie lives in Australia, on the beautiful north coast of New South Wales. She sits in her writing chair and looks out over the tranquil Pacific Ocean.

She writes contemporary romance, outback crime and historical romance. She loves telling stories that always have a happily ever after. She lives with her very own hero of many years and they share their home with Toby, the naughtiest dog in the universe, and Barney, the rag doll puss, who hides when the four grandchildren come to visit.

Stay up to date with her latest releases at her website:
http://www.annieseaton.net

If you would like to stay up to date with Annie's releases, subscribe to her newsletter here: http://www.annieseaton.net

All Annie's books are available in eBook and print at

eBook links:

https://www.annieseaton.net/books.html

Print Store:

All books are available in print at Annie's store

With FREE postage

https://www.annieseaton.net/store.html

Look for Annie's bestselling new series:
THE AUGATHELLA GIRLS

Awards

Winner - Book of the Year, Long Romance, RWA Ruby awards 2023. (Larapinta)

Book of the Year (Whitsunday Dawn) - Ausrom Readers' Choice Awards 2018.

Finalist (Whitsunday Dawn) – ARRA romantic suspense.

Finalist - NZ KORU award 2018 and 2020.

Winner - Best Established Author of the Year 2017 AUSROM.

Longlisted - Sisters in Crime Davitt Awards 2016, 2017, 2018, 2019, 2021, 2022, 2023.

Finalist (Kakadu Sunset) - Book of the Year, Long Romance, RWA Ruby awards 2016.

Winner - Best Established Author of the Year 2015 AUSROM.

Winner - Author of the Year 2014 AUSROM

Printed in Great Britain
by Amazon